A WOMAN'S WRATH

Ruby,

I am very glad you asked all the questions you did.
I hope I was helpful.
I enjoyed your questions and you
will enjoy my book.

Enjoy!

Dm C

2/15/07

A WOMAN'S WRATH

a novel by
DENISE CAMPBELL

Q-Boro Books
WWW.QBOROBOOKS.COM
An Urban Entertainment Company

Published by Q-Boro Books

ISBN 0-9776247-7-3
First Printing January 2007
Printed in the United States of America

10   9   8   7   6   5   4   3   2   1

*This is a work of fiction. It is not meant to depict, portray or represent any par-
ticular real persons. All the characters, incidents and dialogues are the prod-
ucts of the author's imagination and are not to be construed as real. Any
references or similarities to actual events, entities, real people, living or dead,
or to real locales are intended to give the novel a sense of reality. Any similarity
in other names, characters, entities, places and incidents is entirely coinciden-
tal.*

Cover Copyright © 2006 by Q-BORO BOOKS all rights reserved
Cover Layout & Design—Candace K. Cottrell
Cover Photo—Jose Guerra
Editors—Melissa Forbes, Candace K. Cottrell, Stacey Seay

Q-BORO BOOKS
Jamaica, Queens NY 11434
WWW.QBOROBOOKS.COM

DEDICATION

For my daughter Cheyanne. Hoping that you will always have a choice, that you will never know the pain of abuse and the trauma of being victimized. Dreaming for what I visualized since your conception, that you will always be an alpha female; strong, intelligent, and powerful so that you can stand alone in your faith and values, yet gentle and feminine so you can choose when to compromise.

A WORD FROM THE AUTHOR:

First I wanted to thank you all for taking the time to read these words and support my work. I want to take a moment and talk to you about why I chose to write about this topic. As you read, please remember that the women depicted within these pages are symbols of real life, of a system that created the need for the imagination to take authority into its own hands.

I hope we will take the time to look beyond the entertainment and read between the lines for the true reasons why rage and pain would be manifested through the whim of *A Woman's Wrath*. Women have been abused and violated for centuries. Some women, losing self-worth and respect for themselves, become "turned out" sexually and are promiscuous and even express bi-sexuality (though this is not the case all the time). Others become reclusive, hiding away in the shame and taking blame for something that was not their fault.

Being a survivor of such abuse myself, I have experienced being afraid and embarrassed, uncertain of who I am and once faced the confusion as to my body, not wanting to share myself sexually and dealt with major insecurity. I feel this book has forced its way into existence beyond my will. I did not realize I was still dealing with the effects of this experience, and didn't plan on writing about a topic such as this, but once I started, I found I was still very resentful.

You would be surprised how many women and men have told me the stories, many still refusing to talk about it publicly because they are still afraid.

Even more recently in our world, we see headlines that crush us with the reality of this type of victimization:

"Pedophiles Prey on Tsunami Orphans: Boy missing? Predators threat to orphans by Cindy Wockner and Jamie Walker 06 Jan 05.

http://www.nbc5.com/news/4045556/detail.html??z=dp&dpswid=1167317&dppid+65193

Rape and incest have become so common that it seems we are desensitized to the true horror of it. That's why stories like this can be in the news and no one is shocked or appalled or even talk about it anymore:

THE NEW WORLD DISORDER U.N. accused of rape, pedophilia, and prostitution. Civilians, staff in Congo under internal investigation.

http://www.worldnetdaily.com/news/article.asp?ARTICLE_ID=41627

It seems no one pays attention to the dramatic and traumatizing affects of rape, abuse, and incest until a disaster strikes, and sometimes not even then. The big question would be why? Problem is, much like you, I don't know. I am only another victim, an author, someone who knows that pain intimately and would like it to all to STOP.

In writing *A Woman's Wrath*, I wanted it to have some tangible information, something to let you know that you are not alone and that there is help out there. There is a glossary of terms, links, and definitions as well as names and phone numbers of places who specialize in helping victims of rape crimes and domestic abuse. Hopefully this information will help to lead you in the right direction to understanding the pain and shame manifested through different individuals.

I hope *A Woman's Wrath* will entertain you. I found it therapeutic in the ways that predators are repaid for their injustices. So instead of us all going out and becoming vigilantes *(which is wrong and there is no logical justification for such behavior)*, I hope that women and men everywhere who share this tragic experience will delve into this book and enjoy vicariously the demise of the evil that have so drastically affected our lives, our children's lives, and the lives of our loved ones.

PROLOGUE

Hate planted the seed

She stared at the blood, body fragments, and urine that surrounded her. Her hands were shaking uncontrollably while still holding the murder weapon. "Oh God, oh God," she whimpered to herself, still sitting on the hardwood floor where she fell in that final moment. Tears blurred her vision as she moved back against the wall. "I am so sorry," she said to no one in particular. "It was self defense," she told herself adamantly as she replayed the scene before her, the scene that forced her to now sit where she was, the visuals tormenting her as she shook on the floor, pressed up against the wall.

"Don't touch my child, you bastard," Carissa screamed fervently, pleading for her husband not to rape their eight-year-old. Carissa pulled at his pants' leg, trying to hold him back, but the pants were already coming down his hips and over his thighs to release the poisonous predator that would violate the innocence of her daughter Serena. The little girl cowered and looked bewilderedly at the only father she had ever known. Serena blinked back the tears that were keeping her voice mute, her frail body petrified from fear.

"Leave her alone, please," Carissa begged. But her words fell on deaf ears. With renewed vigor she screamed, "Let her be, you son-of-a bitch!" Carissa demanded, but he just swatted at her hands like they were more of an annoyance than a hindrance. He missed her hands and caught her in her face, causing a steady stream of blood to flow from her nose and down into her mouth.

"Bit—ch, you will get some of big daddy next," he slurred drunkenly, mocking her openly, his words dripping with sarcasm. He chuckled at his attempt at humor and was sure Carissa would give up, but the fear in Serena's eyes propelled her mother to keep fighting. Serena backed into the far corner of her small bedroom and shivered with fear. Carissa watched as the floor became laced with a stream of piss that ran from between her frail child's legs.

"It's OK, baby. Mama is not gonna let nothin' happen to you," she promised, knowing in her heart that there might be very little she could do.

When she saw John forcefully spread Serena's legs apart, Carissa began to cry frantically. She held onto his legs, but was not strong enough to stop him. He dragged her body with him and her clothes and skin became baptized in the pee that ran from Serena, and had also soaked John's hands and clothing. Almost blinded by her pain and tears, Carissa could barely look at her daughter. But when she did, she saw something positive in Serena's eyes. There was a silent determination in her gaze.

Tears poured down the child's cheeks, but her gaze was steadfast and unforgiving. She refocused her eyes on her father, willing her mother to continue to fight for her. Carissa wanted to fight, but instead she watched, petrified. She kept her eyes planted on every move her husband made. She watched as he pulled his manhood from his open zipper and pulled Serena toward him. Her heart broke into a million pieces, but she felt weak, frozen where she stood. Finally finding her voice again, she called out.

"Please, please, John, I beg of you. Leave her be." She fell to her knees as if in a prayer, her arms wrapped around his legs and her eyes looking up into the heavens.

"Nawww," he responded nonchalantly. "Let me taste some of this sweet, young thing before she becomes a worthless piece of ass like her mother."

He snickered and tried to kick his foot free of Carissa, but she held on for dear life, hitting and punching him. Unfortunately, her punches were about as effective as the pestering of flies. He kicked her again in her face, this time breaking her nose. She cringed when she heard the cracking of her bones like a loud explosion. The impact caused blood to gush from her nose.

"I can't let you hurt my baby, John. I gave you everything," she cried. Again her words fell on deaf ears.

Suddenly something was awakened inside her—a final reserve of energy from a place deep within the core of her womanhood. She regained her composure and released John's leg. She quietly dragged herself from the room, and once outside, she got up and sprinted to the kitchen. She had killed a man before, a gang member who tried to rape and abuse her in the grim alleyways where she made her home as a homeless girl. She would do it again to save her daughter.

Carissa rummaged though the kitchen drawers and found nothing that could help her. She gathered her wits about her and thought quickly, running though the house like a wild woman. Her thick, curly locks flooded her shoulders and her eyes were crazed. Blood ran down her face and neck as if someone had drenched her in water, causing the fabric of her shirt to cling to her breasts. Suddenly, a feeling of defeat came over her. She had no idea what was going on in Serena's room. All she heard were indiscernible sounds that could only be coming from John.

Then it came to her. John kept a gun inside the sofa, a sawed-off shotgun he kept there for when he pimped his wife and watched. He had taken her through sexually transmitted diseases and other pains, all of which she had endured out of gratitude, but not this. He could not have Serena.

Carissa had done everything she could think of to keep her child when she became pregnant. John said the baby could be his or any one of the men who shared their bed on a daily basis. He wanted her to get rid of the baby, but she begged and pleaded, and he allowed her to keep the child, promising that he would love and nurture it. But now he was Serena's biggest threat.

With all the strength she could muster from her five feet five inch, 110-pound frame, she pushed the sofa until it was lifted to the side. She stuck her hand in the hole in the underside of the sofa and searched frantically for the weapon, gasping with relief when her hand touched it. She wasted no time. She ran back to the girl's room to find John's penis in the mouth of her eight-year-old daughter. Tears streaked Serena's face while John's penis widened her mouth into unaccustomed positions. His hard-on was prominent and threatened to choke Serena as he grabbed the back of her head and rammed his penis into the back of the small child's throat, causing her to gag. Spit dripped from her mouth and her coughs were muffled.

Carissa's heart sank to the pit of her stomach and tears and pain, worse than she felt during childbirth, consumed her. Anger from all the abuse and frustrations she had endured from her childhood to this day surfaced. It seemed that her life was to be repeated in her own daughter's life. Fear gripped her as her own memories threatened to make her weak. Her knees buckled as she stood there, a spectator to what seemed like her own past experiences.

Carissa watched ecstasy appear on John's face and she listened to his moans of pleasure as her baby suffered. With his engorged manhood in Serena's mouth, he released one hand from behind her head and inserted his index finger into the girl's vagina. Serena cringed and her eyes squeezed shut, tears raining down her face.

Carissa refused to allow this man or any other man to mutilate the only family she had, the only true goodness in her life. Having moved more times than she could count to escape the law, she eventually lost touch with any blood relatives and made friends with prostitutes, runaways, jailbirds, and thieves. It seemed her entire life had become a ritual of running, trying to escape something. At the tender age of sixteen, she met this man who promised to protect her and take care of her. He was her savior, and he delivered her out of the darkness of teen prostitution and setting rattraps for food. John was her everything, and there he was, taking everything from her.

He was jabbing his finger in and out of Serena's vagina so hard that blood began to run down her legs, staining her already urine-soaked dress. Yet Serena's eyes never showed submission. They only beckoned to her mother, as they filled with a pain and shame no child should know. At that moment, Carissa decided she would die before allowing John to do to Serena, what her father and so many other men had done to her: steal her pride and womanhood, leaving her no choice but to live with abuse, sell her body, and then do it all over again to please her own husband.

The sounds, the thoughts, her reasoning all came down to this moment. She became enraged as she found the strength to lift the gun from where it originally hung at her side so it was in full view.

"I won't let you do this, John," she admonished. But he only saw her weak, pathetic stance as a joke and laughed, a moan getting caught in his throat as his body jerked, an orgasm emerging.

"I am so sorry, baby." She spoke now to Serena, and then quickly pulled the trigger. She didn't know much about guns or how many bullets were in the one she held. She only knew it was a gun, and it had bullets. The impact of the gun was a shock. Her eyes widened in dumbfounded panic as the gun spewed and sprayed at the target who raped her daughter. The pellets ripped at John's body and she watched as Serena fell, blood splattering all over her face. John's six foot six inch frame fell with a heavy thud to the floor, barely missing the small child's body. His two hundred-fifty pounds of flesh echoed throughout the house. There was disbelief in his eyes as he reached for Carissa, but she held her stance, stood far away from him, and watched as he labored to breathe.

The girl was blown to the ground from the impact of John's falling body. Carissa was glued to the floor. She couldn't move closer in fear of what she would find. She called to Serena from where she stood when she fired that deadly shot.

"Baby, please say something to Mommy," she begged, but the girl had lost consciousness. White, orgasmic fluids stained her face, causing a red and white collage when mixed with the blood. The odor of bodily fluids mingling with gunpowder nauseated Carissa, and she fell to the ground.

Everything had come down to this moment, and the daughter she tried to save had died at her own hands. Everything she thought she was escaping, surviving, trying to give to her daughter, had ended by her deed. Her Serena, whom she swore to protect, was gone. She had failed again. Carissa sat there mumbling to herself, her tears falling like the flowing stream of a powerful waterfall. Taking one final look about her, she knew what she had to do. She raised the gun to her temple, and with her final breath she spoke to her child.

"I am sorry, baby. Mommy failed you." And she pulled the trigger for the last time.

THE AFTERMATH

It was about a week before the neighbors noticed the foul smell of decay in their neighborhood. No one saw anyone coming or going out of the normally busy semimansion property. The young girl who was taken to the bus every day at seven AM by her mother was not seen either. The lack of activity was highly suspicious.

The neighbors, who were always complaining about the music and activity in the detached house that sat on one and a half acres of land, became restless and concerned. Everyone feared "Big John," as he was called. He would threaten whoever would call the police or complain about the endless parties that blazed from the house on a nightly basis. Some feared for the young girl who always seemed so filled with life, but who was kept locked up and not allowed to play outside of school time.

"We all cannot just sit around and say nothing," one neighbor said. He wore a mustache that made him look like a character out of Charles Dickens's *The Pickwick Papers*. "I can understand him being upset about us reporting him about his business or whatever he has going on in that house, but a child is involved, and there is no one around."

"He has most of the cops on his payroll anyway. He ain't gonna get but a slap on the wrist for our benefit and we gone be left with hell to pay," another neighbor who always wanted to be in everyone's business, but pretended he didn't care, said.

"I think you're right," the big lady who weighed more than three hundred pounds chimed in. "But we haven't seen Big John or the little wifey in days. Is it just me, or is everyone here just plain chicken? Either we are going to do something or we're not." She flung her hands on her hips and stared at the growing audience. "So what we gonna do?" she huffed.

"I don't care what you people say, something is going on in that house," the fat lady's nineteen-year-old son volunteered. "I say we break in and check it out."

"Hush your mouth, boy. You don't have any sense," his mother admonished and swung her arms at him playfully.

"I agree with her, so we need a game plan. What are we going to do?" the first man with the moustache asked. "Should we go check it out for ourselves or should we call the cops?"

By now a small crowd had gathered in the upper middle-class neighborhood. Everyone was interested in what they would find, not to mention they had never seen the inside of the most prominent house on the block. Anxiety built inside of them, the desire to probe and pry taking root. Eventually, curiosity made the decision. There were whispers and hushed chatter among the neighbors, all speculating on what was happening. The blazing sun, mixed with the humidity during July in Florida, caused perspiration to form on their brows, and sweat to run from arms and faces.

"Know what? Enough is enough," one neighbor commented. "We cannot just sit around wondering what is going on. This is our neighborhood. We raise our children here. If Big John has a problem with the police coming to his house, then maybe it's time for him to clean up his damn house and leave."

"Amen," the crowd agreed.

"I say we go in." The scrawny, white lady from across the street motioned toward the home. Everyone turned to look at her in shock because she was the type who was blind, deaf, and dumb. She never wanted to get involved. She would see someone being beaten to death and she would say she didn't see anything, go in her house, lock the doors, and turn up the radio. "What, cat catch y'all's tongue? I say let's call the goddamn police. There's that pretty, half-white baby ova there that needs help. I love that pretty lil' half nigga," she said before she realized the majority of the people in the group were black.

Her eyes flew open and she slammed her hands over her mouth. The racism spewing off of her tongue and the hatred in her attitude betrayed her. Anger flared in the crowd.

"You ol' bitch," the big, fat lady from down the street yelled. "Who you calling nigga?" Everyone turned to look at the old lady.

"Whoa, hold up. She is not our concern right now. Like it or not, she is right," the young, mulatto teacher who took pride and joy in little Serena's brilliance said. She didn't want any more trouble than they were already going to be in, going into the home of a suspected KKK man. She focused her attention instead, on Serena. She taught Serena's first grade class, and she too was concerned for the little girl. The little girl reminded her of herself.

"The teacher is right, man," the fat lady's son agreed. "We can't pay attention to this little ol' biddy right now. We have to help the little girl." Everyone murmured their agreement.

"OK, I will call the police," the man with the moustache decided. "Some of you grab a bat or a stick or something. We're going in."

"YEAH!" the crowd joined in excitedly, as everyone scrambled to find something to protect themselves with just in case Big John was not in the mood and decided to use the rifle he usually displayed.

It seemed as though even the trees swayed menacingly, leery of the dread that the neighbors were about to face. The sun seemed overcast in the hot, noonday weather. People pulled at their clothes, which were clinging to their sweat-drenched bodies.

The crowd marched two houses down to where the Kowtow family resided.

"Are you sure you called the cops, man?" the young teacher's husband asked. "I don't want this knucklehead John to pick anything with me because I might have to flatten his ass," he informed the crowd, causing a slight chuckle to erupt.

"Don't worry, I explained what was going on and they said they were on the way," the farmer who lived right next door to the family assured. He was usually privy to a lot of the beatings and heard all the bawling from Carissa. He tried to mind his own business, but he feared the worst. He and his wife sat close with their ear to the wall for fear of getting too close to big John's estate, but even the acre and a half property couldn't disguise the abuse that Carissa sustained; it wasn't even two weeks before when they heard her yelling and screaming for her life. Yet, no one did anything to help. The house had been dead quiet since then.

They pushed the gates open and crept as quietly as they could, up the steps to the large, wooden door with the skull doorknocker facing them as if to say, beware. They touched the door tentatively and it eerily swung open. The stench inside immediately violated their senses and everyone pinched their noses to stop the invasion, but they couldn't. They nervously walked into the house, which was buzzing with flies. The mulatto first grade teacher flinched and screamed when flies, angered at the intrusion, swarmed around her. She started jumping around frantically while her husband and others swatted at the bugs.

"This is just plain-ass nasty," the three hundred-pound lady said. She was a cook and was known for her cleanliness and immaculate kitchen. The others nodded at her comment, not wanting to say anything or remove their fingers from vigorously pinching their noses.

"Oh my gosh! What the devil is that?" one lady whom they hadn't noticed before asked. They all walked closer. It appeared to be a cat that was obviously starving to death. The cat looked scrawny, malnutritioned, and was licking away at a sore that was infested with maggots. Seeing the skeleton of the animal clearly imprinted in what used to be its skin sent shivers down their spines. The animal was on the verge of death. The smell only got worse as they approached the stairs that led to the second floor.

The old, white lady from across the street started to cry.

"That poor chile. Oh, Lord, that poor nig . . ." Everyone turned to look at her and she stopped in mid-sentence and blew her nose. Her face became distorted and contorted from the stench and she quickly replaced her fingers to close her nose and hold her breath.

"Let's just hurry up and get this over with," the man with the moustache said. "I don't think we're going to like what's upstairs, but we came this far, so let's just go."

He led the way up the spiral staircase of a home that was obviously a beautiful showcase. They all felt a little envy toward the Kowtow family. To them it seemed like Carissa and Serena had everything. Big John was well-to-do and the kind of white man they all respected more out of fear than anything else. It was suspected that he was a Klan member, and everyone was shocked when he brought Carissa, who was rich mahogany brown in complexion, to his home. She was well-built and voluptuous with perky, full breasts and wide, curvy hips. She was only a teenager when John brought her into his home and claimed her as his wife. Though there was talk in the town and gossip about what Big John really wanted with Carissa, nobody dared say anything. And so it went for all those years until this day that brought them sneaking through Big John's home, following an odor.

The first person to notice Carissa's body was the three-hundred-pound cook, who gasped and fainted. Everyone moved out of the way so she could fall, except for her teenage son. He tried to catch her, but was careful not to get caught under his mother's weight. There were some snickers and laughter before the rest of the group realized what caused the woman to faint, and for a brief moment, the group was distracted from the foul odor. When their attention was turned back to the reason why the cook fell, everyone was shocked. Carissa was barely recognizable. Half of her brain was filled with maggots and flies. Worms seem to have nestled themselves against all the walls, the floor, and the furniture. Flies buzzed happily around the room. Everyone tiptoed as if the dead could hear them and peaked around the corner into Serena's bedroom. The first grade teacher started to cry.

There they were—Big John and Serena lying on the floor. John and Carissa appeared to be dead, but not Serena. The little girl sat morbidly in deathly silence with her knees pulled into her chin and her arms wrapped about them in desperation. There was feces and piss everywhere. Roaches and flies seemed to have found a feast that helped them procreate and bring about second, third, and fourth generations of their kinds.

Nobody wanted to go farther. No one wanted to move except to turn and run. The nineteen-year-old started to heave and vomited all over his mother, who was still passed out on the floor. The guy with the mustache covered his mouth to try and prevent himself from regurgitating his last meal. No one noticed when the little racist ol' lady left, and the farmer and his wife just held each other in fear. Just then, they heard a slew of sirens. They heard when the squad busted into the house and rummaged through. They heard the footsteps and the voice of one commanding officer yelling, "MOVE."

By now, the fat lady had come to, and her son was apologizing profusely for vomiting on her. The crowd parted to allow the police through to the scene. Immediately, the paramedics ran to the little girl, who said nothing. Her eyes looked wild and bewildered, and she made no move. She seemed to be dead, sitting without blinking her eyes. They checked her heartbeat, which was faint and fading. She was half-starved and had begun to look malnourished, having only barely survived due to the dead rodents, feces, and maggots she ingested when hunger overtook her small body.

"What they lookin' fo', Mama? Ain't it obvious that they dead?" the teenaged boy whispered to his mother. But no one answered him, spellbound by the gruesome scene surrounding them. The child, after a quick examination, was rushed to the nearest hospital, because the minute she realized there were other live bodies and that she was no longer alone, she passed out from shock. She was starving to death and had been hit in her shoulders by the bullets. Her hip was scraped, and her thigh and side had bled from the spraying of pellets from the shotgun her mother fired at John in order to defend her. At the hospital, they could not get her to wake up, and she seemed to have fallen into a coma. She had become so skinny that her body seemed like just the skeleton of an eight-year-old. They feared she would not survive.

1

"Let me go, please," the woman whimpered, begging the man she was so attracted to only hours before not to violate her. Her pleas fell on deaf ears. His hands reached up and powerfully landed on her, eliciting a scream so eerie that Serena's heart fell to her feet.

"Noooo!" The screams came from the dark, secluded streets of downtown Miami and startled her. She knew what she had to do, but she wasn't prepared for the heart-thumping, blood-flowing anxiety that would rush through her body.

"Bitch." The verbal assault moved her to act. She knew she had to move fast. It had to be quick and deliberate. In downtown Miami, with the fast nightlife and excited tourists, no one would look twice at a woman being manhandled by her man. Serena cringed at the thought of what was happening to the woman. This was her first night out and she had been counseled about this many times, but she couldn't help the feeling of nausea that built in her chest, and the feeling of disgust that boiled in her belly. She was afraid, but she had to go through with it, so she walked up the alley and moved with the determination and focus of a lioness to her prey.

"Well, hi there. Looks like I'm interrupting something," she cooed with sultry eroticism that made the tall, gorgeous, Latino man pay attention. He restrained the woman's hands behind her head on the cold, concrete pavement as he rammed himself in and out of her mutilated flesh, her whimpers causing Serena's blood to boil. She was afraid for the woman, but one wrong move could cause the predator to hurt her or the woman, so she proceeded with caution.

"What the fuck do you want?" he asked her, the venom and anger that raged inside of him spilling out in his words.

He removed his throbbing hardness; it had also been unnerved by the sudden presence of their intruder, so he tried to pull himself together. As Serena walked closer and approached the violent scene he had created, she could see that blood slowly ran down the woman's thighs. He was disarmed momentarily, but he was a red-blooded Latino man, and he couldn't deny what was in front of him. He was almost hypnotized as Serena swayed closer to him, and something in him was revived. Her alluring eyes and sensual vibe made him aware of another feeling. He was aroused, and it was obvious as his manhood rose once again, this time to show Serena appreciation.

"You see, that's just it."

"What do you mean, 'that's just it'?" he yelled, annoyed that his voice came out as a squeak instead of the manly growl that he wanted to come rushing out at the beautiful woman who was aware that she had evoked something in him other than anger.

"Well, you see, baby, you told me to get the fuck out of here, and I am telling you that I will, as long as I get to get out of here, and fuck you." She smiled. He was shocked, disarmed, and taken aback. He looked twice at this tall, slender, caramel beauty who was stacked in all the right

places. She had a body that only the gods could have created. Her bosom rose and fell with each breath she took,
and her breasts seemed to scream at him as they attempted
to bust free from her bustier.

She watched as the man dropped the arm of the small,
frail woman. The woman immediately scurried to the corner of the pot-holed street in an attempt not to be noticed
by him. Her eyes were black and blue and her clothes were
ripped. She tried fruitlessly to hide the bleeding that was
staining her legs and clothes. Serena kept an eye on the
woman while she also watched the corrupted suitor. She
saw the woman quickly pulling up her panties. *Maybe she's
a prostitute*, Serena thought, but that did not justify any
man hitting or taking a woman's body against her will. A
woman could do and wear whatever she wanted without
warranting any violent acts.

Serena boldly walked to him, fueled by the hatred and
anger she knew would be quenched once she had him
where she wanted him. She was no longer afraid; the natural insecurities and fretfulness that follow one during the
first time of anything released their grip on her. For now,
the venom she felt had become her companion on this
quest.

Before he was fully aware of what was happening, Serena's tongue was in his throat and she feverishly tried to
tell him with her mouth and body what she couldn't find
the words to say. She wrapped her body into his with the
passion of a lover, hungering with desire.

"Let's go," she said with enough yearning that he could
only follow her lead. The lady who was victimized by his
charm and charisma only moments earlier, stared on in
shock. She had known the gorgeous Casanova for a month.
Watching him daily at the office could not have prepared
her for this brutal attack. He had courted her and wooed
her for two weeks before she agreed to go out with him on

this night. The violence in his temper brought out the Mr. Hyde in him. Yet she stared on, traumatized as the couple got into the uniquely shaped, customized Lamborghini that waited at the side of the road, until they vanished.

He looked around inside the car sheepishly before getting into the vehicle. He was in awe of the lavish roominess inside. It seemed to be a one of a kind vehicle, and he couldn't remember ever seeing anything like it before.

"Wow," he exclaimed as he climbed and started to get comfortable. Serena sat beside him nervously fiddling with her fingers, unsure of what to do next, but a hard glare from the driver told her she needed to follow the plan. She reached over the man and began kissing him fervently. "You are my type of woman. You know exactly what you want," he mumbled through their fervent kisses. Serena moaned, pulled her skirt up to her waist, and slipped her leg over his thigh, straddling him.

"Yes, daddy, I am any woman you want." The man was so into the moment that he didn't hear the pain in her voice. She wished the night would end, but she knew there was no turning back. Suddenly, her curly, red, dangling locks were yanked, inducing a surprised shriek from her lips. The sound of pain sent his manhood on overload and he wanted to ram himself inside her. She grabbed his crotch and massaged the tip of his erect penis. The whimpers that were released from his lips didn't sound like the animal he was. Regret stabbed at her as she realized what they were about to do.

"You want me to fuck you, right? That's what you said back there, chica," he reminded her, ready to collect on the goods, pushing his finger through her lacy, crotch-less underwear to find the entryway to her warm haven. She squirmed and rode his finger until he felt as though his dick would burst right through his pants.

"Yes, I want to fuck your brains out, daddy, but not here,"

she said, looking up to the front seat to see the back of the head of the female driver. The driver was maneuvering the car through I-95 from downtown Miami and onto Dixie State Highway 1, which led to the ritzy neighborhood of Coral Gables.

"We have company, and I don't want any witnesses to the deadly, erotic, naughty things I am about to do to you," Serena explained. She panted, losing herself in the sexual abyss that she had worked herself into; shame gripped her for enjoying any moment of it at all. She could tell he was very well endowed and the thought of him forcing himself into an unsuspecting female made her even more angry. She closed her eyes and focused on the matter at hand.

"Fuck that bitch," he panted. "I don't give a shit who sees. Matter of fact, the more the merrier." He snickered, and a horrible flashback bombarded her senses. She shook her head in disgust. She wanted to jump off his crotch and snap his neck on the spot, but she restrained herself. She knew she had to follow the process. She would enjoy it so much more if she could see him suffer like the rabid dog he was.

"Yes, I would like that, too, but she will join us when we get to our destination. You can have as many of us as you would like." She moaned in his ear, taking her tongue and flicking it across his temple, sticking the tip of her heated oral member into his ear.

"I like that. I got lucky with you bitches tonight, huh?" he panted in pure animalistic amazement. Removing his hands from between her thighs, she held them behind his back and stuck her tongue down his throat. She pulled on his tongue and lips with heated passion and reached for the metal rings that sat inconspicuously on the backseat next to him. He became suspicious and struggled for her to release his hands, but before he could do anything else, he was handcuffed.

"What the fuck is this?" he demanded, realizing he had been tricked. The cold iron restraints now imprisoned his hands and kept him from exploring her curvaceous hips and passion hole.

"Easy, daddy. You are going to like this." She consoled him, stroking his ego and the tip of his shaft simultaneously. She stuck her tongue in his mouth again and ripped the buttons from his shirt so she could toy with his nipples. He groaned softly, building momentum as she lowered her mouth to his love stick. What she wanted to do with him was far from making love. Serena wanted him to sample the black widow's ambrosia in the most horrific sense of the word, and she smiled when she thought of Elizabeth's gifts and the black widow spider's mark, which enhanced Elizabeth's dangerous characteristics. She would make him pay.

"Oh, you feel so good," Serena muttered as her tongue tantalized his shaft and her fingers pulled his zipper open. With his hands handcuffed, there wasn't much he could do but surrender to the will of her expert demands.

Moving her heated mouth over his cock, his hips shifted and angled his swollen member to explore her oral orifice. She allowed him to plunge deep into her throat until he could almost feel her tonsils, and to his surprise, she didn't gag. She took it as if her mouth was her pussy. He couldn't help the shattering thrill that ran through him, and he trembled. She flattened her tongue and allowed it to attack his senses by massaging the sides of his shaft.

"Holy shit," he grunted. "Holy shit," was all he could say as she swayed her body and moved her ass, squeezing her thighs as the overwhelming urge to mount him consumed her.

"How much time, Cath?" Serena asked the driver.

"We are on Sunset Drive, love. Two minutes. Just hold down the fort." Moving swiftly, Serena pulled a silk scarf from her cleavage and tied it over his face. She could feel the car pause briefly, waiting for the gates to open. The car doors opened and they swiftly got out and moved inside the house. Jason, the manservant, wasted no time. He had everything they needed laid out in the underground lair, and he watched as this victim enjoyed his last taste of pussy euphoria.

"This is it, daddy. You ready to experience the time of your life?" the voice cooed in his ear. The sensuality and excitement that oozed from her caused his manhood to rise again. He was rock hard, scared, enthused, and impatient. He couldn't tell who had spoken to him since he could hear hushed whispers all around him.

"Hell, yeah. I am going to give it to you good, bitch. Real good," he stammered in an attempt to sound macho and in control. But he was slowly becoming aware that he had no control. He felt hands all over him, pulling his pants down around his ankles and cutting his shirt away without the removal of his handcuffed hands from behind his back. Suddenly there were mouths all over him—sucking and licking everywhere—and hands fondled and massaged every part of his body.

"Hey, what the . . ." he started to say when he felt the clear, cool liquid squirt over his backside, and the soft, delicate hands that began to knead it into the crack of his ass. He felt the sensual woman press against his back, and felt the hair on her mound as she pressed into him made him sigh. Cathalina, the driver from earlier, gyrated against his backside and massaged his spine as she prepared him for a very special treat. The heated lips that devoured his cock and slobbered on his balls pushed him into a sensual overload. His senses tried to decipher what was going on, who was in front of him, and who was behind, but soon these thoughts drifted from his mind. His body and the desire for passion took over, and he yielded to himself.

It was at that moment that he felt smooth fingers slip into his anus, and this time, he didn't object. He leaned his body over, and strong, delicate hands pressed his head toward his knees, assisting him. He groaned, and the sighs and whispers of female voices heightened his arousal. He could feel breasts on him, and smell the sweetness of excited, womanly aromas.

"Oh, put it on me. Give it to me," he begged. "Oh God, how many of you are there?"

The hands that finger-popped his anus and rubbed down the crack of his posterior began to spread his cheeks apart, squirting oil to make sure it was fully lubricated for entrance. Before he realized what was happening, he felt himself being mounted from behind. Soft, feminine fingers kept his butt cheeks wide apart, but it was a very masculine dick that was piercing him from behind, sliding in and out of his anus. He was in such shock that he couldn't even breathe. His head was being forced into his knees from the butt-thrusting pressure behind him, and he squeezed his eyes shut to resist the tears from building in his eyes. Pain saturated his body, from his hips to his head, and his head seemed to explode into excruciating pain. He wanted to moan and scream out, but his pride wouldn't let him.

Soon the slipping in and out sounds from his now lubricated anus and Elizabeth's dick making contact with his ass began to feel good. Fear took hold of him and she bit his tongue to prevent him from making sounds of pleasure. She pulled out and slapped him playfully.

"That's it, baby," Elizabeth coached. "You took it like the bitch you really are," she shot at him, using her words and the slaughtering of his body to show him the deep dislike she felt for him. "You like that, don't you?" she teased, but he only responded with disgruntled and painful grunts.

"You fucking bitches are crazy. I didn't agree to this. Let me go."

The laughter that echoed around the room startled him. It sounded like hundreds of women, but he knew there couldn't be more than four of them. Even the cynical laughter excited him, but his fear began to climb.

Before he could get another word or insult in, he felt his legs being pulled wide apart again with steady hands and a penis that felt twelve inches long, and at least two-and-half-inches wide, being rammed into his asshole with such force that his screech was like that of a banshee, and the ripping of his flesh caused blood to gush from ruptured blood vessels and run down his legs.

"Is that what you wanted, you little man slut?" Elizabeth hissed. "I was trying to be nice, but since you can take it like a man and talk shit, I am going to give it to you like a man." The pleasure they vowed to give their victims before death would now be denied him, and he would just feel a bitch do her thing as her soft and delicate hands became as strong as lions' paws, pulling him from all angles.

"You didn't ask for this?" a soft, low voice whispered in his ear. Tears that he could no longer restrain streamed down his face. For the moment, he was paralyzed by the surprise that entered him and the hands that held him in place. One woman was practically sitting on his neck to keep him folded in half, and his legs were held tightly by female hands he couldn't believe possessed such strength.

"Did she ask for what you did back there in the streets?"

"Oh God, no, please help me. This is crazy," he whimpered.

"Crazy?" the voice spat at him again, and the laughter resumed.

"I wasn't doing this to her. I didn't do anything," he pleaded, still trying to hold on as he felt the throbbing of a penis four times the size of his stroke him deep and hard, surrendering nothing, and showing no mercy. He tried to talk a few times, but his voice caught in his throat. He couldn't believe he was getting aroused.

"Fucker, what do you mean you didn't do this? Didn't you just rape a lady only moments before we picked you up?" But he only snickered a weird type of laugh no one could understand.

He could feel the momentum build and the thrusts got deeper, stronger. He was on the verge of a feeling he had always enjoyed, the mounting pleasure.

"You are turning me into a faggot? Is that it?" he had the nerve to ask, but this time he felt a lash, a stick so deep and quick he jolted and tried to throw the women from him, but he couldn't move. He knew they drew blood because he felt the slow trickle of a wet droplet slide down his spine.

"Oh, yeah . . . this ass is good. Fuck," he heard the voice behind him shout. And as she exploded inside him, they removed the blindfold so he could see what it felt like to be fucked without one's permission.

"So this is what a chick with a dick looks like." He laughed sarcastically in an attempt to muster some pride and maintain his manhood.

"How about this is what a chick with a dick tastes like?" she asked as he was released to stand upright enough so that his face was in her crotch, and she stuck her limp penis in his mouth. "Bite me, motherfucker, and you are gonna wish you were dead," she warned.

His eyes flashed around the room quickly and saw he was outnumbered. One lady, as beautiful as he could imagine stood in the corner of what seemed like the belly of hell. She was dressed in nothing but a gun sling and had two guns straddling her hips. Hanging from what looked like a bee's nest, one woman hung from roped chains. Even the woman before him—woman, man, he didn't know what to call her—was a cool cinnamon complexion with flawless skin. Her lustrous, long, straight black hair hung to her shoulders, and her eyes glowed red. Were those real or contacts? He didn't care. He wanted out.

"OK, so you had your fun. Let me go." He slurped and spoke in barely audible words.

"What did he say?" Cathalina smirked.

"The fun is just getting started," the man/woman replied. He watched the luscious lips of the girl who had just fucked him like he was a piece of pussy as she pulled her dick from his mouth and walk away. Suddenly, he felt crawling all over him. *Spiders?* he wondered. But that question was soon answered.

Running wild all over him were three of the most deadly spiders known to humans—a black widow, a brown recluse spider, and the Brazilian wandering spider. He simply stood there because after being bitten by the deadly Brazilian wandering spider, he was rendered paralyzed.

Cathalina and Elizabeth moved away from him and left him in a circled area.. His eyes widened with fear as a glass cage quickly lowered over him. He was locked in with the spiders, handcuffed and helpless, blood dripping from his ass, and the laughter of the women mocking him. This was some shit. He was bitten so many times that he collapsed to the floor, his body becoming a cobwebbed mass as the spiders fought each other for territory. As he slumped over within his cage and his eyes rolled to the back of his head, he heard them walk away.

"You did good, Serena. Next time, though, you get to fuck him," Cathalina said.

2

"Your honor, your honor." The bailiff knocked persistently on her door. "The lawyers are ready for you to hear their petitions." The bailiff spoke as loudly as he could within the walls of a judge's chamber. The presiding judge was lost in thought. She couldn't stop the violent headaches and anger she felt every time a case such as this came before her. She looked at the case in front of her again and shook her head. It never ceased to amaze her—the women, their fear, how reluctant they were to testify against their predators, their abusers. In this case, a woman had to die in order to get justice.

She slammed the folder shut and pulled herself together. She picked up her robe and stared at it momentarily. All this time, all her hard work to try to make a difference, it all just seemed to have been a waste of time. All the late nights studying to be at the top of her class as a black woman rising through the ranks, and then being appointed to the seat of a Florida State Judge hadn't made a difference. All the obstacles she had to overcome, and here she was again, feeling helpless.

She chuckled lightly as she thought of her predecessors,

her heroes. All those who came before her, Thurgood Marshall, the first African-American to be appointed to a Supreme Court seat, and Charles Hamilton Houston, the first black lawyer to win a case before the Supreme Court. They had accomplished so much good, even in a time when things were so much worse for blacks, first because of slavery and then segregation. History inspired her, her own pain and the pain of others inspired her to succeed, yet she felt her personal passion to help and fix the dire situations in society was worthless. She felt helpless. In spite of having been appointed as a judge at only twenty-seven years of age, the work began to weigh on her and she felt twenty years her senior.

She wished she didn't feel like her hands were bound by the law, and as though her seat was worth nothing at all. Her anger flared as she carefully pulled the robe around her, transforming herself and restoring the false ideals and image that the black cloth carried. The weight of it hung heavily on her shoulders, and she felt it had become more of a burden than a blessing.

She spun with the graceful stride of a runway model, collecting her full, auburn, curly locks from her shoulders and placing them in a bun. She thought of how all the attorneys drooled in her presence. She would be celebrating her thirty-second birthday this year, but she still felt empty, alone, and unsatisfied with her accomplishments. The powerlessness she felt began to consume her. She had begun to despise the honor that had been bestowed on her.

She snapped her hair into place, collected the folder containing the case she must now rule on, and walked out the door. She stood behind a screen, patiently waiting for the bailiff to do his job of introducing her.

"The Honorable Judge Serena Kowtow presiding," the bailiff announced proudly, and as she glided to her bench, her beauty radiated from the sternness of her face and her rigid, locked cheekbones. Her complexion was smooth and flawless, and somehow the lack of a smile made her even more stunning. The bailiff was only one of her many admirers. She sat slowly, and her hazel eyes glowed with the angry fire she struggled to contain.

"We have the same paperwork, I presume?" she asked almost rhetorically, and both the prosecuting and defending attorneys nodded their heads in reverence.

"Good!" Judge Kowtow exclaimed. "Let's start with the defending attorney," she instructed firmly, "then I will hear the prosecutor. Be quick and precise about it, gentlemen," she demanded, looking from one man to the other, her eyes resting on them and firmly holding them in a dare. Both attorneys couldn't quite describe the chill that went through them, nor the immediate stirrings in their loins for this dangerous looking beauty before them.

Serena zoned out like she normally did during cases like these. She could imagine the slime bag who raped and murdered his wife, his attorney now before her claiming that he was reformed and a new man, and had just been temporarily insane when he committed his crimes. The respondent's attorney then explained how the victim had left behind kids and a family who mourned her.

"This is a waste of my time and taxpayers' time," she mumbled quietly under her breath. This was the part that really disgusted her. Sitting there in a place where she should be able to help, a place that should give her the power to wipe away the heart-wrenching pain she felt as the respondent told how a husband had raped his children and allowed them to watch as he murdered their mother in cold blood with his bare hands. The murderer and rapist was previously convicted and he was now fighting his conviction in an appeal.

She struggled with the tears that threatened to saturate her face and wondered how the case had gotten this far.

But there had not been enough evidence to convict the bastard, so she knew she would have to let him go. She forced back her own tears and replaced them with a stoic expression.

Serena's day wore on until it was time for her to drive to her home in Coral Gables, one of the most historic and beautiful districts in Miami, Florida. She relished the big, spacious homes in the area and the way the streets were marked with rocks on the ground that looked like carved gold. One could get lost in the sheer beauty of the quiet streets filled with beautiful homes and lush landscaping.

The giant oak and weeping willow trees grew tall and majestic for hundreds of years, rising high into the sky from each side of the street like a fence, and then touching in the center to create the illusion of a bridge. She let the convertible top of her Porsche midsize SUV collapse into its secret place as she sped home. The one of a kind sports car was made especially for her, to her specifications. It allowed the sun to sprinkle light onto her skin and radiate through her curly, auburn hair that was now free and flowing from her shoulders. Her dark, Calvin Klein sunglasses blocked the anger in her eyes, and the ruby rouge she wore on her lips gave her the impression of a seductress.

Her mind raced a thousand miles per minute when she thought about her hatred for men and the system. They were both demanding and confining. She was almost at the brink of losing it when her cell phone rang like clockwork.

"Yes," she greeted.

"Looks like I called right on time. It sounds as though you were going into one of your rage sessions." It was her therapist and friend, Cathalina. She had noticed a pattern of anger developing in Serena over the past year. Her journey was one of contempt, and during sessions she would go into tirades on how she could truly help the helpless.

"No, I am fine, Cathalina dear. You underestimate the

power of self-control and an active imagination," Serena retorted amicably.

"I don't believe you, Serena. You say the same thing every
time, yet there is no smile in your eyes and no glee in your
voice."

"How do you know this? You are simply on the phone."

"I don't need to see you to know that you are not smiling. And I know this, because I know you. You are my
friend, and I love you," Cathalina said, calming her friend
with her soothing voice and passive approach. Serena was
like that shy plant they have in the islands. Beautiful and
dangerous, but if you reach out to touch it, it becomes shy,
closes its petals, and shrinks away until danger has passed,
then it reopens.

"OK, Cath. How about you tell me about your day?" Serena asked, changing the subject.

"Well, I am sure it was not as exciting as yours. I had a
couple of female patients today who are deeply disturbed."
She hesitated and waited for Serena's response. But she
said nothing. Serena listened for what she knew would
come, the truth that a man had brutally raped or abused
these women, and that their mental health problems began
in their youth as a result of an abusive parent. This was routine for her. She had done enough studying of cases and
overseen a few of her own to know the rhetoric.

"But you know the story, hun. It's always one thing or another," Cathalina told her without getting into details. She
too knew and was aware that Serena understood what had
not been said.

"So, who are they?" Serena asked as she pulled into her
driveway, which was almost a quarter mile from her home.
She stopped in front of the driveway and pressed the
buzzer on the visor of her car. The wrought iron gates re-
tracted into the walls quickly, to allow for entry. As the gates

closed behind her, Serena removed her sunglasses and placed them on the dashboard. The sunglass case was embedded there and opened easily for access by the motion detector that only reacted when she put her hand directly above the case.

"Cath, sweetheart, I'm home. Are you stopping by for drinks tonight?"

"Yes, I thought about that. Let me call you. It's still three in the afternoon and I have a few more patients. You seem like you need me, so I will try to rush over." Cathalina smiled and chuckled to herself.

"Do you feel like having some fun tonight?" Cathalina asked after a brief silence. There was mirth in her voice and it danced like a soothing lullaby.

"Whatever you like, Cath. Whatever is on your mind." Serena smiled and hung up the phone. She really liked Cathalina. She was the only person she trusted. Serena grabbed her sweater, which shielded her thin frame from the slight chill of early spring mornings in Florida. It was always warm in Florida, but at five in the morning when she was out and about, the cool, crisp scent from the trees that she loved and the chirping of small birds were not the only things that greeted her. The slight chill in the air was never welcoming.

Serena walked to her door, swaying effortlessly in her mid-thigh, black dress that flattered her curves. The nude stockings she wore extended to her toes and into her imported stiletto heels, making her legs rival those of any runway model.

Serena dropped pieces of her clothes from the moment she entered the door. Her house was immaculately kept. She had a manservant who greeted her with champagne in a crystal glass, crackers, and caviar. By the time he entered from the servants' quarters, which were set up like a home

within her home, she would be completely naked, heading
to her long, ascending staircase that led to her private bedroom.

"Hello, Serena. How was your day today?" he asked in his
sexy, baritone voice, smiling at her seductively.

"Hello, Jason. My day was the same. And yours?"

"My day has just started, Mistress, now that you are home."
He winked at her and she blushed. She loved Jason in a way
she could not describe. He was different to her. "May I help
you with these, Serena?" he asked, looking from the door
where the first article of clothing was, then following the
trail of clothing that preceded her to the staircase. His eyes
landed at her toes, then climbed up her long, curvaceous
legs and landed on her ass. She turned around, exposing
her cleanly shaven mound, and he smiled, revealing deep
dimples that enhanced the dark richness of his mahogany
complexion and exposed beautiful, even teeth that had a
small space in the front. It was as though when he smiled
and revealed that space, he had allowed her into the gate of
his soul.

"I would have nothing less," she responded, giving him
the command to clean up after her. Jason was about six feet
tall, which was about the same height as she was. He was
slender and powerfully packed. His six-pack abs glowed
from the oiling down he did before approaching his mistress, which is the way she liked him. He wore nothing except a loincloth covering the secret to his manhood.

Serena stood there, watching as he bent over to pick up
her garments. He was posing for her, and the daily ritual
was like a dance. He would gyrate his waist in a seductive,
circular motion, and flex his pectoral muscles as well as his
ass cheeks to entice her. Serena became wet with anticipation as he got closer to her. Piece by piece he retrieved her
clothing until he was on the staircase now bowed at her

thigh with his mouth opened like a Pavlov dog, ready to do the licking.

He waited for the signal that she was ready for him, and when the deep sigh came with the throwing back of her head, he launched at her in slow motion, holding her gently and laying her back on the staircase as he licked and caressed her mid-sized, perky breasts with his tongue. She relaxed in his arms and allowed herself to be carried away. He tantalized her areola until she moaned with pleasure. He watched her movements, which were specific instructions for him as to where he was allowed to touch her and when. Serena's hands grabbed at his dreadlocks, which were neatly twisted and hung down the middle of his back. The crimson-colored dye he used to highlight his locks added to the allure of his beauty. Her hands traced his back, feeling the hardness that flexed from desire and passion.

Jason's strong hands led the way down below her breasts and lingered on her torso, gently kissing and moving southward, tonguing her belly button while his right hand requested permission to enter the wetness that screamed for him to plunge something deep within her. They both moaned deeply when his index finger teased her swollen clit.

"I love you, Serena," Jason whispered, staring deep into her eyes to ensure that his sincerity was not missed. His eyes danced with the image of a lovesick child and he looked upon her face passionately, still waiting for the response that never came.

He returned to the task at hand, pressing his body into her as she sighed sweetly, arching her back and writhing her waist to meet the thrusts of his finger as he moved quickly. Moving down the trail that her navel swallowed, and then falling into the triangle of her womanhood, he allowed his tongue to replace his finger in the secret place that released her love juices.

"Ahhhhh, you are wet!" he exclaimed, tossing his head back in pure ecstasy. His hair coming loose, he shook it sensually in an attempt to move his hair from out of his face. But with his face buried in her snatch, his hair indulgingly showered over her torso, teasing her breasts and falling over her thighs with the slightest movements of his head.

"Come on, lover. Eat my pussy, you piece of shit," she yelled. The onset of her verbal assault sent a shiver through him. This was her way, and he knew it, so he moved, allowing his hands to cup the curve of her ass, pulling her cheeks apart and fingering her anus. Then he moved directly between her legs, which were wrapped securely around his neck and threatening to suffocate him. She urged him to plunge his tongue deeper, and her sighs became more fervent.

"Oh Jason. You want this pussy, don't you?" she asked rhetorically, lifting her ass from the stairs and pulling her legs on his neck simultaneously, forcing his head, lips, and tongue to assault the wetness and urgency that was building in her abdomen. Jason used his teeth and took small nips at her outer lips, which had swollen pink. He loved the smell of her when she was on the verge of coming. Nestling his nose into her hairless mound and breathing hard to prevent himself from succumbing the grief of knowing he could never truly have her, never truly satisfy her, he continued with his onslaught.

Her fingernails assaulted his back with crazed scratches that he endured each time they had this intimate interchange. Jason braced himself for the orgasm he knew would come any second, and the pain he would endure for the pleasure he had bestowed upon her.

Serena grabbed his hair and pulled at it as though she were riding a horse, pressing her hips into his face and throwing her head back in anticipation of her volcanic proof of satisfaction.

"Yes, yes, yes!" she sighed softly, prodding him to keep at that single pace. Jason's fingers pushed into her anus as if he was digging for gold, and his tongue did the same to her pussy, licking the crack between the two spots, and from time to time hoisting her ass above his eyes so his tongue could taste the dew and sweat drenched finger that her love hole housed.

"I want it. Now, you bastard. Put it in," she demanded. But he kept licking her. It drove her crazy when he tossed her salad right when she was about to cum, pulling her cheeks apart and causing the chill of the thrill to run through her, from her neck down to her toes, until she was caught in a whirlwind of uncontrollable spasms.

"Now, motherfucking asshole. I want you to fuck me now," she begged and grabbed at his loincloth, which covered the place that once boasted a proud ten inches in length, and almost two inches in circumference. He heard her, he wanted to, he could feel the desire to enjoy the excitement of their exchange build inside him, but there was nothing he could do about that.

"Fuck," she yelled in anguish, realizing what she had forgotten. "You don't even have a damn dick. You are nowhere near the man you used to be," she spat at him.

The torture was sometimes unbearable, but this was the price he paid for his life, the price to love her. He choked back the anger that was raging inside him, a battle he fought daily.

Jason licked softly, soothing her clit as if to ask it to relax, tempering it, allowing her ass cheeks to fold neatly back into themselves and using his hands to caress her outer thighs as he kissed her inner thighs. Her legs relaxed and she moaned lightly in the afterglow of her orgasm, and tears began to stream down Jason's face.

He pulled away from her in a submissive posture, preparing to be devoured like the black widow devours the male spider after mating. Then standing, he walked to the center of the grand living room. The cathedral ceiling was laced with chains that came uncoiled at the press of a button. She stood, her skin glowing with sprinkles of sweat that twinkled on her body like stardust. On the wall in the stairway where she stood, she waved her hand in a circular motion and a panel in the wall opened, exposing her cat-o'-nine tails and the spiked dog collar she would tightly squeeze onto Jason's neck.

"So you like to eat pussy?" she asked as she descended the stairs, walking with the attitude and grace of ten thousand Egyptian pharaohs. She approached Jason, who now stood in the midst of linked chains that hung from the ceiling as if they were lynching tools. There were seven of them and each was linked differently, some with spikes and others with cuffs.

"Only your pussy, Mistress, and I would die for it," he told her submissively, unemotionally. His back was turned to her and the whip marks that had been burnt in his skin from previous whippings were visible. The raised hue of scars had healed and reopened and healed again. This was her way of loving him. It was the only way she could love him, and he accepted that.

"Is my hot pussy worth dying for, Jason?" she asked seductively, nurturing the web of hatred that had built itself up inside her for years, starting with the scar of the memory of her mother's death and her father's cock in her mouth.

"I live and die to fuck you, Mistress. If licking the shit out of your cunt gives you pleasure, then that's my bidding."

With those words, Jason stretched his limbs, his legs apart, hands outstretched, and she latched the chains on his wrists and ankles. Serena's naked body threw the whip back and swung it forcefully at him. She wanted to cause him pain and hear his cries, and Jason knew this too, so he succumbed to her will. She forced her body to muster the strength of men twice her size and weight, and poured her revulsion into every lash that traumatized his body.

"I am so sorry, Serena. I didn't mean to do it," he said between clenched teeth as he attempted to bear the pain.

"Then why, why you worthless piece of turd?" she asked, as her own tears drenched her face with each snap of the whip. She was reminded that Jason was just a man and not worthy of her love. But she loved him for the sacrifice he had made for her—to bear the burden of those who caused her pain—a memory that had festered and grown more infectious as the years went by. Serena fell to the floor, and Jason unlatched himself. She wailed uncontrollably, curled into the fetal position. His love for her could move mountains, so timidly, he knelt down to her, lifting her into his strong, beautiful arms. He could have protected and pleased her, but her hatred ran too deep. He looked at her as she whimpered, frail and vulnerable, and he released a tear for what they had both lost as a result of her past.

Without words, Jason proceeded with the ritual. He glided up the stairs, holding her securely in his arms as though she were only a baby, and headed to the master bedroom. The room was as large as two small apartments. The crystal chandelier hanging from the center was turned down low, and the light illuminated her canopy bed, which was draped with red, silk sheets and boasted pillows and stuffed animals of all sorts. Her room looked like it belonged to both a woman and child. He walked onto the tan, Italian marble floor in her bathroom, which was the size of a large bedroom.

The tub was designed like those from the 1800s; it was marble-tiled with a replica of the Michelangelo painting *The Creation of Adam* drawn into it. The tub had four legs curved into the floor. There was a full shower to one side with sliding, opaque glass doors that only allowed the vision of a shadow to seep through. Jason placed her in the tub, allowing warm water laced with cinnamon and myrrh to wash over her. He washed her as gently as a baby, while holding her head in his arms, allowing her head to rest gently on his chest.

Lifting her from the tub, he gathered her into his arms, walked back into the bedroom, and placed her in the bed. Walking briskly back to the bathroom, he retrieved her towel and patted her down until the residue of water was dried, then he pulled the covers over her. Bowing, he paid homage to her. He was her submissive, her slave. Taking one more glimpse of her, he turned her over and kissed her beautifully rounded posterior. Then he crawled on his hands and knees, exiting her bedroom and quietly pulling the heavy doors shut.

3

Cathalina's tall, beautiful, five-foot-eight-inch frame walked slowly from behind her desk and she sat next to her patient, who had tears streaking down her face. She glanced briefly at her clock and realized it was already quarter to six. She had hoped she would have gotten out of the office and headed home to shower and change into more comfortable clothes before going to see Serena, but it seemed as though she might have to cancel. She hated making plans with Serena and canceling. Cathalina believed that Serena suffered from some malignant eroticized transference. This was one of the first ailments Cathalina believed had manifested itself upon Serena due to the sexual abuse and over stimulation in her childhood.

The patient seated on the chair across from her reminded her of Serena when she had first reluctantly sat in that very chair. The arrogance she displayed was not one of conceit, but only one of knowing what she had endured to still be alive and able to sit in that chair.

"Lara, I am so sorry about what you have suffered. It's a form of childism, a term developed in 1975 by an African American psychiatrist named Chester Pierce. You were weak and vulnerable and the trauma you suffered as a child has lingered, bringing you the anger you feel today." Cathalina tried to give an explanation to her distraught patient. "You see, it's really not your fault that you have this rage." But her words didn't seem to cause much comfort, and by now Lara had overstayed her visit. She needed to get going.

"I am so sorry, Dr. Shekhar. I know I have been here for close to four hours now. But I just really need your help. I don't understand why people who were supposed to have loved me more than anything else in the world violated me the way they did. I feel deceived and I have become a bitch because of them . . . just a slut." Lara spoke candidly, staggering and stumbling through her words. Cathalina felt sorry for her. It was the same sense of empathy she usually developed for her patients. She could only imagine the rage Serena would feel if she were to hear this woman's story.

"I will tell you what, I'll prescribe a mild antidepressant for you. Whenever you feel overwhelmed with emotions of anger and a sense of loss of control, just take one and it will give you some peace."

"I just feel like killing him, you know? I feel like killing them all. I wish all men would die. Anyone who rapes and abuses a child does not deserve to live, and the men who take advantage of the vulnerability of women are just as bad," Lara blurted out as she walked calmly toward the open window. The serenity that overshadowed Miami at sunset did not touch her heart. Her mannerisms seemed under control, but the look in her eyes and the tone of her voice told an entirely different story. She was ready to kill, and Cathalina recognized this immediately. Serena had the same look in her eyes whenever she spoke of men.

"I do understand. That's why I want to see you back here next Monday. Today is Friday, but if there is anything you need before your appointment, please don't hesitate to call. If you call my office line and state that it's an emergency, I will be paged. OK?" she asked, hoping that would quell Lara Lopez enough to get her out of her office so she could be on her way. "You know I am here for you, Lara," Cathalina told her with outstretched arms that rested on Lara's shoulders.

"OK," Lara agreed, her tears drying as quickly as they had come, and her pleasant disposition returning as though this woman had never been hurt, which was a classic manifestation of trauma.

Cathalina had been seeing Lara for almost six months, which was around the same amount of time she had been treating Serena before actually recruiting her. But Serena was not just a patient; she was also a friend. All the studies Cathalina had performed as a doctor of psychiatry and behavioral sciences, the treatments she was taught, the different scenarios she experienced, and her internship in the hospital of psychiatry had not prepared her for the psychological damage she would encounter in her practice with these abused women. Although she tried not to become friendly with her patients, there were a few she gave special attention to. One of them was Lara, but no one was more important to her than Serena.

As Lara got up and walked gracefully out of the office, Cathalina couldn't help admiring how simply gorgeous her patient was. Her hair was cropped short with blond highlights that brought out the yellow hue in her skin tone and her light gray eyes, which flickered when she was angry. Her body was well-developed with full breasts, a small waist, and wide, childbearing hips. She sported slightly bowed legs that showed off the roundness of her ass and accentuated her walk. It was a shame that this thirty-five-year-old woman could not find love because she was filled with the emotions of an abused child.

The only drawback to her beauty was the facial hair

under her chin that refused to leave. Lara had confided that she had spent years and much money on shaving, plucking, and electrolysis, but nothing seemed to eliminate the problem. The hair just kept returning and coming back thicker, which dampened her self-esteem and forced her to hide from the natural attention a man might direct toward her.

Sitting back in the chair that Lara had just occupied, Cathalina breathed a sigh of relief and looked at the clock that hung high over her reddish mahogany desk with a high back leather chair resting behind it. She loved the calm serenity of the painting that hung on the wall, displaying a waterfall gushing through a peaceful forest. The oil painting was done for her as a graduation present from her then boyfriend, who later decided to have a sex change, and was no longer Brian, but Briana. Cathalina chuckled now as she remembered.

Her mind also ventured back to the day when she had severe uterine burnings in her vagina, and abdominal pains. Then she began noticing a foul order whenever she used the bathroom, and sores began appearing on her labia majora and under the hood of her clitoris. She remembered her panicked rush to the hospital, where she found out Brian had given her gonorrhea, syphilis, and herpes, and then her devastation when she was told that she'd had the diseases for so long, they had damaged her internal reproductive organs. If that wasn't bad enough, she would never be able to have children, because they had to admit her and give her a hysterectomy. She really should have trashed the painting when he broke their engagement and embarrassed her with his nonsense. But she kept it as a reminder of how he had stolen her life and ability to have a child. And the painting also fueled her anger, which was what pushed her to help the women who came to her office every day. The same energy that pushed her to help propelled her into a life of vigilantism, fueled by the energy that caused her to hate so strongly..

It was now seven o'clock, and she wondered if she could still get the girls that she had scheduled from the agency to come over and entertain Serena. She picked up the phone and dialed the madam of "Sex Cell," the most popular underground organization of sex slaves, submissives, and fetish hunters in the vicinity.

"Sex Cell," a seductive voice answered on the second ring.

"Madam Cleopatra, please?"

"Please hold." While Cathalina waited, she was entertained with screams and moans, sensual listening to bring on even stronger sexual urges.

"This is the madam. Can I help you?" came the soft voice that summoned passion and desire over the line. If Cathalina had been on hold any longer, she would have started to masturbate. Her breath caught in her throat as she was caught off guard when Cleopatra answered the phone.

"Hey, Cleo, it's me."

"Cathalina, darling." Cleo said, her voice changing to normal. "I was wondering if you were still going to call. When you called earlier I had everything arranged, and you know my clients get upset when they cannot get their usual."

"I am sorry, Cleo. I was meeting with Lara again."

"Oh, that poor dear. How is she?"

"She is getting stronger. I can feel the anger festering inside her, but she needs to feel that first before she can grow. She needs to feel the power of being in control before she can heal."

"But is she ready?" Cleopatra's anxiety and impatience was obvious in her voice.

"I told you, Cleo, I will let you know when she is ready. Now is not the time," Cathalina said with a soft, but firm voice. Wanting to get on with the matter at hand, she smiled and exhaled softly.

"How about we follow through with that night of fun and passion? I am sure Serena is still waiting for me, and I have never broken my word to her without calling to change plans or reschedule."

"Yes, I know, Cath," Cleo teased, using the nickname that only Serena called Dr. Cathalina Shekhar. She knew she was treading lightly, but she wanted to drive her point home.

"Why don't you send the package on over, and meet me at Serena's?" Cathalina put the plan in motion and totally ignored Cleo's previous comments. There was no need for her to respond. Things were the way they were, and she had no plans of changing them anytime soon, even if it was up to her alone.

"Sounds good to me. I will see you in twenty minutes," Cleo said and hung up the phone. She hated being put on the backburner by Cathalina for Serena. She hated that Cathalina would jump through hoops for one woman and one woman only, and because of her blinders, she could never see how much Cleo loved her, or that there was nothing Cleo wouldn't do for her. Yet, Cathalina was the only person who had her on a string. In her world, she was the feared Madam Cleopatra.

Cathalina hung up the phone and felt that usual uneasy feeling that swept through her body every time she got off the phone with Cleo. She knew what the problem was, but this was no time for her to be concerned with that. They had been waiting for this day since they met Serena more than a year ago. They had groomed her, molded her, and taught her the art, the true passion of what to do with her anger, pain, and hatred so she could function in a some-what normal state in her daytime job. Tonight she would be initiated, crowned, and Cathalina was proud she had found her. Serena was her protégé.

Cathalina walked to her window overlooking the harbor of Biscayne Bay in the most beautiful part of downtown Miami. She looked over at the ocean, which seemed to stand still and may have seemed like a mirage had she not known it was really there. She closed the window and walked to her office door. She looked around her large, up-scale office and breathed slowly. She had done a nice job with the decorating. Nothing was overdone. If anything, there was an undertone of humility to hide just how much Cathalina had. She didn't want to make her patients feel uncomfortable. Most of them were regular, middle-class, working women who worked hard for what they had. She didn't want to seem like she was gloating by brandishing her financial wealth in her office.

She walked back into the now-darkened room and to the far left corner, which housed a twenty-seven-inch plasma television that was embedded into the wall above the beautiful mahogany stand displaying DVDs with medical titles. She knelt down and adjusted the large seven-foot mini tree that cast its branches above the center of the room, giving it an outdoor feel.

All the colors were earth-toned, except for the carpet in her office. It was at least four inches thick, white, and plush. No one was allowed to enter Cathalina's office without first taking off their shoes. Taking off their shoes was the first step to bearing their souls. Her twenty-by-fifteen-foot office had a massaging vibrator tucked neatly beneath the carpet, and walking to the chair in front of her desk was pure ecstasy to their feet.

Cathalina closed her doors, walked out into the warm Florida evening, and got into her car. As the wings to her Lamborghini closed down and locked, Cathalina couldn't contain the excited flutter of her heart. A black woman like her had come a long way to get to where she was today, walking the line of upper white class and having enough power to help her sisters. She breathed in the scent of her uniquely designed Lamborghini, a two-door, four-seater that allowed for a hollow back top, as if there was an egg on top of the back half of the car. The front part was as sleek and narrow as the nose of a fighter jet. She smiled and sped off to Coral Gables where her friend awaited her.

Serena was still lying in her bedroom when Jason knocked on her door. He was not allowed to enter without permission. Serena usually went into a comatose sleep after a session with Jason. Somewhere deep within her, it hurt to think of Jason and what she did to him. Sometimes in the recesses of her mind she still felt regrets.

The moment she heard the rehearsed knock on her door, she knew that Cleo and Cath had arrived. Suddenly, she began to tremble and her heart raced at the idea of what was about to occur. She had prepared for this and she was ready. She was excited and she was not turning back. This was something she had to do.

Rising, she walked to her huge walk-in closet, which was the size of a small room, and pulled out her Victoria's Secret, black, see-through gown with flower patches that covered only her nipples and her snatch. Serena glanced at the gold-embossed grandfather clock over by the fireplace and realized that it was a little past eight. She couldn't believe she had slept that long, but that was not to be a concern right now.

Jason stood next to her wearing his Zulu leopard-printed loincloth. He was standing in a defensive stance holding a shotgun, the same kind of sawed-off shotgun that her mother used so long ago to protect her. She kept reports about the incident locked in her safe with all her valuables, the newspaper clippings, the video archives, and information that the psychologists used to explain her past. She kept them all safely locked away like treasures.

She moved next to the picturesque window looking out into her front yard and pressed the release lock for her gate that allowed entrance to her hidden fortress. She watched as four cars pulled into her driveway, fitting neatly into the spacious parking area in front of her house. She recognized Cath's car, but she didn't know to whom the other three belonged. Not that it mattered. They were with the person she had come to trust more than anyone else in her life. She watched silently as the doors of the other two cars opened, and she didn't stay to watch anymore. Instead she went down the stairs, stood by her front door, and waited to hear their approaching steps.

She opened the huge door that led to the safety of her home and allowed her visitors to enter. First it was Cathalina, who kissed her lightly on both cheeks and stood next to her. Serena blushed and Jason looked at her. She knew he wasn't happy, but that was not her concern. She felt safe with Cathalina's hand snuggled tightly into hers for reassurance. Cleopatra followed her, and Serena was shocked at her appearance. She had never met the madam before. Cleo was a big woman. She wore black leather that covered nearly her entire body except her ass cheeks, which were exposed as she walked by Serena. She had to be just below two hundred pounds. But she was the sexiest, most beautiful big woman Serena had ever seen. Cleopatra was heavy on top with a waist that curved into her torso and thighs. One's eyes would naturally follow the curve of her ass, which was perfectly rounded and flowed into her long, cream-colored, caramel legs. Her skin was as smooth as milk and her smile exhibited deep dimples that made her hazel eyes glow and dance. The black leather against her body was like a second skin gripping and holding everything in its place.

"Cleopatra," Serena sighed under her breath. This woman was a legend among them. Them, those who lived in their underworld kingdom, those women who favored the night and the things that elicit fear and fascination in most, but were treasured among them. Cleopatra was not considered a "true" spider. She was the gatekeeper, the protector of them. She had the information, the cover for their toys and exotic tastes in prey. But she bore the mark of the crocodile, not a spider. It was tattooed on her back and looked as if it were alive. The rough, stubbled skin of the croc was embossed and as brown as the muddy waters of its natural habitat. Cleo was as fast and as dangerous as the animal.

Cleo paused briefly in front of Serena and then waited for the others to enter. When the door closed behind them, there were six women including the exotic Asian beauty Elizabeth who headed to the secret room below Serena's fortress. Serena waited as Jason put in the codes and watched as the wall became animated, transforming into a hidden secret passage that led to a world of sexual delight. Cleopatra was proud of this space, even more so than her own palace of pleasure, because she had a hand in its unique design and location.

"Come," Cathalina urged them all, "let us begin." A sneaky, evil smile crept across her face. She knew these women; they were noted predators of innocent children in their respective countries. Cathalina, who was well-traveled, made deals with the authorities in each of their homelands, where they would have been put to death. But seeing their propensity toward deviance, the officials chose Cathalina's fate over lethal injection. Cathalina looked at Serena with a subtle urgency that told her not to be afraid. She sensed Serena's apprehension, but urged her on. She was prepared for this.

Cleopatra cracked her whip, and the group of women

walked in behind Cathalina. They were to be the entertainment for the rest of the night.

The two women who came out of the Rolls-Royce went in first and lay down horizontally on what seemed like hospital beds, but were made out of stone. They proceeded to take off what little clothing they wore. One girl was Russian with pale, white skin, brown eyes, and long, stringy hair. She didn't speak much English, but her sighs and her body spoke the language they needed to know. She was about five-nine with a medium build, and her body was filled with hair from the top of her head down to her arms, the center of her stomach, and into the mound of joy that she now offered to the inductee. The other was an African beauty who surpassed the mere image of commercialized pretty. Her skin was as smooth as silk and as dark as a black stallion. Her legs were thick and powerful, her arms muscular and strong.

Her body stretched to about six feet tall and she was as cleanly shaven as a brand new baby. She had no hair on her, not on her head, not under her arms, not on the entryway to her love canal, and not in the crack of her curvaceous posterior. She too had not been in this country very long, but her threshold for pain and pleasure was immense, and she was willing to do anything to feel passion that would send her mind into overload. Tonight she would get just that.

Cleopatra went and gathered their tools like a surgeon on the verge of performing surgery, and then squirted scented baby oil over the women's bodies. And as if on cue, they began to massage the silky liquid into themselves.

"Get the pets," Cleopatra coaxed, and Elizabeth slowly marched to the center wall of the hidden room and knocked twice. It was then that the scratching came, and Elizabeth knew that the trained pets were preparing to be released. She walked over to a stone structure that held a large urn displaying condoms of all flavors and colors. Next to it were biscuits. She picked them up and walked again to the door, which she pulled open with the huge ring that hung from it instead of a doorknob.

As the two beautiful wolf dogs approached her, she stood in the command stance that they knew, holding the biscuits in one hand and the whip in the other. The whip was no ordinary whip, because the tip of it was the head of a cobra snake, and the head felt like the biting of fangs as it tore into the skin. They walked to Liz, cowered, ate the biscuits, and waited for directions.

"Ready," Liz announced, and brought a beautiful smile to Cleopatra's face. Her dimples sank within her cheeks and the small space in the middle of her front teeth opened to show the soft pinkness of her tongue.

The two women began to moan and gyrated feverishly in anticipation of what was to come, willing their bodies into excitement. The two wolf-type dogs, as white as snow with eyes that glowed in the dimly lit room, began to sniff as they had been trained. They sought the scent of the female sexual aroma that had been vigorously saturated in their senses. Cleopatra stood over them and spoke softly, almost soothingly.

"Ready to be satiated, my pets?" she asked of the women whose juices flowed eagerly and without restraint. They knew the price they may have to pay and enjoyed this death sentence over their previous one. They had tried to escape twice, but Cleo caught them and made their stay more restricted and uncomfortable.

"Madam, I am. Do what you will of me," she uttered. Her foreign tongue's accent was so strong, Cleo seemed to have been the only one to understand her.

Cleopatra took her hands and reached for the table next to her, grabbing what looked like a pair of circular rings.

The rings were about a half-inch thick in width, and sported inverted needles that were on the inside of the rings, instead of on the outside. Cleo opened each one like a handcuff, and locked it onto each breast of the beautiful, black butterfly. As Cleo closed each ring, the needles dug into the flesh of the woman, causing her to wail in pain. Her screech assaulted their ears. Serena watched, afraid, nervous, and uncertain. Her mind raced a million miles per hour. She knew what she was there for; she had agreed to it. But suddenly, with everything there and it all happening in that moment, she wanted to stop, but she couldn't. So much had gone into this. She didn't want to disappoint Cathalina. So she stood patiently, waiting for her instructions. She had watched as Cleo and Cathalina ripped the manhood off of many a man—voyeurs and other violators who stood before her in court. Cases she couldn't solve were delicately and discreetly handled by her friends.

Now, for the first time, Serena would witness what extreme torture looked like. Once she was initiated, she would become used to these techniques, but for now, she would watch and become familiar with bondage and the tools of hatred she would use to funnel her anger through, and to take revenge for what she couldn't control as a child. A man who becomes a predator and violates God's weaker, more fragile creations were worthless. She felt herself shudder, and unexpectedly, on a subconscious level she began to enjoy it. Her body reacted and her juices began to flow as she watched these women build themselves into a sexual rhythm of anticipation.

Blood rushed from the breasts of the African woman, but she did not ease. Instead, she became even more fervent. Elizabeth stood on the other side of Cleo with the Russian woman, and took hooks from the table that stood next to her. Clamping them between her index fingers as she made a fist, she approached the woman's opened legs and ripped the lips to the entranceway of her womanhood. The Russian clenched her teeth and kept massaging her breasts. The healed scars from her clitoris and bottom told the tale that she was not a stranger to this; she had used these same horrific strategies to mutilate unsuspecting children who died painful deaths before being discarded.

"Oh, you are a fucking bitch. I knew you would like that," Elizabeth stated, enjoying the pain that this woman was gaining sexual pleasure from, her male tool rising in anxious need to plunge into the meaty, pink flesh of these women who had violated the basic moral code of humanity. They hurt children.

The woman looked at her with wild, aroused eyes and licked her lips at the visual excitement of her tormentor.

"Not today, pet, not today," Liz responded as if reading her mind. "Today and for no more todays after this, you belong to them, my faithful pets," she whispered. Then taking the acupuncture needles, she began masterfully slipping them into soft, feminine flesh all over the woman's body. Again the Russian woman clenched her teeth and squeezed her eyes shut, and a smile, as eerie as it was evil, plastered itself on her thin lips. Her head swung from side to side in an attempt to bear the pain.

Cleo soon gave the signal and the women were on their knees, dog collars were placed around their necks and they were chained to the stone fixture that served as their beds. The whip from Elizabeth's snake head lashed out on their backs, faces, legs, and ankles, wherever there was a free space of human flesh, and their cries came mercilessly.

Cathalina gently massaged the tattoo of her mark, the brown recluse spider, on her right shoulder, situated right below her collarbone. She could handle and pet the deadly spider, since during her initiation, she was bitten by it, and she was now impervious to its venom. The spider each woman became bound with was symbiotic with her after they each surrendered to the same ritual that Serena must now endure. Cathalina stood close to Serena, whose black, transparent garment clung to her shapely body, and Cathalina's hands found their way to her spine. Like a spider's spindly legs dancing across its web, her fingers caused the sensory nerves of Serena's sensitive flesh to tingle.

This was to be a very delicate process, because if not done correctly, the poison of the Brazilian wandering spider could kill her. They needed to be quick, and they had already prepared her anti-serum just for the occasion.

"Come now, Serena. It's time to be baptized," Cathalina whispered, taking her hand and leading her into the midst of their vengeful hell. Behind glass cages in the four corners of the room, spawned and bred were four of the most venomous predators in the world. Each cage housed and nurtured these creatures according to their natural habitat.

To the east of the room was the black widow, which spun her chaotic web without design. Hundreds of them hung upside down in their own space from their webs. The males, smaller and without adornment, hid until it was their time to attempt to mate and perpetuate the lifespan of the spiders, and in so doing, most would make the ultimate sacrifice and die.

To the west and north of the room were the brown recluse and the Brazilian wandering spider, two species of spiders who spun no web. These spiders liked the dark-drenched areas that helped them feed and breed. They were loners and would quickly wander and hide among peat moss, green trees, and the dark surroundings of the forest, which offered them reprieve from wandering eyes.

To the south were the scorpions. But their anti-venom serum was being prepared for the one who would be marked with the sign of the scorpion. Cathalina began aggressively and passionately kissing Serena, which drew deadly stares from Cleopatra, but there was nothing she could do.

She wasn't even a true spider, and in a few moments, all going as planned, Serena would be their leader. She knew this; Cathalina had told her on many occasions that they sought someone like Serena, yet the actuality of it was still painful to watch, especially since the Cathalina seemed to have taken so much to her. Cleo knew she had to remain respectful, as there was no loyalty amongst people who would hurt others, even if their motives were justified. Cleo snickered at the thought.

"I hate her," she whispered under her breath.

"Don't be afraid, Serena. I will not allow anything to happen to you. I would die first," Cathalina vowed. Serena was led between the two stone bed structures and chained between the women. Her legs were pulled apart for oral tantalization during the baptism. Elizabeth nervously toyed with a nest of black widows as the tingling of their legs helped to calm and relax her anxious nerves.

Cleo walked over to a small, sidebar refrigerator and pulled a small jar from it. In the clear bottle was white liquid that was sticky and gooey in its natural form. She also took out a large needle. The painful looking needle was the only thing large enough to inject enough of the serum into Serena to quickly counter the poison.

Jason was called in for his servitude duties. He mourned internally for the woman that destroyed him as a man in the physical way that counted, and lamented without sound that his only crime was to love her too much. He was too pushy; he should have left her alone when she refused to date him the first time, but six months of arrogant, forceful courting got him exactly what he wanted in a way he never imagined.

He was made to kneel between her thighs and touch her in that familiar way that quelled her trembling legs. Silent tears ran down her face and she channeled her negative thoughts to the man she knew as father. She poured all the hate into her body as she was taught to do in order help repel the spider's poison and distract her from the pain.

"I am right here, Serena," Cathalina moaned in her ear, her warm breath percolating Serena's nipples. Cleo handed the anti-venom serum to Cathalina and then the poisonous Brazilian wandering spider was given to Elizabeth in a jar. Cleo stepped aside to stand on the opposite side of Serena, in between the two women who lay on the stoned beds dying. They too, had to face the pain that Serena was facing. Jason was afraid for her, so he gently kissed her inner thigh and allowed his tongue to soothe her in the only way he was allowed to now. Cathalina removed Serena's scanty gown and allowed it to hang on her arms, and then she kissed her bare shoulders softly, allowing the warmth of her lips to send shudders of desire through Serena's body while she was carefully being blindfolded.

At the moment Serena was to be bitten by her spider, Cleo and Elizabeth opened the spider jars, releasing the deadly invertebrates, which scrambled onto the sweaty surface of the two women's bodies. One move from each woman as they squirmed in anxious astonishment and the deadly fangs of the spiders plunged into their flesh. Their screams were beyond description. Their screams only echoed the visual of the scene, as the spiders seemed to be amalgamated with the women in the way they held steadfast in their venomous bite.

It was in that terrifying instant, when the screams burned their ears and Jason's tongue melted between Serena's thighs, in that moment when Cathalina, careful not to get bitten herself, released the Brazilian wandering spider onto Serena's shoulder. The anxious, belligerent predator wasted no time. Serena was on the verge of orgasm and Jason held her fast as her legs began to vibrate and her body shuddered from the convulsive eruptions of pleasure. The spider perched itself with aggression and prepared for its hostile maneuver. Just as her sighs and moans of pleasure escalated into a climatic peak and Serena uttered Jason's name, the spider's fangs found the sweet taste of her flesh and kept biting. Her body shook both from the pain of the spider's bite and from what Jason was doing to her, and she was quickly losing coherency as fear replaced pleasure.

Serena seemed faint now and her eyes rolled back in her head. It was hard for Cathalina to snatch the spider from Serena's shoulder because she was shaking so hard. She didn't want to yank out the spider and leave the fangs in Serena's flesh. The spider was left on too long, but Cathalina remained strong, not wanting to show her dread because their experiment may have gone wrong. Hesitation, for even a fraction of a second, could be deadly. Cathalina carefully reached for the spider's back, urging it to return to its jar. Jason held onto Serena's weak body as Cleo, Liz, and Cathalina hustled to release the restraints from her hands and legs. The other two women were sacrificed, and now dead to the world. Their bodies were ruthlessly shoved to the side, and Jason was bid to throw them into the spiders' lair. The spiders clung to the bodies of the women, whose pain threshold could not withstand the spiders' attacks in addition to the torture they had previously endured. Jason quickly opened the glass-caged entrance and disposed of them.

"Quickly," Cathalina urged. "Give me the anti-venom serum." Her voice cracked as she could not hide her emerging fear as she spoke. Her eyes were wide open with both terror and hope. As she reached to take the needle from Cleo, she dropped it in her panic that they might not save Serena. Cleopatra bent down to pick up the needle.

"Cleo, move faster for crying out loud." Cathalina's eyes were huge and she was growing increasingly agitated.

"Here," Cleo told her after picking up the instrument and squirting a small amount of liquid from the tip to test it.

"Elizabeth, hold her hands. You are stronger than the both of us," Cathalina demanded.

Jason looked on in disbelief, keeping his thoughts to himself. *These bitches are crazy.* But all he could do was stand by helplessly, knowing that to cross these women, who hade already crossed so many lines, was useless. They were quickly growing beyond the realm of reason.

Serena had begun foaming at the mouth and puking when the serum was administered, and she passed out soon after.

"Take her up to her room and clean her up. Make sure she is comfortable and stay with her until I return." Cathalina belted out orders, commanding Jason to take action, and he wasted no time. Again, he effortlessly scooped Serena into his arms and rushed out of the underground lair.

Cathalina, Cleopatra, and Elizabeth worked fast, cleaning the room until it sparkled, and looked and smelled as if nothing had happened there. It was now the wee hours of Saturday morning, and dawn was upon them. They needed to change out of their clothing into everyday attire, and put the secrets of the dangerous things they did and their future malicious mission behind them for this night.

4

"How is she?" Cathalina asked Jason, who had diligently stayed by Serena's side, leaving only to go to the bathroom and to wet the cool washcloth that he used to usher away the fever that sent Serena into a fitful sleep and tormented restlessness.

"She had a fever all night," he growled, unhappy with the charade of the women, knowing he might be the only man who might live to tell it, and scared to show his contempt too openly, knowing they wouldn't hesitate to hurt him as well.

"Leave us," she told him, and Jason stood slowly, not really wanting to go, but knowing that Serena's wrath would visit upon him if he didn't obey Cathalina. His hesitation angered Cathalina and she began to fume, her eyes narrowing to slits and her hands clenching into balled fists. She had no idea why Serena tolerated this man who was seemingly useless to her, though she was there to aid Serena in saving his life after Serena's uncontrollable anger caused her to reach for the nearest butcher knife and castrate him as easily as if his male parts were swiss cheese. Serena had freaked out, and Cathalina hadn't wanted to lose her mentally, so she had assisted, securing the medication, pain killers, and all the things necessary to stop the bleeding. They could not take him to a hospital, that would have garnered too much attention, and for some reason, Serena couldn't let him die. Serena seemed to need him. It signified weakness to Cathalina and that bothered her beyond reason.

"I said, get out!" Cathalina demanded, and this time, Jason did not hesitate. He placed the washcloth on the nightstand next to Serena and backed out of the room, not only because that was the way Serena preferred it, but because he knew to turn his back on a woman like Cathalina could be deadly.

Once he was gone, Cathalina took off her clothes and snuck in bed beside Serena. She had to survive. She was running a high fever and she tossed and turned in pain and anger. Taking some homemade herb concoction that she solicited from a doctor friend, Cathalina opened Serena's mouth and gently released the sweet liquid on her tongue. She continued this routine for hours, and at midnight when Serena's fever broke and she began snoring lightly in a peaceful slumber, Cathalina left, content that their mission was successful. She hoped that her dream that Serena Kowtow would reign with such horror and vengeance upon those who violated women and children, that it would leave heads spinning. This was something she had planned for years, through her studies, and her pains—that one day she would be able to make right all the wrongs that had been done to her and so many women before her.

Late that Sunday evening, Serena was greeted with breakfast in bed. Jason had gotten up and prepared for Serena's breakfast later than usual so she was able to sleep in after having such a rough night. He knew she would be starving, as she had been sleeping since she passed out from their Friday night ritual and was only now waking up.

"Good morning, Serena." Jason smiled brightly, happy to see Serena up and about. She was so beautiful, standing there naked at the window that gave her a panoramic view of her estate. He basked in the glow of her complexion and fell silent as he was reminded that he could never make love to her the way a man was meant to. He felt the tingle in his groin area that he had become familiar with, a tingle that would have sent his once proud manhood on the rise. He allowed his eyes to drink in how exquisitely created she was, and he permitted his gaze to linger on the sight that was not there before—the scar created by the spider bite. He could see the scar on her left shoulder, or at least what seemed like a scar, as it was a webbed design created from her flesh, leading above her shoulder blade and disappearing. He walked slowly to her, cautiously, so he could get a closer look. His breath caught in his throat as he neared her and stood by her side. The mark of the spider was more than a web. It was the image of a raised spider, five inches in length, and it looked as real as if he was looking at the culprit crawling across the floor. Serena turned to look at him and smiled.

"Hey there," she said warmly. "Guess I had a close call, eh?" she stated unemotionally, as though her life hanging in the balance was nothing more than night turning into day.

"Yes, my love. I was concerned," he told her honestly and let his gaze drop to the floor.

"Well, now you see that your worries were unwarranted," she said matter-of-factly. "I am as fit as a fiddle and feeling better than I have in years." She grinned, her smile warming him as she took his chin within her hands and lifted his eyes to hers. Before he realized what was happening, she kissed him softly and lovingly on his lips. Her eyes danced harmlessly and sweetly upon his face. This was the reason why he had fallen in love with her. Tears of regret fell from his eyes.

Serena ate and took a long bath, aided by Jason as she relished in his recounting of the weekend. She mused as she took the soapy sponge and lovingly caressed the image of what she had now become. Her skin pulsated in that area on her shoulder, to her surprise. It seemed impossible, of course, but she could swear that spider was inside of her. She could feel its life and its soul surging through her.

At the sounds of the phone ringing, Serena jumped up, leaving wet spots all over the floor as she ran to catch the phone. She picked it up on the fifth ring and was glad that she did.

"Hello?"

"Darling!" the voice greeted

"Cathalina," Serena shrieked with excitement. "Where are you? I thought you would be here," Serena said, knowing full well Cathalina had left her side only hours before. Cathalina began to laugh.

"I am actually treating myself to a late dinner on the beach." Serena sighed disappointedly at the thought.

"I wanted to make sure you got your rest and that you were awake and doing OK," Cathalina continued before Serena said what Cathalina knew she would say.

"But you know that I would have loved to join you." Serena pouted.

"You were ill, and no doubt have just gotten out of bed. Besides, I know Jason has told you that I was there. You know I would never leave you to fare alone." Hearing this, Serena relaxed and went to sit on her bed in the nude, dripping wet, listening to the soothing words that came through the phone.

"When will I see you?" Serena asked. "I am sure there is much work to be done."

"Yes, we need to do a little cleaning in your spare room. There are things there that it is almost time we dispose of," she told her, and Serena knew what, better yet, whom she was talking about.

"Yes, I understand. When do you think?" she asked again, still unsure of the way of the women's routine, but she was soon to learn all of her duties as their leader.

"Take today and rest, my queen. Tomorrow is Monday and there is much to be done. The team will meet on Wednesday to proceed. Do you work tomorrow?"

"I just told Jason to check my schedule. I think I only appear twice this week with some basic duties and paperwork," Serena told her. "But I can confirm that for you later today."

"Sounds wonderful. So we will meet on Wednesday again. Get some rest and let the spider acquaint herself with you," Cathalina told her. At the mention of the spider, her skin began to pulsate again in that specified region of her body. Serena's mind began to swim with thoughts of anxiety, and an uncontrollable urge to attack came over her.

"All right," Serena panted. "I will rest and wait. Somehow I feel a little out of place, like my body is no longer mine and I am a guest in my own skin." Serena shook off the thought that she might indeed be in for more than she had bargained for, but she felt this was her life's purpose, and so she contained her emotions. "I think your idea to relax is a good one." Serena submitted and smiled deeply, a smile that Cathalina returned, knowing and sensing it through the telephone.

"Well then, my lady, I bid you good night, and I am excited about our new destiny." Cathalina shuddered at the thought. She couldn't believe they had done it. They all had a close encounter which lingered on the borderline of death when they were injected with the deadly flavor of their chosen specimen. These women were chosen through anger, fear, and similar circumstances. All the ingredients had to be right. And so it was with Lara Lopez. She had the ingredients, and now she only had to agree.

"I will talk to you soon, Cath." Serena's voice cut through her thoughts. "Bye now." She saluted and Cathalina hung up the phone.

5

"You need to stop shutting down. This is only going to hinder your progress." Cathalina urged her. "You need to let it out, let yourself feel the anger and distress, allow the torment to consume you. It's the only way you will be able to let go, the only way you will know the power within you." Cathalina tried to soothe Lara, but she was afraid. Whenever she felt herself on the verge of a boiling point, she would stop and let herself simmer. Then the deadly calm that she had exacted over the past fifteen years of her life would overpower the hatred. Her passive-aggressive behavior had become a habit. After years of abuse, she used this method to deal with the pain, giving herself a moment, a small space where she could seek peace.

But this was not good in Cathalina's eyes. She wanted Lara to learn to grow angry. In her opinion, Lara needed to let hatred seethe within her soul and guide her. But most importantly, Cathalina wanted her to discover the power of control, and when it was appropriate, to unleash the wrath of her pain.

"I am a slut, doctor. That's what everyone calls me just because I like to express myself, just because I take advantage of the opportunity. That's the only time I am not afraid to have someone look at me, at my body. Why is it that a man can do this—screw around with ten women at the same time and claim to love each for what they bring him, and it's OK. But a woman does it and she is suddenly a bitch?" Lara asked calmly.

"It's hypocrisy," Cathalina responded with the same serenity that Lara reached out to her with. Changing her tone above or beyond her patient's could disrupt the flow of their conversation. "Just because they have a dick between their legs does not give them divine right to pussy intervene on every post of the playing field. Women like you even that field out, and that scares them. The whole proper image, the whole philosophy that they teach baby girls about keeping our legs closed for that one man—that's for them, not us."

"In all honestly, Dr. Shekhar, is there a way to fix this? To fix me? I don't want to be like this anymore. I cannot help but want sex. The very thought of a man sticking his tongue or cock up into my pussy is all it takes to make me excited. I love the feel of every opening in my body being filled with two, three, or even four dicks up inside me. Does this make me a nymphomaniac like they say?"

"You have got to stop beating up on yourself. Embrace who you are!" Cathalina became excited with who Lara was, and how much of a benefit her mind would be to their team. "It is not your fault you were raised by two women who loved each other and who fucked each other. Not your fault that you met your gay father on his deathbed, his life being sucked from him by AIDS. It is not your fault that you love men."

Cathalina paused to allow the words to sink into Lara's head. She wanted Lara to find a loophole. It was obvious that the patient did not want to stop. She wanted permission to be who she was, to continue to do as she wanted, and Cathalina wanted to give her that freedom, give her that space to free her sexuality and rid herself of her one and only inhibition—the restraints of society, the box of conformity that the world tried to paint women into. *Fuck conformity*, Cathalina thought. This was the time for women's liberation.

"In my heart, I know you are right." The tears flowed slowly down Lara's face, and she took her hands and ran them through her closely cropped head of hair. "But . . ."

"But nothing." Cathalina reached for her hand and something sent a shiver through Lara. She sensed a power about this woman that she could not describe.

"But," she continued, placing her other hand on top of Cathalina's and refusing to allow her thoughts to be dismissed, "I cannot get over this dirty feeling I get every time I have sex with these men. I know they are only using me. They look at me with scorn and disgust until they need to get laid again. Then I am their first choice. If I could change that . . ." She hesitated, her rage hitting a boiling point, and she could feel herself falling into her safety net, her protected place of harmony where she was still and nothing hurt her.

"Snap out of it, woman," Cathalina snapped, pulling her hands away. Her voice was stern, but her face remained soft, her brown eyes dancing with vibrancy. "Don't you know the power within yourself? You should snap a man's neck who dares to disrespect you." She saw the look of confusion on the petite woman's face, and began to rephrase her statement. "They wanted to be intimate with you as much as you wanted it, right? Did you force them?"

"Of course not," Lara defended.

"Then why should you be scorned? You are not asking for payment for your services. You deserve respect. They empty themselves inside the heavens of your euphoria and then you are suddenly not good enough?" Cathalina stood now, pacing. She moved to her desk and touched a shielded door. It opened to reveal a few buttons.

Cathalina pressed a button and the light hum of the massager beneath the carpet purred, rippling along both their feet, pulling the tension from their bodies.

This session was taking a lot from Cathalina, and she would have to move fast before the anger of her spider senses was disrupted.

"This is nice, Dr. Shekhar." Lara complimented, getting up and walking to the huge window that overlooked Biscayne Bay. With the plush, white carpet pulsating under her feet, and the visual of the calm, greenish-blue water beyond, Lara was starting to make sense of it all.

Looking at her watch, Lara realized that their hour was up. Cathalina wanted to keep going, but she didn't want to scare the woman off. They had been meeting now for more than six months and she felt she knew Lara pretty well. She harbored anguish and dismay at the injustices of this world. She had been abused too many times. Lara came to Florida illegally, like most of the Cubans and Puerto Ricans in South Miami, and like others she was able to blend in because of the huge population who made their home there. She had subjected herself to the orgies and group sex that she thought she wanted, but always left feeling dirty when it was all over.

Lara remembered all of this as she walked to the waiting area in Dr. Shekhar's office and crossed her legs primly to slide on her open-toed heels. She shook her head and squeezed her eyes shut at the memory of hanging out with a guy she thought she liked, a guy that she planned to allow to sniff the essence of her juicy womanhood.

But before she knew it, he had friends over, all guys, and one by one they took turns plunging their dicks inside her. Did one of them ask her permission? Did even one refuse to fuck the creamy moisture that she felt compelled to make available? Did they care? No, they didn't! And the guy she really wanted, the one she really liked, had just used and taken advantage of her. This would not happen again, she decided at that moment. Just two nights before she had again succumbed to her desires as the premiere guest in a threesome to fulfill one guy's whim and fancy. Enough was enough.

Cathalina watched as Lara left her office. She knew she had pushed her, but she hoped she had gotten her point across. Lara was to complete their circle and accept the blessings of the scorpion to aid her. She would take the will and respect from those who took it from her. She would avenge her sisters and brothers who had their voices and choices taken from them. She was the one.

Lara walked to her car trying to contain her anger, the re-sounding sound of her Puerto Rican accent shattering her eardrums as she got into her old, beat-up, 1988 Mazda 626. She hated the way her rage would just come to her as calm as the rising moon and consume her like the burning sun at high noon.

She opened the car door hard and slammed it shut be-hind her. She sat at the wheel staring off into space toward Dr. Shekhar's office building.

"I hate this shit. I wish she could help me already," she murmured to herself through clenched teeth. "Two more weeks and I am out of here. If she cannot help me, then I will help myself," she decided and then put the key in the ignition. She couldn't help or stop the memories from in-vading her mind. She thought back to that gang rape, the day that guy and his friends ran a train on her. Even to say his name brought her blood to a boiling point.

Her drive home was reckless and unfocused. Watching her drive on the Palmetto Expressway to Hialeah Gardens one would swear she was on a racetrack or a player in a video game. She entertained dangerous thoughts and turned the radio on to see if she could drown them out.

"No. If I killed him then I would be locked up. That's not practical," she reasoned with herself. "But then again, maybe I need to be locked up. That fucking Mariposa! Maybe I need to get people like him off the streets and then my purpose is served." Lara snickered uncontrollably down the highway. Her beat-up car with the loud muffler that needed fixing and the old engine that had always been overheating surprised her this day. Her car took on the challenge, fueled by the hatred in her heart, and sped steadily down the highway to take her home.

The twenty minutes it took for her to drive home was not enough to quell her seething rage. Lara tried to follow the techniques that Cathalina had taught her—to breathe, relax, and think of a time and place that brought her serenity. But today that would not work. Today, she needed something more and she did not know what it would take.

"Hey, Lara," a handsome young man in his late twenties called out to her. She had seen him around plenty. He had made it obvious that he was interested in her and admired her beautifully sculptured physique. At first Lara tried to pretend she didn't see him, lowering her eyes as she placed her car into her parking spot in the apartment complex where she lived. From her car she could see the pool. It was beautiful. She was fortunate that her apartment balcony also gave a good view of the pool and recreation area, and it always seemed to offer her some measure of peace to look at the stilled reflection of the aqua water. But today this view failed in its promise to her as well.

Buried in her thoughts, she believed that the man had continued on his way so she could continue on hers, but she was wrong. Turning to open her door, she stood face to face with the six-foot, muscular body of a gorgeous man.

"Are you OK?" he asked her as she stepped out of her car.

"Yes, of course. Why do you ask?" she stuttered slightly and maneuvered her way past his hard flesh. She felt her nipples harden involuntarily and she silently cursed the natural reaction of her body.

"I know that we have only seen each other in passing, but I was hoping to change that by asking you out to dinner." Lara just looked at him, studying the movements of his mouth, the way his wavy, black hair curled into his face, his eyes that softened as the greenish-blue color hypnotized her, and the way his even, white teeth seemed to casually bite and tug at his bottom lip. His creamy, tawny complexion blended into his body as he made subtle movements to enhance and flex his muscles as he spoke.

She watched as he spoke to her, and she listened with more than her ears. This is what Lara had become accustomed to with men—listening to what they are really saying, which was always, "Let's just drop the formalities and go right to fucking."

She smiled then. She knew that her overactive imagination was getting the better of her, but more often than not she was right about what men wanted from her.

"I don't think that's a good idea, uh . . ." She didn't know his name, and at that moment she realized that he had called her by her name before he came over. *How did he know it?* she wondered to herself before the sound of his voice broke through her thoughts.

"Leslie," he finished for her. "Leslie Thomason at your service." He took her hand as he said it, and without his eyes leaving hers, he kissed the back of her palm.

"I am really not in a going-out mood."

"It doesn't have to be today." He was quick to offer a way out, while leaving a way back in the door. "It could be tomorrow, next week, or even next month. There really isn't a rush." He flashed her a devilishly handsome smile then, watching his prey weaken under his powers. "I am sure there will be a day when you wouldn't mind some company." He meant to drive his point home, but his insistence just added speed to Lara's legs and she squirmed from in front of him and was on her way to her apartment as fast as she could run.

Leslie looked after her helplessly, and was about to feel rejected, but his ego, like most men's, kicked in and soothed him. After all, Leslie was a man who had any woman he wanted. Never had he been denied the sweet juices of the woman he craved, and so he let her go, knowing he would not let her be the first to break his impeccable record.

Lara opened her door quickly and just as quickly she closed it behind her. The deadly calm came over her again. She felt in control again, blocking out the evils of the outside world that threatened to aid her in losing her mind. She leaned her petite, slender frame against the door to her apartment and looked around. Her thoughts went wild just thinking about the audacity of these men. Their entire existence, it seemed, was to harass, violate, reproduce, and annoy.

She could feel her palms becoming sweaty. Though she maintained her outward composure, her internal collectivity was long gone, her eyes glowing with pure rage. She looked around her one bedroom apartment and her eyes searched the kitchen. She looked from the bar table to the kitchen cabinets. She looked, her eyes searching frantically, and she was propelled forward. Walking through the dimly lit living room and feeling the rigid, gray carpet below her feet, she clenched and unclenched her hands and fists. Tears ran down her face as she made it to the bedroom door, walked to the bed, and laid herself flat across it on her stomach.

She closed her eyes then, and suddenly felt the loving snuggle of her cat Peter as he nestled against her cheek, his tail swooning over her head and his gentle purr urging her to wake up and pet him. Her eyes shot open like bullets, and her mind vaguely remembered or recognized her pet. She knew he belonged to her. She felt that she cared for this animal, but the inner urge to destroy overwhelmed her. She calmly took the large, well-fed, gray-colored cat into her arms. The more she touched him, the more he purred. His joy and excitement irked her.

Rolling onto her back and then sitting up, she looked at him as he lavished in her touch. She struggled to find the sensibility she knew was in her, the reason. But as her hands stroked the animal's head and landed on his neck, all she remembered was that he was male, and like all males, he was interrupting her peace and time, demanding attention so he could have his needs met.

A smile of pure ecstasy appeared as she quickly found the strength and ability to snap the cat's neck in one quick motion. She held him up and looked into the petrified, unblinking gaze of the dead animal, and she felt a surge of thrill she had never known. It was as though she was hungry and was given a taste of her favorite food. Her elation transcended all the orgasms and pleasure she had ever experienced with men.

Lara allowed herself to lie back on the bed, taking her treasured pussy with her. He lay on her chest and she stroked him, although this time he didn't purr, nor did his tail caress her. Suddenly, she felt her body come alive in the most unlikely of places. She felt the tingle in her toes rising up to her calves and into her thighs. She felt her body shudder and tremble, and she grabbed the bed as though there was an earthquake beneath her. She felt moisture between her legs and her wetness seemed to flow down her pantyless thighs. She could not control the explosion that followed, grabbing her and throwing her legs open. The tingle of a breeze hit her clit and she moaned loudly. Her nipples hardened and she grabbed them, kneaded, and massaged. She felt her groin thrust and gyrate as the swelling within her vaginal muscles exploded and she became possessed, aching and gyrating as she was used to doing in the arms of a man. But a man could not have brought on what she felt. Her own anger had given birth to the kind of sexual satisfaction she had never known.

Leslie Thomason had a date. He allowed Lara to run off to her apartment, but he was not concerned. Not only was he convinced that she liked him and was playing hard to get, but he lived in her apartment complex. How much longer could she possibly resist? Not much, by his calculations. So he continued on, admiring himself in the rearview mirror of his indigo blue, convertible PT Cruiser. He found that he had been thinking of Lara a lot lately. Her body called out to him, and she had an allure that he couldn't resist.

Speeding from his designated parking spot to the electronic door that secluded the community, Leslie took one glance at the second floor apartment window that exuded very little light, and imagined what he could do with that woman. He sped off, jumping on I-95 to North Miami Beach where he was meeting the girl he danced all night with at the club the night before. He would feed her at the café outside of the mall so she couldn't get distracted, and then return home with her.

6

As soon as Lara was gone, Cathalina picked up the phone and dialed Cleo's number. She wanted to tell her that Lara was almost ready, but she didn't really want to see Cleo. She knew Cleo would be happy to hear the news, but Cathalina didn't want to meet in person because being with her would bring back stuff she didn't want to dig up. Unfortunately, spending time with Cleo was not something she could ignore or avoid.

Cleo sat in her empress room in the dungeon in a miserable mood. She just couldn't get over how this whole situation made her feel. She couldn't help the feeling of wanting to kill Serena, to get rid of her. Adding her to their team was supposed to make them stronger, especially because of Serena's career status. She had just kind of fallen into their laps miraculously. But all she had done so far was disrupt the relationship she knew she would have had with Cathalina had Serena not come into the picture. Cleopatra, Madam, Empress of Sex Cell was the center of everything before.

Now Cleo's anger grew and boiled, not only for the torturing of men who are filled with rage and hurt women, but also for Serena Kowtow. Cleo sat back in her leopard-printed recliner and looked around her special haven. The hammock that hung from the ceiling brought back many a sexual memory and she shook her head at the many broken handcuffs she hung as memorabilia around her.

Cleo closed her eyes and sniffed at the powered drug next to her as she thought back to the many murders that she and Cathalina had orchestrated and pulled off without a hitch, all the disappearances and half-eaten victims found in the Everglades—the work of her beloved crocodiles. That's how she knew she wanted to be branded with the image of the crocodile. She smiled as she reminisced about the descriptions of the brutal deaths that were plastered across the newspapers in Miami. The news had all men on their best behavior for many years. She smiled eerily as she thought of the rush of the moment that would consume her, and the way she and Cathalina would release each other's tension by violently sucking the nectar from each other as an act of rebellion. She remembered wrapping her body around Cathalina, sheltering her frailer form, and having her breasts sucked and licked until she was into full rapture. Now she would be lucky if she could get Cathalina to smile at her.

A knock on the door jolted her from her thoughts, and her light brown skin burned bright red in rage for the disruption. The girls knew not to interrupt her when she was closed off in her private quarters.

"What is it?" she demanded more than asked.

"It's me, Madam. Natalia." She identified herself so as not to bring on the wrath of Cleo. Natalia was Cleo's favorite girl. She brought in the most customers and they were usually high profile clients. Besides, she had a talent for using her body in ways most women never mastered, and Cleo herself had found herself a victim to the sweetness of Natalia.

"What is it, Natalia?" Cleo asked, softening her voice some, but no less angry.

"Cathalina is on the phone," Natalia said slowly. She and everyone else knew how Cleo felt about Cathalina, even if she had never said a word about it.

"What line?"

"Ten."

"Thanks, Natalia. You have customers?"

"Yes, I do. I'm on my way to get into costume for Trump Dupree." She giggled openly and Cleo couldn't help but laugh too. Everyone knew who this financial tycoon was and they were surprised every time he would fly down from New York to visit with Natalia. They enjoyed his tips even more, so they accommodated him even if he was not scheduled.

"Go do our thing, Natalia," Cleo urged happily as she picked up the phone. She wished all her girls were like Natalia. There was only one other who was better than Natalia. But she was not all female. Before picking up the line, Cleo took a deep breath as she wondered why Cathalina hadn't called her private line directly. *Maybe she was hoping to get the voicemail instead of me*, Cleo thought before she answered. It pained her to even think of it.

"Hello, Cathalina. Do you miss me already?" she joked half-heartedly, really wanting to know the answer, but not willing to push Cathalina.

"Hello, sweetheart. How is business today?"

"Awesome. Just sitting here waiting for our next move." Cleo chuckled nervously at the small talk and wondered anxiously what Cathalina was getting at. "Cathalina, why didn't you call my private line?" she asked before she could stop herself. She didn't want to come off sounding resentful before the conversation even got started. It just bothered her so much. There was a time when she didn't have to second guess whether she should be honest with

Cathalina, and it saddened her that so much had changed between them.

"Oh I didn't?" Cathalina smirked, trying not to let her mirth drift through the phone lines. "I didn't realize that I didn't call your personal line. I was just in a hurry to talk to you."

"So, here I am. What's the news?"

"I think it's almost time to make our move on Lara," she told Cleo, almost whispering. "Her anger is at peak levels and I think she would be receptive to the mark."

"Are you sure?"

"A few more weeks and she will complete the circle."

"So we must prepare then. We must meet and join together in council to decide on our initiation process for the mark of the scorpion." Cleo knew this was something that had to be done. She loved the sisterhood they shared in their anger and vengeance, though they held no other loyalty toward each other, other than to protect each other while they worked. She wouldn't trade the secrets of their wrongdoings for anything. The taste of blood, pain, and anguish pleased her, although she wished she could please Cathalina as her own.

"That's an excellent idea. Have you spoken to Elizabeth since Friday? I think she was supposed to be out of town. She is starring in that play *Man Killer* in Atlanta. Being an actress keeps her busy and informed." There was something special about Liz that Cathalina liked, special beyond her physical attributes and unique contributions to their team. Not only was Liz a hermaphrodite with a fully functional penile sexual organ, but also, unlike most hermaphrodites, her vagina was also fully developed. Elizabeth was a woman true and through. She was sexy and curvaceous. She was slender with silky, olive skin. Her hair, a mixed hair pattern that was intermittently curly and straight, was jet-black, and hung down her spine, tapering off where the roundness of her derrière met her spine. She was stunning, with high cheekbones and slanted eyes with pupils almost as black as her hair. She remained neutral on all levels, though her anger seemed to have gotten worse over the years. She still had not healed from the wrongs that were done to her and seemed, even through it all, to feel some remorse. Tears would usually glaze her eyes during each painful encounter she exacted.

"No, I haven't heard from her, but you know how Liz can be. She's an artist. She likes her space and her privacy. She will come to us when she needs us, I suppose." *Or when we need her*, Cleo thought.

"Yes, I guess you are right." Elizabeth had always been the quieter of the threesome once she came on board. She was their first pick and her methods were daring and on the edge of crazy.

It was growing late, and although Cathalina didn't really want to, she decided to spend some quiet time with Cleo. She cringed when she heard herself make the offer.

"So what are you up to for the rest of the evening here in Miami where the possibilities are endless?" she smiled a forced smile, willing her voice to submit and echo the sounds of flirting instead of the repulsion she was steadily developing for this beautiful seductress.

Cleo thought for a second, holding her breath. It'd been more than six months since she and Cathalina had spent some time alone. Always their time had been spent organizing, planning, and punishing those who deserved punishment. She was afraid to hope for alone time.

"I am as free as free can be, Cathalina. Why? Did you have something in mind?"

Cathalina chuckled knowingly and allowed herself to continue.

"Well, actually I was hoping that maybe we could go grab a bite to eat. I haven't eaten, and maybe we can do some catching up then," she lied, wanting to offer some sort of peace offering to the volatile dungeon mistress. She always wanted Cleo to have a sense of hope. Hope was what gave Cleo the strength for the tasks at hand.

"Sounds inviting," Cleo said, not hiding her sarcasm. She would take this offer nonetheless. "Name the time and place."

Cathalina thought for a moment about the most public place she could find, and where they could probably find some action. But she couldn't think of anything.

"You pick. I can't think right now for the life of me," she admitted, knowing that by giving up her advantage of a location, anything was possible with Cleo.

"I know just the place. Meet me here, and I will take it from there," she uttered excitedly.

"That's fine. I'll see you in a few minutes then." Cathalina exhaled and hung up the phone. No use in prolonging the inevitable. She knew Cleo wouldn't let it just drop there. Something had to give, and if she wanted to pacify this tyrant, she was going to have to present her with a real peace offering.

Cathalina tried to keep the conversation to a minimum as they sped to Aventura Mall in North Miami, blasting Matchbox 20's most recent CD, and singing along to the tunes.

"I'm not crazy, I'm just a little impaired I know, right now you don't care." Cleopatra looked at Cathalina oddly but appreciatively. One thing the two always had in common was music. Cleo had just picked up the same CD on Saturday, the day after Serena's initiation, and she was not aware that Cathalina had also purchased it. She loved the way Cathalina drove, speeding down I-95 in a vehicle that was made to go. Cleo allowed the music to sear her soul while enjoying the presence of her secret love.

They pulled into the huge Aventura Mall exterior parking

area. The place was huge and gorgeous with plants and trees from the surrounding neighborhood complementing those that acted as decorative enhancements to the shopping and eating areas of the mall. Not to mention that it's a hotspot for couples making out at night. Cleopatra was glad that she got to choose the spot for dinner. She was ready for an anything-goes kind of moment, and if the mood struck and Cathalina decided to give her a taste of that memory that was slipping away from her so fast, she could take it right there. This was Miami, and anything was possible.

Cathalina cruised into a familiar spot toward the front. There was special parking for handicapped guests, and so Cathalina reached in for her handicapped parking sticker and flipped it up onto the dashboard so they could pack closer to the mall entrance. As she moved, Cleopatra watched the sheer sleekness of her movements and the way Cathalina's skirt hiked up to reveal her beautiful, long, brown thighs. Cleo's mouth watered and she allowed her hand to accidentally slide down the length of Cathalina's luscious invitation as she reached for her purse that lay at her feet. The car was small in the front and roomy in the back, so Cleopatra used that to her advantage just to touch Cathalina in hopes of stirring the same memories she harbored.

Cathalina looked at her and smiled knowingly, not wanting to shoot Cleopatra down and hurt her feelings. She reached for her hand and gently fondled her fingers, allowing her caress to linger and then creep up to Cleopatra's forearm. Cleo shuddered and trembled. Just the thought of what it might be like to bury her face between Cathalina's thighs again had her juicy fruit melting into a watery existence.

"Com'on, hot stuff. Let's go eat. I'm starving." Cathalina broke the trance of her thoughts and smiled at Cleo reassuringly. Her eyes twinkled with promise and Cleo hoped that promise would be realized this night.

"Hummm! Smell the fresh scent of the ocean. The breeze. It's a beautiful night, Cathalina. Thanks for inviting me."

"Now who else would I enjoy a night like this with, if not my partner in crime?" Cathalina laughed out loud at her own remark, her slender frame jerking from the sheer pleasure of it. "No pun intended." She winked while giving Cleopatra a playful shove, then took a long stride toward their eatery of choice.

Cleo bubbled with joy from within, thinking thoughts of the possibilities and taking quick, subtle, sidelong glances at Cathalina. Her heart drummed to the beat of passion as she brushed her arm against Cathalina or fondled her fingers while they walked. Cleo sashayed her beautiful, voluptuous body and felt her thighs rain the sweet juices of an excited woman. Anticipation filled her and held her body captive in a way that she didn't want to end. As they neared the popular pasta eatery that was nestled outdoors with peaceful plants and palm trees surrounding it, Cleo noticed that there was a man palming a young woman hard. His hands were everywhere and his feet played footsie under the table. The girl, seemingly shy and timid, tried fruitlessly to dissuade him.

Cleo watched as the man reached for the girl's shirt and unbuttoned the top button with one easy snap of his nimble fingers. His index finger trailed down the center of her chest to her bubbling cleavage. Cleo heard Cathalina rambling on about Lara, who Cleo desperately wanted to be ready for the team, but this time her interest was elsewhere. Her sexual desires heightened and she began to breathe harder. She was hot for someone, yet she felt the repulsion that the thin, voluptuously-shaped young girl felt for the man who would not stop touching her.

The two friends instinctively slowed their pace when Cathalina realized the source of Cleo's distraction. They found themselves being led in the direction of the couple. Glancing quickly around the restaurant, they saw waiters and waitresses flirting shamelessly for their tips, and women and men engaging each other in tireless persuasion for that well sought after sexual release. The voices mingled into noise, and the crocodile plastered on Cleo's back began to breathe. Cathalina took her hand and squeezed it tightly, sensing the urges that were building within her friend.

"It's OK, Cleopatra. Let's go eat," she urged, gently pulling her toward the eatery. As they neared the restaurant, the voices of the patrons became louder and more mingled together, sounding to Cleo like a high-pitched frequency that she just couldn't stand. She wanted to go over there and grab that man's very soul from his body and suffocate it so that he couldn't even ascend into purgatory. He would be unrecognizable as ever being human.

"OK," Cleo submitted, "but please, let's sit somewhere where I can keep my eyes on him," she insisted. The open-backed tank top she wore was a visible display of her internal anguish. She wanted to hurt this man.

"Are you OK?" Cathalina asked, bidding her to sit at the seat where the hostess had led them. She noticed the grimace on Cleo's face and became concerned. She knew the amphetamines inside of her were surging. "Maybe it's a better idea for us to leave, Cleo. I don't think this is a good time to take on anything," Cathalina urged, but Cleo was already too far gone. Her mind was made up. She wanted to get involved. She was already involved emotionally, psychologically, and in the way of the guardian.

"We are already here, Cath." She smiled eerily and calmly, using Cathalina's nickname reserved only for Serena, but tonight she knew she needed no excuse to use it. "We will have a nice, quiet dinner as planned," she stated flatly. Cathalina knew that the night was on whether she wanted it to be or not. And whatever happened or was about to happen had to be done right.

"Can we have a couple glasses of Chardonnay to start, please?" Cathalina smiled warmly at the server, a tall, thin, Caucasian man with blondish-brown hair who couldn't be older than twenty-one. They watched as he walked away and then simultaneously their eyes reverted back to the couple being overly sexual. The guy had gotten up and roughly grabbed the arm of the petite, blond, Latino girl. His hand moved from her arm to behind her neck, ruffling her neatly-pinned hair, which fell down to her shoulders. Cleo clenched her fists and held on to the edge of the table.

She stood tensely and watched as he led the girl out of the restaurant and toward the dimly lit parking lot. They followed the man as Cleo's hairs stood on edge and every hormone in her body was at its peak. She surveyed the cars parked neatly in vertical rows, but at this particular moment, they seemed eerily taunting. Cathalina tried to hold her at a distance, but her spider, now sensing the thrill of a hunt, writhed under her skin.

"Leslie, this is not at all necessary. I think you have had too much to drink." The young lady pleaded to his sensibilities, but the only sense he was thinking with was the one in his pants. He responded with a grunt and pulled her into him so closely that they seemed as one. She struggled against his body, but then gave up, falling limp.

"Now that's better." He praised her submission. "It would feel so much better if you relaxed." The keen hearing of the crocodile in Cleo caused her to spring into action, but the mindfulness of her companion held her back.

"Let's just walk up on them. He'll let her go and this whole episode will be over," Cathalina compromised. But at that moment, he threw the woman face down on a Volvo in an attempt to violate her. The space was semi-dark and no patrons were around to notice the couple.

As the man hoisted the young woman's skirt and pulled her panties away, she began to whimper. He took his finger and gently rubbed it alongside her clit and vaginal lips. He stood still for a moment, an electrical charge of anticipation flooding his already engorged penis in preparation for entrance. He took his fingers from between her legs and licked them, closing his eyes to the pure ecstasy of his desires. He whispered something in her ear. Cleo cocked her head in an attempt to listen, but he was speaking too low, too softly. Holding the girl, he quickly released the threat from his pants and rubbed the tip against her opening. She moaned and he took that as permission. He slipped it in an inch and threw his head back from the pure pleasure of it. Without being able to control himself, he plunged himself deep within her and she screamed, throwing Cleo into action with Cathalina following closely on her heels.

Before he knew what was happening, Cleo's two-hundred pounds was on him, beating him. For a second, he saw a light flash before his eyes and thought it was the excruciating gratification of what he was sampling between the legs of his unwilling lover, but when it hit him that he was being attacked, he pushed off of his victim and began to swing wildly. Cleopatra's fist connected with his jaw and he staggered back. The frightened young woman who was being molested grabbed at her clothes and ran off into the distance. Cleo tried to go after her, called after her, but she just kept going and refused to stop.

A crowd had now gathered to watch as this beautiful, fair-skinned woman pinned him by his neck to the same Volvo he was using as a bed. Cathalina ran back to Cleo and pulled her off the man. She managed to get Cleo off the man and through the crowd before the police got involved. She shoved Cleo into her very high profile and noticeably unique car and sped off before things got any more out of hand.

"What did you do that for, bitch?" Cleo shot at Cathalina. The shock on Cathalina's face rendered her speechless. "I almost had that sonofabitch, Cath!" She spewed anger from her very soul, and Cathalina realized that this was more about Cleo than the situation, so she tried to contain her urge to respond in the same volatile manner.

"Cleo, you were out of control, love. We must remember where we are and not behave this way in public. I know that your nature is different. But we have to be careful. Did you see the crowd?" Cathalina asked her as gently as she possibly could without raising her voice. Cleo was wiping her ringed fingers over her face, and her long, black, polished nails dug into her temple in frustration.

"This feels like an unfulfilled orgasm." Cleo laughed shakily like a junkie needing to get a fix. But she wasn't joking. The thrill of the kill was always exciting. It brought with it a very special kind of satisfaction that could not be measured. If she were lucky enough to get "lucky" after such an adrenaline rush, she would enjoy the bliss so much, it would be worth it. She could only remember such a moment now. Actually experiencing such a moment had occurred almost a year in the past, but no such opportunity had arisen recently. The very thought of it brought tears to Cleo's eyes.

Cathalina watched her with concern. Cleo was becoming very selfish and absorbed in what killing was doing for her. She seemed to be forgetting the purpose and reason in the first place. It wasn't for self-fulfillment, it was for justice, it was for the greater good, and soon Cleo would have to be controlled. This concerned Cathalina.

Cathalina, speeding down the I-95, noticed her friend's anguish, and pulled over by the Fort Lauderdale Airport and parked. That area at night was very deserted and quiet, with only the illumination of the runway lights to give the descending planes guidance to land. Cathalina pulled onto the deserted grassy area and turned off the car lights. Turning slowly, she looked at Cleo and reached for her hands, which were clutching her face.

"Cleo, you helped that girl. It was enough," she told her softly, but Cleo only shook her head in disagreement. "Yes, you did. She got away and he will probably never do such a thing again."

"You are wrong, Cathalina. He did get away with it. By the time I acted it was too late," she mumbled under her hands; they were now covering her face. Cleo was unable to stop the flow of tears that had crept up on her. Cathalina removed Cleo's hands and wiped at the tears that had seared her flawless mascara.

"That was neither the time nor the place. We don't want to become hot again, not now while we are just fortifying our team." Cathalina sighed and reached out to hug Cleo. As she got nearer to her, Cleo grabbed her like a life vest, buried her face in the tattoo of Cathalina's spider and shuddered while crying dry tears.

"It's OK, hun. Everything is all right," Cathalina soothed and softly stroked Cleo's hair. Then she kissed Cleo's temple, then her forehead, her nose, and her closed eyelids. She knew this was what Cleo needed, what she wanted most—the comfort of Cathalina's arms and the softness of her touch. Cathalina thought about where things were obviously leading. She knew it would happen, but she didn't know how. She chuckled softly as Cleo pushed away from her shoulders and pressed her lips into hers. Hindsight was amusing to her.

"What is it?" Cleo asked, blushing.

"It's been so long," Cathalina lied.

"I know. I have missed you, Cathalina," she whimpered before pressing her lips into Cathalina's again, forcefully pressing forward to touch the delicate frame of Cathalina's lean body.

Cleo reached for Cathalina's head and pulled it deeper into her kiss, caressing her tongue and frolicking with her teeth and gums. Cathalina moaned softly, and then deeper, relaxing her mind to what she knew she would not be able to resist tonight. They shared horrible secrets and bore the marks of their sisterhood as a reminder. Cleo needed her tonight, and even though she really didn't want to, she needed to make a sacrifice tonight for the greater good of her comrade, so she submitted to her.

"Cleo," Cathalina moaned, "you drive me crazy," she lied, allowing Cleo to take full control of the moment. Pulling Cathalina across the gearshift and simultaneously releasing the seat so that it reclined back, Cleo had Cathalina right where she wanted her. She slipped her hand under Cathalina's skirt and found her soft cheeks already moist from the excitement dripping between her legs. Cleo's fingers sought out her clitoris, and with agile flickers, she brought a soft sigh from Cathalina that pushed for her to continue.

"You missed me too, didn't you, baby?" Cleo asked. And to hide the disgusted sarcasm on her face and in her voice, Cathalina just moaned. Yes, she was excited, but it was the thought of Serena that turned her on, the idea of being loved by purity. Cathalina allowed her mind to wander to a resting Serena. She felt her abdomen quiver at the thought of Serena's tongue licking the life sources from her thighs, and she trembled when Cleo's fingers masterfully and knowingly brought her to full orgasm. She clenched Cleo's back and bit into her shoulders so she wouldn't call out Serena's name in her blissful delirium.

Allowing her mind's eyes to guide her, Cathalina ripped open the tight knitted top that barely concealed Cleo's double-D bosom and buried her face between the soft mounds of her cleavage. She inhaled and started to cough, but she forced it to come out as a muffled sound of pleasure. She allowed her hands to roam over Cleo's pierced belly button, and allowed her face to follow, planting soft, butterfly kisses as she went. Cleo was impatient to have her desires quenched.

Cathalina proceeded to return the satisfaction that Cleo gave to her and repositioned both she and Cleo for better accessibility. The stars shined brightly as the two women shared one more secret of pleasure. Cathalina touched and fondled Cleo's vital sensitive areas until she heard the expressions of satisfaction croon from Cleo's lips. Only Cleo was not faking it when she told Cathalina that she loved her, and that she didn't want to ever again forget the sweet touch of Cathalina's body against hers.

Cathalina pressed her face deep into Cleo's belly and wept softly. She knew this was a dangerous connection. She felt the caution within her as a silent alarm warned her of what was to come.

7

Lara awoke just after eleven at night and wrapped her arms around her body, experiencing the after effects of murdering her innocent cat. She looked next to her on the bed where she lay and saw that the cat was still there. His tongue hung to the side in an unconcerned expression.

The wetness between her legs seemed to tell of an unfulfilled desire as thoughts of her earlier episode caused her to squeeze her thighs tightly together and moan deeply, wanting to feel the swellings of a male counterpart inside her. She rocked herself unsuccessfully in an attempt to comfort her body, but she knew from past experience that the only one thing that could give her the comfort she really needed was a man.

Her mind ran wildly through her little black book, wondering who she could call on at this time of night to come to her aid. Most of the men she was intimate with had wives and girlfriends and were otherwise occupied at this hour without previous planning. The urges sent a pang of sexual hunger through her and it shot her up from the bed. She searched through her clothing and found something sexy— a red, lacy, Frederick's of Hollywood teddy with a feathered boa, crotch-less matching underwear, and matching white and red stiletto heels. She squealed with delight at the thought of dressing up and ran to the shower to get cleaned up.

"Who can I share all of this lusciousness with? Damn, I am horny!" Lara said out loud as she stepped under the piping hot water and allowed it to wash away any guilt or concern, for anything or anyone, from her mind. She allowed her body to fully focus on the need that was boiling like an untamed volcano between her legs.

I wonder if Mark is still hanging out with that bitch Pauline, or that slut Patrick for that matter, she mused to herself. *These two-way niggahs are starting to get on my nerves,* she thought devilishly, lathering the soap all over her and lingering over her throbbing pussy.

She rubbed herself dry after exiting the shower and looked around her small apartment.

"Damn, I have more sexy lingerie than food," she said to herself. "You really are a bitch, aren't ya?" she asked herself as she swayed toward her mirror and modeled the flimsy pieces of fabric that she had just put on.

Quickly thinking back to earlier that afternoon, her mind lingered on the gorgeous creature who introduced himself to her as Leslie. He was scrumptious. Imaging what might be hidden in his pants caused her to squeeze her legs together again.

"So you wanted some of this, Mr. Leslie?" she asked the mirror in a seductive voice. She inhaled, trying to recapture the scent of him. Again she imagined the length of him, which caused a second soaking that dripped from the crotch-less panties she wore. She quickly ran to the door and looked up and down the open corridors that overlooked the parking garage, the swimming pool, and the main building with the rental office. Florida was unique in its apartment designs, allowing for breathtaking views from each individual apartment. She glanced at the clock that was now chiming midnight.

The place was empty, so she took the two flights down, still in her sexy lingerie, to where she parked, and tried to survey the area where she thought he might be. Then she spotted it, his PT Cruiser. *He had a PT cruiser earlier. Black convertible top and it looked like it could use a new paint job. Couldn't be more than a 1999.* Usually she wouldn't consider giving up the punani to a guy driving such a dump, but desperate times called for desperate measures.

She hustled over, timidly at first, and then in an urgent dash, kneeling on the ground to check out the number marked on the parking space underneath the car. It was marked 405. She stood up, brushed off her knees, and sighed a sigh of anticipated satisfaction.

"Apartment 405, I'm coming, baby." And she began to laugh. "No pun intended." She sashayed her overheated body back to her apartment and ran to the bathroom, reaching for the washcloth and wiping the liquid that was running down her thighs. She grabbed her favorite perfume, Obsession, and squirted a tad on all the female vitals; her neck, her chest, belly button, inside of her thighs, and behind her knees.

Still wearing nothing but the teddy and her boa feathers wrapped around her shoulders, and feeling the heat permeating from her body, she was propelled to his door where she stood for a good five minutes before knocking.

Leslie lay in his bed thinking back to his incredible night. Who was that woman who had attacked him? His thoughts pressed into his mind for answers, causing his head to hurt and his jaw to throb and ache. He thought he heard a knock at his door, so he went into the living room to investigate.

Leslie's apartment was definitely a bachelor pad, boasting a black leather sofa and loveseat and getting-busy red lights that only slightly lit the almost dark room. He had a big, sixty-four-inch, stand alone television with all types of sports videos and DVDs displayed on each side. Porno movies, stacked at the very bottom for convenience, sat opposite the sofa. His refrigerator was loaded with liquor, beer, and dips for chips, and a jar of glow-in-the-dark condoms sat on his nightstand.

He looked at the clock and saw that it was 12:30 AM, and then he looked at his door as another knock came. He looked at the clock again. *Could it be that those crazy bitches followed me home?* he wondered. His curiosity got the better of him, so he rose to go look through the peephole. As he neared the door, he stopped and turned back toward the kitchen. He got the baseball bat that he kept hidden behind the kitchen door, just in case he had to defend himself.

"Holy shit," Leslie said as he peeped through the peephole before opening the door. He then tried to compose himself, willing his immediate erection to subside, and attempted to conceal the look of surprise on his face.

"I knew you would come around," he crooned, smoothing out his wrinkled, silk shirt and trying to act smooth.

"Yes, I came around," Lara said and smiled at him. He placed the baseball bat behind the door and opened his arms so that she knew she was welcomed to come inside.

"No," she said.

"What do you mean 'no'? You are the one who came knocking on my door at one in the morning." He was becoming agitated and his libido was rising again at the sight of this gorgeous, practically naked woman right in front of his door, a woman he had fantasized about on more than one occasion.

"I meant, if you want me, take me. Right here." The

words came out of her mouth and she was somewhat surprised. Usually guys came on to her and she would give in. But to solicit a guy was a first for her. She felt this bold new energy consume her, as if she was being pushed by some unknown entity within her.

Leslie laughed and stepped to the threshold of the doorway, reaching for her waist. As he stepped forward, she saw that one of his eyes was partially closed and that his lip looked as though it was bleeding, but she ignored that. She had an urgent need to have the cavern between her legs filled, and right now he had what she wanted to fill it with. She allowed him to pull her into his body and begin to kiss her neck and shoulder. She unbuttoned his pants and sought out what she craved. Grabbing his shaft in her hands, she didn't have to do much before he was fully erect and ready for action. She lifted her legs around his waist, and thrusting her hips into his groin, she felt the tip of him pierce her. He groaned and moaned as he felt her guide him inside of her already soaking pussy. He grabbed her legs and braced himself against the door posts for balance

"Shit, oh fuck. Bitch, your pussy is so fucking wet." He was so excited and so ready. She had taken him by surprise. She didn't seem like the bold type, but more like the kind who would have to be coerced, so this was a pleasant surprise.

"Yes, I knew you would like this," she stated blatantly. She heard the words coming out of her mouth, but couldn't believe they were her words, her thoughts. She wrapped her legs around his thighs and braced her arms between the doorway, holding on for stability. He held her tightly and hoisted her up so he could thrust himself deeper within her.

"Yes, that's it, daddy. Oh yes!" she screamed at the top of her lungs.

"Shhhhhh," he begged, knowing he had other mistresses in the same building, and he didn't want to be caught out in the hallway doing her.

"Don't tell me to shut up, you bastard. Fuck me if you are going to fuck me, and let me enjoy the shit." Realizing what she had just said, and seeing the look of shock and newfound respect for her on his face, she began to giggle and then laugh. She grabbed his neck and met his stabbing thrusts by slamming her buttocks downward and pulling him into her with the back of her calves.

"I'm cumming, I'm cumming!" she exclaimed louder and louder as her passion rose within her and creamed all over him. But she wasn't finished. She adjusted her panties and walked into his dimly lit apartment. *That was not good enough*, she thought to herself. Killing the damn cat was a better orgasm than what she had just had, and she needed something more powerful. She felt like a junkie seeking the high she had hours earlier.

"Damn, what about me, Lara? I didn't come yet," he whined.

"Don't worry. I will take care of you," she promised, taking him by the hand and leading him to the sofa where he willingly sat down. Pulling his pants down below his knees, she spread his legs and fully exposed the meat that she wanted to please her so badly. Slowly taking the tip of his love stick into her mouth, she played with his pee hole until he felt the need to ram himself down her throat.

"More," he grunted deeply from within his throat, the pleasure almost choking him. She moaned as she slowly took him into her oral cavity, and with swallowing motions she allowed her tongue to bathe his shaft, consuming the full length of him. "Ohhh, shit." He sighed, enjoying the pure ecstasy of the experience. "I want to cum, baby. Oh gosh, I am going to blow right now," he told her, grabbing the short tresses of her hair and pushing her head into his crotch. But she wouldn't allow it. She pulled off of him and straightened herself out. She could feel her juices sliding down her legs and her pussy throbbing as though it was about to explode.

"Where is the bedroom, love?" she asked in a sexy, sultry voice. It didn't take a second for Leslie to respond, because before she could complete her request, he was on his feet and heading down the short, dark hallway. They entered a room and he threw himself on the bed.

"Baby, where can I go to freshen up a bit?" she asked almost hypnotically. She had dropped the boa and revealed her hourglass curves, rendering him speechless. He watched her as he pointed back down the hallway. "It's OK, hun. I'll find it," she assured him and swaggered out of the room. As soon as she was out of sight, she dashed stealthily to the kitchen and searched for a knife. She couldn't find one, but she found an ice pick, which was better. She needed her fix like an addict, and she was going to get it by any means necessary.

Placing the handle in the waistband of her underwear, she glided back into the bedroom and slid into the bed next to him. With his eyes closed, he reached for her. She took the pick out of her panties and put it under the pillow. She moved so quickly that she didn't notice that the space under the pillow already had an inhabitant.

"I cannot believe that you're the same woman I tried to kick it to earlier," he whispered in her ear as she lowered her body on top of his now fully naked one. He grabbed a firm hold on her arms and wanted to hug her tightly. She was like his dream woman. She felt his manhood rise.

"You feel so good against me. I wish I had followed you here from the first time I saw you wave at me a year ago when I was moving in," she told him genuinely. He fit her so well. She knew she was on a high, and that she was feenin'. *Maybe that was it?* she thought to herself, but she just couldn't shake the feeling. It was something powerful.

"Yeah, baby, I been trying to get your attention for a good minute, but you always seemed uninterested and on the go."

"Don't make out like I'm a saint now." She giggled.

"I would be stupid to do that. I noticed all the brothas you had creeping up in your crib at nights. Sometimes I thought it was only you and your girls hanging out, but I see that you know how to play the game."

"I wish those times were as nice as you make them seem," she said sadly. "Anyway, I am here now, and there is only one thing on my mind, and there is only one man who can give it to me."

"Now you talking, sweetheart. You are my kinda woman," he told her, wrapping her into his arms and burying his tongue down her throat. He flipped her over so he could be on top, and then he ripped the rest of her clothes off. He inhaled her scent and licked her nipples, nibbling until they were hard and taunt.

"Just like that, baby." She urged him on, encouraging him not to stop until his face was buried between her legs. She squeezed them shut over his head and he gasped for air. She released him and then wrapped her thick, shapely legs under his buttocks and pulled him up to her. She could feel his hard on pressing into her midsection, and she arched her back and shoulders, pressing her thighs to meet his thrusts.

"Oh, girl, you've got heaven and hell between your legs," he confessed as he moved gently at first, and then faster, meeting her in an erotic rhythm of pleasure that they both surrendered to. They sighed and danced the horizontal mamba until he felt the urge to explode inside her. "Girl, let me stop and put on a condom," he told her, not really wanting to stop. But she didn't respond. She felt her body tingle all over. Her tummy fluttered with a thousand butter-flies and her toes curled. She got flashbacks of the after-shock waves she had experienced with the cat, and she wanted to know what it would feel like to have that experi-ence with a man. She figured it would be ten times as pow-erful.

"I hear ya, and I feel ya. You don't need a condom. Trust me. Just keep moving. I don't want you to stop," she begged, and he gave her what she wanted. She could feel the length of him grow longer and the width of him in-crease. Heaven help her, she was about to cum.

As she pushed him to bring on an explosion, she felt her-self reaching under the pillow for the gift she had placed there earlier. She couldn't wait. She felt the insides of her thighs ache that beautiful, powerful pain, and she opened them wider, inviting him for a deeper feel.

As she grabbed the handle of the ice pick, he grabbed her hand, noticing that she was up to something, but he couldn't stop himself from the primal pull that he was engaged in. She was ready to cream all over herself, and she braced her-self to experience the orgasm of a lifetime. He did not see that she had the pick behind him, ready to plunge it into him, until it was too late. Then she noticed that he had a gun hidden under the pillow and within his reach. *How did I miss that?* she wondered. She was surprised, but the pos-sibility only heightened the excitement of her ecstasy.

"What are you doing?" he asked her, as she shifted, mak-ing his maneuvers uncomfortable. But she only smiled a grimace so scary and ugly that he thought she seemed al-most demonic.

"Are you possessed or some shit?" he asked her, still mov-ing.

"Now this is one fuck worth dying for," she whispered, so he would come closer to hear what she was saying. As he pressed his body into her and she heard him say, "Oh shit, oh shit . . . O," she removed the weapon from its hiding place, knowing he was completely distracted, and rammed the pick deep within his shoulder blade, puncturing through to his heart.

"What the fuck?" he screamed, blood running down his already beaten mouth. She let go of the pick, grabbed his ass, and wrapped her legs around him so he couldn't move, forcing the cum to come before his dick went limp.

"Oh YESsssssssssssssss!" she screamed. "Fuck this pussy, baby. Isn't this pussy worth dying for?"

"You are a sick bitch," he gargled and placed the gun next to her temple. Her body convulsed so hard from her orgasm that she closed her eyes. Her legs trembled so much that she released them from around his body. She shook so much she could have suffered a seizure, and with his last breath he pulled the trigger of his gun, splattering her brain on the bed, her body still feeling the aftereffects of her orgasm.

"I hope that was an orgasm worth dying for," he whispered. Leslie realized that he couldn't move and that he was badly hurt. He allowed himself to rest on top of her and lay down, trying to gasp for air. He closed his eyes and chuckled to himself. *What a fucking way to die!* he thought, and his eyes went blank.

8

As Cleopatra and Cathalina drove leisurely back to Miami, still reveling in their lovemaking and the toe-curling aftereffects that riveted their bodies, they heard bustling sirens in the distance.

"Oh boy, another tragedy. Looks like something huge happened somewhere close," Cathalina observed. Cleo didn't want to hear about it or even think about another person at that moment. She was only concerned with how she felt at that very moment, and that she was with the woman she wanted, the woman who had denied her for so long.

They cruised on I-95 and watched as ambulance and police cars sped past them, sirens blaring and screaming so loudly that they could not conceal their curiosity.

"I think we should go see what the problem is or where they're going. After all, I am a doctor," Cathalina said while steering the car in the direction the police went. She didn't want Cleopatra's input. All Cleo cared about was that she was sexed up and satisfied, and that's all that concerned her now.

"Why can't we just go back to your place and relax, Cath?

People are in accidents all the time. We should know. We have orchestrated quite a few of them ourselves." She chuckled at her own humor.

"I just have this really eerie feeling about this one. I don't know what it is, but I feel that we should go." Cathalina dove in and out of traffic behind the police vehicles, trying to keep up before traffic reorganized itself behind the moving emergency vehicles.

"What kind of feeling? You are always feeling sorry for these no-good, lowlifes that get themselves in trouble. Can't you see by now that you cannot save the world? This is why we do what we do, set things right that have gone drastically wrong." Cleo bitched about Cathalina's choice to be concerned, but Cathalina was used to it. She was a doctor, a psychiatrist. That's what she did—care about people, feel empathy, want to fix things. It was who she was.

"I am not going to have this conversation with you again, Cleo. This is who I am. You want me to be this unfeeling, callous bitch, but that's not who I am. I would much rather not be running around at night fucking and destroying God's perfect creation. Men and women were made to be soul mates, the opposite of each that should be whole, but somewhere along the line we screwed that up. That does not make what we do right. It's just a small way of appeasing what I feel is an injustice. Now if you don't mind, could you shut the fuck up so I can concentrate on driving?" Cathalina told her. Cathalina's clear annoyance brought Cleopatra to attention.

"So is it my fault that things got screwed up by assholes who only think of themselves? It's my fault that creation has become undone by nasty, psychotic freaks who think with what's in their pants, rather than with their brains." The venom and revulsion Cleo felt escaped her mouth as easily as the air she breathed.

"We are not doing anything by dealing with it the way we do. I personally feel that it's so messed up that what we are doing is the only way. But if we think about it . . . and notice I said we, what we are doing is adding to the problem, not fixing it," Cathalina said.

"Well, you can WE your own damn self, Cath. You talking as if you have regrets, like you want to throw in the towel after all the shit we did, turn us in to 5-0 and just say forget it. But it won't be that easy, trust me! We are going to do what we star . . ."

"Oh my goodness!" Cathalina exclaimed, cutting Cleo off as she pulled into the apartment complex behind the police officers, ambulances, and detectives.

"Really, Cathalina, stop with the theatrics already. We already have dramatic Liz. We don't need you acting too," she spat brazenly. "What did you do that for?" Cleopatra screeched as she felt Cathalina's fist connect with her shoulder.

"Keep your fucking mouth closed for a change and use your damn brains. Sometimes I wonder how I got mixed up with your stupid ass." Cathalina allowed her anger and resentment toward Cleo to get the best of her. And although she realized what she said, it was too late to take it back. Besides, she didn't want to take it back. It was about time she said to Cleo what was on her mind.

Cleo just stared at her. She hung her head and silent tears flowed down the side of her face and under her chin. Cathalina's words hurt her. She felt the truth in the words and was dumbfounded. Cathalina didn't even look at her. She just parked the car off to a corner and watched the police.

"This is where Lara lives." Cathalina's cadence was soft and soothing, but fear had her almost paralyzed. "When I pulled up behind the cops just now, my stomach did flips," she almost whispered, as she felt the churning in her abdomen telling her something was deadly wrong. She felt like she had connected with Lara already, and although Lara was already groomed, now something was fatally wrong.

"Do you think this is about her?" For a moment, Cleo stopped thinking of herself and her own insatiable ego. For a moment, it hit her that the time and energy they had spent, seeking out the right person for the fourth spot, and the months of preparation, might all be lost in a moment.

"I don't know what it is. I just feel that something has happened to Lara."

"They are coming from the second floor," Cleo observed

"I know. She is on the second floor, but I just don't know where her apartment is located." Cathalina wrapped her arms around herself and sighed deeply, in solemn hope that this was not what she thought it was.

"Oh God."

"Don't call God now, Cleo. Stay here. I will be right back."

Cleo watched Cathalina as she walked briskly toward a group of medics taking instructions from the police. She watched as police explained something to Cathalina that made her shudder.

"I don't understand? Why can't you tell me what's going on?" Cathalina asked with more urgency than she wanted to express.

"Because this is police business," the detective snapped sharply. Seeing her reaction, he relaxed and spoke in a more caring voice. "I am sorry, ma'am, we are in the middle of an investigation now and I cannot reveal that information to you. Are you related to the deceased? Because if you are, you can go to the precinct for further information."

"Excuse me, sir. They would like to bring the bodies out now," one young, uniformed officer interrupted. "What would you like to do?"

"Wait, Detective," Cathalina said. "I was seeing a woman in this building who was ill. Could you possibly explain to me who the woman was?" she grabbed the sleeve of the detective who had begun to walk away and make his way toward the coroner, who had already separated the bodies and was bringing them down to the ambulances.

"Seeing her how?"

"My name is Dr. Cathalina Shekhar. I am a psychiatrist. I was seeing her for anger issues and sexual aggressiveness." Cathalina spoke the words slowly, as though she wasn't sure if she should really say them. She hoped she had not compromised herself by identifying who she was. But she knew that sooner or later there would be an investigation anyway, and somehow they would find their way to her office to find out the same thing she was telling them now.

"How did you know that something had happened here tonight?" The detective turned to her suspiciously. "Why are you here?" He turned toward her in the mid-stride and stopped to look directly into the tall, dark-skinned woman's face. He could see she was in a lot of pain from the expression she bore. *Damn, she is stunning!* he thought to himself, willing his face not to blush and appear on his olive-colored, Italian complexion.

"I was on my way home from dinner with a friend. She is waiting for me in the car right now," she told him as she shied away from him when he reached out to touch her shoulder.

"What is that? I think you are hurt. You're bleeding on your shoulder," he informed her with gentle concern and bit more suspicion.

"Oh, it's nothing. I accidentally hit my arm on the car door in my rush to get out and come speak with you."

"We have medics here. You should let one of them take a look at that for you before you go." His humor was lost on Cathalina.

"I am all right. Really." She decided to leave before he prodded any deeper.

"Fine then, come with me and you can take a look for yourself, see if this is your patient or someone else. After all, she had no identification on her, so whatever you could help us with would be greatly appreciated," he told her and then he stopped again and looked at Cathalina with deep concern. "There is one other problem." He paused and waited for her to focus on him.

"What is it?" she asked, impatience bubbling within her.

"The woman was shot in the head. Half of her face has been blown off. You may not readily recognize her," he warned, trying to be sensitive to the woman's possible inexperience with dead bodies.

The detective turned on his heels and strutted away quickly, forcing Cathalina to keep pace as she approached the two dead bodies on the stretchers. Cathalina cringed and braced herself as they reached for the white sheet and rolled it back from over the female victim's head. A squeal escaped her mouth. The part of Lara's head that remained made her identity evident. Cathalina doubled over as the brown recluse churned and raked its legs into the wound on her shoulder in response to the situation. She began to vomit the dinner she had shared with Cleo only hours before. The peppered garlic Alfredo sauce with fettuccini, chicken, and shrimp did not look as appetizing as it did when she devoured it earlier.

She heaved again as she turned her face away from the blood and gore of the gray mass of brain that had settled in a clustered mass to the side of Lara's head, face, and shoulder. Lara seemed happy, a smile on her face in death. Cathalina recognized the blond mass of hair left on the right side of her head, and the butterfly tattoo on the right side of her neck that she had once admired and made a mental note to compliment Lara on.

"Are you all right?" the detective asked, extending his white handkerchief from his blazer pocket.

"I'm fine," Cathalina reassured him, thanking him for the offer with a shake of her head, The thought of what she had seen grabbed at her insides and forced her to try to bring up what no longer existed inside her body.

"Did you recognize her?"

"She is Lara Lopez. She was my patient. She lived in Apartment 225. I am not sure which direction that is in. I have not been here before. But she spoke of it often during our sessions." She began walking back toward the car where she knew Cleo would be irate and impatient.

"Wait. Dr. Shekhar, here is my business card. Please feel free to contact me if there is anything else you can think of that might explain why this happened."

"OK." She took the card from his hand and continued walking.

"Dr. Shekhar, if you are not busy tomorrow, could you please come to the office and make a statement? I will fill you in on the details once the report comes back, which should be sometime tonight."

"If that's what you need me to do . . . he . . ." She paused and stopped to look at the card to get his name. "Detective Isaac Taylor," she finished as she locked eyes with him for a brief moment and smiled. She paused a moment longer as she watched the white drain from his face at her smile. She also knew that the black was draining from Cleopatra's face at the same time, since she was back within range of the car, and she knew that woman well enough to know she was on pins and needles waiting for her to return.

"Thank you," he mumbled bashfully. Cathalina did not turn around again. She just waved her hand goodbye and proceeded toward the car where a litany of questions awaited her.

* * *

Serena sat in her judge's chamber wringing her hands and pulling on her hair. She just couldn't stand it. It was almost the end of her general workweek, and only a week since she had received the mark of the Brazilian wandering spider. She wasn't sure if it was just her normal repulsion with her job, or if she was simply growing restless of the repetitions of failure in her job. She just wanted to be free.

She felt trapped every time someone came before her and got off with a just a slap on their wrist. In the past few days, she found herself taking notes, writing down names and addresses of every vagabond, every lowlife, every woman beater, and every pedophile who got off on a technicality, while simultaneously silencing the voice of so many innocent children. She made notes of the who's, what's, where's, and why's. She would research their locations and follow up with their parole officers. Every day she caressed the words transfixed on the papers bearing the information that would make her lethal to those whose names were on the list. It took everything inside her to restrain herself from jumping over the bench and strangling the life out of these useless members of society—predators. She felt renewed and invigorated with each thought of their deaths. The spider sense in her was powerful, fresh, and new, waiting for the moment to emerge and blend fully with her. She wanted to hunt.

The urges she felt were unreal. Leaving the courtroom for the day, Serena got into her car as though in a trance. She wore a sadistic smile on her face and was propelled to move forward with a will she felt she didn't control. She drove aimlessly north toward Broward County, moving toward Ft. Lauderdale on I-95, headed in the direction of Coral Springs, which led to the Everglades off the 441. As she drove she glanced at the list of elusive predators who had violated the essence of the women who had trusted them, preying on the vulnerability of women like her and children, innocent children.

"Yes, I know." Her words drooled off her tongue. "What? What was that?" she giggled sadistically. "Yes, those bastards think they are messing with idiots? Nincompoops?" She drove steadily, doing eighty miles an hour on the highway and gaining speed as her mind locked on to her destination, her goal.

"Marcus. Marcus what? Yes, his last name." She listened as though waiting for the answer from an invisible friend sitting with her, and she responded as though that person had given her what would be considered valuable information.

"Marcus Cummings, yes. That would make sense." She snickered as she associated his name with the act of an orgasm. The thought was intoxicating.

"Don't worry, they will not get away with it." Her mind melted as one with her now closely guarded emotions. She was talking to herself and on a dangerous brink of losing her mind. She began to feel as if the spider was speaking to her, feel as if it was telling her what to do, and forcing its reckless anger and aggression on her, multiplying her already existing confusion and the pain that had festered and grown from her own.

She saw that she was nearing the home of Marcus, and she wondered why he had made his home in Sandalfoot, Florida, so close to the Everglades. As soon as the thought registered with her cognitive senses, she sneered.

As she drove, she became more and more delusional, and paranoia proliferated and gained strength in her fragile mind.

"Duh, of course he made his home near the Everglades—easy disposal of bodies, willing alligators and crocs to eliminate evidence. Bastards are nuts!" She was almost flabbergasted at his audacity. "Yeah, I know, as if no one would figure that out," she said in response to her own thoughts. She was completely disturbed at his flamboyant disrespect for her and for the law. "I mean, they swear that they have changed, that they didn't do it, that they are now rehabilitated and productive members of society, but it's all a damn lie," she bellowed so loudly she jumped and looked around to see who had said that. She was alarmed because although she knew the voice must have come from her, it did not sound like her normal voice at all.

As she neared Sandalfoot, she could almost smell the earthiness of the vast piece of land. It spanned for miles and contained muddy waters with reefs peaking above the plateau. She could almost see the wide space with all the creatures that had made the Everglades their home, hosting and procreating and bringing it to life. But she saw something else—a man—walking toward a resort that housed and entertained tourists visiting the Everglades. He was a nerdy looking Caucasian male with weak, frail-looking limbs, and big ears. She heard herself laugh.

"That's it? That's all you are? Taking lives and destroying what you don't even have the brains to develop in yourself!" The look of him appalled her.

"Look at the puny, little wimp!" She couldn't believe it, but her disbelief soon faded. She no longer saw the frailness of his physique, but rather, the image of a man who had hurt and destroyed her. She embodied the emotions of those he had killed and violated as she began to hear screams.

She drove to the parking lot of the tourist shack and parked. As she became impaled with visions, in her mind she thought she could see the spider move and curl up with feistiness, egging her on, pushing her to move her legs and get into motion. She no longer saw herself as a woman. She felt as though she was growing extra legs, had talons extending from her back, shoulders and sides, and the elongated limbs were lifting her from the ground and placing her face down to the floor. She felt like she was in a vision, locked in a trance. She heard herself emit a sound that she didn't recognize, but she knew she was laughing.

"Too fucking cool!" she thought she heard herself say. Her coherency remained focused on one man, one target who must feel the wrath of a woman scorned, taste the bite of the bitten, and face the consequences of his actions.

She felt her arms grow additional muscles that attached themselves to tendons and ligaments that were not there before, her legs folding into a crevice like a kangaroo's pouch, her back flattening to the ground. She felt huge and strong. She felt herself spring with the wind as she took motion, moving toward the man, and she heard one word emitting from her senses—Cummings!

"What the fuck?" the man shouted as he turned around at the sound of his name. She ducked as she positioned herself for an attack, wanting the attack to be a partial surprise. She needed him to be afraid, to feel powerless and overcome by something one would think to be harmless. She stared at Marcus who now seemed vulnerable.

"That's right, Mr. Cummings, bet you don't feel that powerful now?" she knew she was thinking this, felt she was saying it, but the words seemed to come from someone else, somewhere else.

"Who are you!" He laughed, wondering why this clean, together-looking lady was sneering at him. He thought maybe she was lost or something. "Do you need directions?" he uttered under his breath as he continued to walk toward the path that led to the pond, focusing on his own destination and somewhat ignoring Serena.

"You have no conscience," she yelled at him, feeling brave.

"Lady, I don't know you, and I have no idea what you are

talking about." He snickered at Serena. He thought she was obviously insane, so he began to laugh.

Serena was tired of the game. She wanted to hear him screech in pain, she wanted to rip him limb by limb, and she wanted to get him where it really hurt. She was hurting and she felt no one understood her pain, understood how she felt watching rapists and domestic abusers get away with so much. She envisioned that she was something dreadful and she lunged at him. He slapped her and she backed away holding her face.

"You don't recognize me do you?" The cynicism in her voice caused the man to look closer.

"Wait a minute." He stated, recognition forcing its way on him.

She laughed.

"Wait for what? For you to hurt and abuse more women and children?" She could see herself pulling him into her and using another one of her talons to rip his pants open so his genitals were exposed.

"Oh no, gosh, please," Cummings pleaded as tears made their way down the man's pale cheeks. He kicked and screamed and he tried with everything in him to loosen the grip of the thing that held him. She thought she had him where she wanted him, she thought she would make him beg for mercy. Her mind became jumbled with thoughts of revenge.

Serena sniffed again, this time excreting a saliva-type foam, and allowing it to slowly drivel on him. The secretion fell from her jaws and dropped below his waist, burning into Marcus's groin and melting away his penis like they were ice cubes exposed to the summer sun. The hair on his pubic area singed and smelled like fried flesh and dead animals, yet the smell was intoxicatingly sexy to Serena. She felt her vulva swell with longing, so she regurgitated again, letting herself slobber this incredible spit upon his arms and legs. Excruciating pain galvanized his body and he shook as shock chronicled his pain. As his brain registered that his body parts were disintegrating, his skin melting and making him unrecognizable, he began to shriek.

She coughed as though trying to bring up a festering cold from her chest. Then in one spitting motion, she spat the yellowish foam on his face. It saturated his mouth and like acid, began eating away at his face. He opened his mouth to holler again, and the secretion dripped onto his tongue, leaving it hanging out and his tonsils visible to the world as his flesh was eaten away and his eyeballs began falling out of their sockets.

She laughed, but it was a sound she could not, and did not recognize. She peered over at him as he dropped into the grassy mounds of a hidden swamp. He now resembled the scum that he truly was. The thought came to her that she should rest her body on him. She was surprised at her actions as she spun a web around the half acid-decayed body.

Serena woke up in bed, not knowing how she got there. She was still wearing her Donna Karan suit, which was now shredded to pieces. Her body now displayed muscled contours that ached as though she had worked out for the first time. Jason sat across from her, staring at the woman he had serviced now for almost two years. He had watched her go through transition after transition since having met this Dr. Shekhar who was supposed to be helping her. But that was not the case. Day by day she got increasingly worse. He was becoming scared for her.

He watched as she trembled. She was sweating profusely, but she was not feverish. He ached for her. He ached to reach out to her. But he couldn't touch her. He couldn't clean, change, or go near her. She dragged herself into the house without following her normal routine. He followed her to her bedroom where she curled into a ball and emitted a painful sound that was so eerie that it brought tears to his eyes. She was in pain.

"Jason, what's happening to me?" she reached for him.

"I don't know, a man brought you here, said you fainted and was saying a lot of terrible things."

"What do you mean, terrible things?" she coughed.

"I don't know. He said he was walking behind his home near the everglades. You pulled up and started saying stuff about him being a predator."

"And what else?" she grabbed Jason's hands, urging him to go on. Jason looked down not knowing how to feel, and horrored by her psychotic changes.

"He said you tried to attack him, you thought you were some giant animal and you wanted to punish him."

"Oh no, oh no. He knows who I am?"

"He recognized you from court. He confirmed it with your wallet in your car. He brought you home."

Serena held her stomach and cringed. Shame and confusion filled her. Jason took her head and placed it on his lap. He caressed her and rocked her until she fell into a fitful sleep.

In another part of the city, another woman tossed and turned in her sleep until she suddenly jumped from her bed. It felt so real. Dyania got up from her bed and stumbled over the pile of clothing that she had been meaning to take to the laundry for the last two weeks. It was dark and she squinted to adjust her eyes to the darkness. She got up and walked to the bathroom to pee. She sat on the toilet seat, and when she got up, her pee had curded to the top of the water in the toilet bowl like french onion soup. She turned to flush and screamed.

"Oh, my dear Jesus. What have I done to deserve this?" she flushed the toilet and ran back to her bedroom, knocking over her night lamp and hitting her chin hard on the foot of the bed. "Damn," she exclaimed, hopping on one leg and falling back under the covers. Then the tears began falling down her face.

Slowly, she got up and moved toward her footlocker. She then went back to the bed and reached under the mattress for a purse that was locked to the bedspring. She opened the purse and retrieved a key. She used the key to open the locker, then pulled out her journal and began writing.

The dreams have started again. I don't know what I did or ate to trigger them. I haven't had these nightmares since I was twenty. Why would this be happening now nine years later?

She hiccupped and coughed, then placed her face in her hands and had a good cry. She had to keep going, she needed to journal the account of these attacks or whatever the hell they were. The journaling had helped before. The doctors had used it to chronicle the episodes as they came.

What is happening to me? Why is this happening again? Why am I having dreams of spiders? Why am I imagining things—that I am sick, animals, and weird feelings that keep throwing me off?

The thoughts ravaged her mind like before. The only difference this time was that they were stronger, more powerful. The dreams were manifesting themselves into hallucinations.

She didn't understand all the conflicting emotions that riveted her body and her mind.

*What did I do to deserve this? I mean, for crying out
loud I imagine that I have puncture wounds magi-
cally appearing on my body as though I am being bitten again and again. But . . . but that's impossible.
But then the marks disappear almost as immediately
as they appear. I know my mind is playing tricks on
me, but how do I stop them?*

She laughed at her growing insanity. Dyania had always
been level-headed, always been smart and focused, logic
being her compass. Yet, she found herself lost in the sur-
real.

She continued writing in her journal, trying to make
sense of things that had no logical reason, and then new
tears formed in her eyes as she remembered her parents'
deaths.

They had told her over and over again that she had imagined that her parents were in Brazil on some government,
scientific expedition. She wondered why anyone would lie
to her, especially the people who she trusted, people she
loved, who her parents loved and trusted. Family. She had
no reason to think they had, yet she felt that something
happened that they were not admitting.

She put her journal back carefully at the bottom of the
footlocker and reached for one of the only photos she had
of her parents holding her proudly. She looked at her thick
afro-puffs, her slanted Asian eyes, her high Indian cheekbones, and smiled. She held the frame close to her heart
and heaved as new tears forced their way from her body.

"Why did this have to happen to you? Why did this happen to me?" she questioned the smiling images of the last
memory she had of the people who brought her into this
world, and she held the photo close as the remnants of the
nightmares passed. She drifted back into a peaceful sleep.

*   *   *

Another day at work and Serena experienced the same erratic sensations. She couldn't control her thoughts and had no memories from the previous day. She left work again with the same uncontainable desires to wipe clean the face of the earth from the predators whom she felt castrated her.

She drove back to her Coral Gables home feeling unsettled and confused. She hadn't felt like herself or had any semblance of normalcy since she took the mark. She hated the way she felt and wished that Cathalina would offer her some form of comfort by helping her understand her chaotic emotions. Her pulse raced and she was sweating abnormally. She clutched the steering wheel and crumbled the paper in her hands that held information of newly released serial killers, murderers, pedophiles, and other predators of society. She couldn't understand this sudden need to go and do something about it. She thought she was doing something about it all this time through the career path she had chosen, and quietly she would harbor secret thoughts to annihilate the bastards, but this was different. She felt desires so real she could taste the blood of her victims. She knew she was being irrational, but the more she met with the ladies, and the more they talked of the sad condition of the world, the more she felt herself being pulled into their need to be violent and her suppressed anger had gradually risen to the surface.

"Why am I going through this? Don't do this to me; I wish I could take it all back," she lamented. Suddenly, she began to laugh as she drove homeward. Sporadic flashbacks of various thoughts she imagined, her hallucinations of the way she had liquefied Marcus in the Everglades amused her. She still didn't know, couldn't tell if she had dreamed that or not. She had not heard anything about the incident on the news or anything else to verify the reality of it.

"I must be going crazy," she whimpered sadly to herself.

She absorbed these thoughts and feelings until she noticed she was instinctively slowing down. It was three o'clock in the afternoon and motorists had begun to show their impatience for her casual driving. With each drop of her speedometer she could feel the ambition of the spider. Then she felt something, a sensation of crawling on her left shoulder where her tattoo was, and she almost shrieked.

"OK, this is just way too crazy. I have to get home. I am beginning to feel things and see things. I have got to get to Cathalina." She shook her head and released the bundle of her curly locks, allowing them to fall on her shoulders.

She was almost at a full stop in the middle of traffic when she slowly moved a portion of her white, silk top to see what had crept under her shirt. There was nothing there. She signed and relaxed.

"My gosh, I must be on some powerful drugs to be thinking that I am feeling spiders under my clothes, and have things crawling up my back." She wondered if the others felt the same way. Maybe she did the wrong thing going forward with this situation that Cathalina convinced her would make her feel better. She felt no better now with the idea of actually hurting the predators than she felt letting them walk out of her courtroom.

Looking up from where it seemed she had sat for hours, she surveyed her surroundings and had a sense that she was someplace familiar. She looked at the crumpled piece of paper in her hand and opened it. She noticed that as she opened the paper, it seemed to stick a bit with some mushy, white, gooey stuff. She chuckled, not really knowing why, but was amused and truly fascinated.

"The mind is a powerful thing and I am quickly losing mine."

She ignored what she thought she was seeing and opened the paper to take a closer look. Her attention was immediately diverted as her eyes were suddenly drawn to one particular address, that of a Mr. Vincent Ratigan. He had just registered as a pedophile with the local police department after getting off practically scot free for the murder of a little girl who was found beaten to death in Hialeah Gardens in Miami.

Serena touched his name on her list and somehow she was able to see that this man was indeed guilty of a crime for which he was not adequately punished. She got flashes, glimpses into the reality of what he had done, like movie clips, shooting images into her mind, but she knew she was just replaying the evidence that was heard and shown in court, the images that were splashed across the television screen for all the world to see. She saw him take the child from her own backyard. She seemed to go with him as if she knew him, running and smiling, her beautiful, thick, black afro bouncing along with her. Her black, trusting eyes lit up like fireworks, and her arms swung freely as she ran to him.

Serena blinked back, the honking of motorists behind her bidding her to get out of their way. She realized she was still in the middle of the street.

"Oh no, it's happening again." Panic stricken, she stepped on the gas and pulled over. The images made her want to vomit.

"I need a vacation. I am starting to internalize my job." She had parked not too far from the lavish home that was clearly the address of Vincent Ratigan, the home he had made for himself.

She began to cry as she remembered the faces of the children, the crime in motion, the atrocity. Her anger multiplied as she remembered the headlines.

The man took the little girl down by the swampy lake areas of Hialeah. He played with her clothing until she was almost naked. Serena squeezed her eyes shut as she saw him unzip his pants. The images skipped. *Then the man was punching the girl on the side of her temple and knocking her down. She couldn't have been more than four-years-old.* Tears began welling in Serena's eyes.

"Latoya." She uttered the girl's name and something stabbed into her shoulder. She looked again toward her shoulder and there was a small drop of blood seeping through her shirt like a needle had pricked her, but it hurt as badly as the punch that put Latoya's lights out. She knew she was only seeing things, but it felt so real. Something pushed Serena forward and her body was thrown into the steering wheel with a thud. The horn started beeping. She regained her composure and looked again through the mirror of images that her eyes were showing her.

He threw her in his trunk, sat in his old car, and smoked a cigarette.

"Stop it. Stop, please stop," Serena said out loud, silent tears streaming down her face. *Latoya was suffocating. After hours of being in the truck she came to. She coughed. He opened the trunk and unzipped his pants again. He punched her in her mouth until a tooth fell out and she spat blood. Fear and shock took over her helpless body.*

Serena couldn't take it anymore. Her anger was so great it was as though her very life depended on what she did next. She wished she could make him feel pain in so many ways that her own body ached. When she couldn't withstand the pain any longer, she cried.

She must have stayed like that for hours, because it was now almost eight in the evening and a darkened hue had come over the sky. The sun was beginning to set, and she must have blocked out everything because her phone registered that there were seven missed calls, three of which were from Cathalina. She picked up her phone and called her. Cathalina would know what to do.

"Serena, where have you been? I have been trying to reach you." Cathalina asked excitedly. "I was so worried."

"I am OK, Cath. But I have been experiencing some very strange side effects from the ceremony. I think the spider bite is having an adverse effect on me."

"OK, slow down. What do you mean adverse effects?"

"I don't know how to explain it. It's just strange." Serena sighed deeply.

"Listen to me, hun, just concentrate. Are you feeling sick, light-headed, dizzy, nauseated? What?" Cathalina tried to help her with the words to describe how she was feeling, but Serena just kept saying no.

"It's a little more complicated than that, Cathalina." Serena whispered as if there were eavesdroppers nearby. "I am seeing things, feeling things."

Cathalina laughed.

"Oh Serena, stop it. You are pulling my legs." But her gaiety was quickly extinguished when Serena remained quiet.

"Cath, I feel like my emotions are spiraling out of control. I am having thoughts and feelings about things that are wrong beyond what we have done in the past and what we are planning to do. I am afraid."

"Serena, you are overreacting."

"I am not overreacting, Cath, please listen to me. I keep imagining that there are spiders crawling on me, biting me, I see blood. And I think that I attacked a man the other day."

"What are you saying?"

"Marcus Cummings. He is one of my cases. I attacked him and he recognized me. Took me home."

"Oh my."

"Exactly. And now I am sitting here seemingly losing my mind."

"Don't be afraid, Serena. Where are you now?"

"I stopped for a while. I was on my way home and I think I have subconsciously arrived at the home of another one of my past case files—a convicted, reformed pedophile." The words sounded weird and unbelievable coming from her lips.

"I think all our talks and plans have become a highly sensitive situation for you. Maybe you need some Ativan, something to calm your nerves."

"Yes, maybe you're right." She smiled a smile of relief. "You are always right, Cathalina."

"Not always." Cathalina spoke so softly that Serena couldn't hear. "Don't give me any accolades yet. We have to make sure you are OK." She spoke louder into the phone. "I will see you as soon as possible."

"That would be nice. I will speak with you then." Serena hung up the phone feeling a lot better. She knew all she had to do was talk to Cathalina. She thought Cathalina was amazing.

In that moment, Serena had an overwhelming urge to look up. And there he was—220 pounds and six feet, four inches of hard muscle. His bald head looked as smooth as satin, and he was wearing a cotton top and Sean John jeans. His rich, dark skin seemed to glisten against the hues of the falling night sky, and his eyes, light and agile, seemed to dance as he made eye contact with her. His face was cleanly shaven except for the goatee he sported with an attached moustache. His smile exposed full, delectable lips and beautiful, white, even teeth that seemed to dare her to come kiss him. She swallowed hard and took a deep breath. If she didn't already feel such repulsion for him, she would find him stunning. She could feel herself getting wet between the knees, and she squeezed them shut to stop herself from putting her hands there to soothe the ache he had brought on her with just his attentive stare.

"Do you need any help, miss?"

"No, thank you," she said, almost choking on her words. Her body was screaming "Yes, yes, yes, get in here and take me right now." But she knew better. He was a gorgeous man and in many ways reminded of her Jason. Her palms were so sweaty and sticky that she couldn't let go of the steering wheel, and her mind just kept seeing little Latoya's body through his eyes.

"I think you need help, miss," he insisted. "You are blanking out. Did you just hear what I said?" he asked after standing there looking at her for a moment. He moved closer to her car and stood at the window, bending down slightly to look inside.

"No, I am fine." She tore her eyes away from him; afraid to see more when suddenly her vision got fast-forwarded or rewound. She couldn't tell which it was, but flashes of children in varying age groups appeared before her, each under fifteen-years-old. She couldn't tell how many of them there were, but they were hurt, in pain, crying, dying, and bleeding. She couldn't focus on just one. They just kept coming and coming and she wanted them to stop. She put her hands to her temple and pressed hard when she suddenly found some control, some power within herself to calm down, to stop, and to focus.

Oh gosh, did he see that? See me flipping out? she wondered. Thoughts flooded her mind, struggling to find some sense in what was happening to her, but she pulled herself together and felt the spider on her shoulder curl up. She was pacified for the moment.

"How about a drink of water, ma'am? I live right here. You could come in if you like. I won't hurt you. I promise."

She surveyed his disarming smile and the sincerity that danced behind his eyes. *Is this the way you lured those poor children?* But looking at his outstretched arms—the strength of them, the gentleness of them—she somehow found the strength and reached up, allowing the power in him to guide her out of her car. As he opened the door to help her out, he almost wet his pants when he saw her license plate, which was an official plate.

"Are you all right?" Serena asked, looking at him cautiously. The blood seemed to have drained from his already dark skin, leaving it looking ashy. It was as if he had seen a ghost.

"I'm fine. I'm sorry. For a moment I thought you might be someone I knew," he told her. She wasn't here for him. She was just driving and happened to be someone that needed help. He was being paranoid. "Have you been sitting here long?" he asked. "It's late." Serena smiled warmly at him and her knees almost buckled when he smiled back.

Thick, full lips curled into a curvaceous and flirtatious smile, and glistening eyes twinkled with sex appeal. She could feel his thoughts in her most private erogenous zone. She struggled to find her voice, and almost chuckled at her own awkwardness. Suddenly, she felt a sharp piercing in her abdomen. She was hungry.

"Honestly, I don't know. I guess I could really use that glass of water."

"Are you sure? Have you eaten? You look faint."

"No really. I don't want to be an imposition. A glass of water would be fine.

"It's not an imposition at all. How about a sandwich? I just made some. I could share, no problem, really."

She smiled.

"If you insist, I could use a bite."

"Great, follow me." He took her hands. "Here we are," he announced as he led her up three short steps and then into a vast living room where he seated her on a large, sectional sofa. She looked about her environment quickly and noted that this man was the rugged type, from the bear rug replica on the hardwood floors, to the moose's head hanging from the wall. There was a huge fireplace and an abstract painting hanging on another wall, and there was not much else.

"I'll go get you some water," he said. And before she could look up at him, he had walked away, disappearing between two huge double doors. She couldn't help noticing how his tight, perky ass swayed in his denim, and how his calf-high Timberland boots hiked up one of his pants' legs. He moved swiftly, like a man with purpose and calculation, and she was able to survey him in peace without being plagued by visions and delusions. The thoughts still seemed like a dream to her, something she fantasized. But right now, for the first time since this whole thing started, she just wanted to feel normal, without all the delirium.

"Here you go," he said, returning and seating himself next to her on the arm of the sofa, leaning in a bit with his left arm outstretched on the back of the sofa seat. Swallowing hard, Serena looked up at him and smiled.

"Forgive me. I know you told me your name, but I forgot." She hung her head, feeling a bit shy and awkward. She knew all this other stuff about the man and here she was acting like a love struck school girl. She chuckled. How ironic. Some things just had to be done the old-fashioned way.

"Actually, I hadn't told you my name." He smiled at her, showing gorgeous white teeth and sparkling eyes.

"Oh."

"Don't be embarrassed. It's Vincent." Serena was jolted by the deep rumble of his voice, but forced herself to look into his eyes again. "Vincent Ratigan." Her smile brought one to his lips and they both locked in a momentary gaze. He reached for her glass with the water in it and placed it on the end table next to the sofa.

"Now, I want you to try my world famous, all meat, no healthy stuff sandwich."

She laughed.

"What? Never heard of that?" he asked her, trying to get her to relax a bit.

"No veggies?"

"Nope. Every now and again, I treat myself to a pure meat, all junk day. And it's your lucky day because you get to join me." He winked playfully at her. "And my lucky day because I get to enjoy the company of a beautiful damsel in distress. You have made a gentleman of me."

He went to the kitchen and returned with the sandwiches. "Well, here you go. Dig in."

"No, I can't."

"Don't tell me you are one of those women watching your figure. You know you don't have to do that. You are way too thin as it is."

"Really, that's just too much."

"Please, you are my guest and you are really hurting my feelings." He was happy that she seemed to have perked up. He found her exquisitely beautiful. She was a goddess and he wondered what could have gotten a woman like her in the state he found her in. She took the sandwich and took a small bite, her face lighting up.

"Humm!"

"Good, eh?"

"Yes. Wow." she said between chews. "How did you make it? This is the best sandwich I have ever had"

"I bet you wished you knew." He laughed out loud, a rumbling from deep down causing her to stare at him in disbelief. Maybe she was wrong. This couldn't be the same man on her list. He was wonderful.

Their laughter died down and they spoke quietly for hours. The time just seemed to slip away from Serena; they grew closer over the course of the night, and she felt very comfortable with him as he told her about his hobbies, dreams, and ambitions. How he had no children and had never been married, and how he yearned to one day have children.

"How about you?"

"Oh no, not me. I think children are a blessing, but I don't think I have what it takes to be a mother."

"Are you kidding me? An exquisite woman like yourself?"

She looked up and realized it was almost midnight.

"Vincent, it's late. Thank you for being so wonderful, I think this was exactly what I needed. But maybe I should go now." Serena clasped her hands, and adjusted her knee-length skirt.

Sensing her sudden discomfort, Vincent got up and sat across from her in the loveseat so she wouldn't feel threatened.

"Why don't you sit a while longer? You were really out of it back there. Do you feel feverish? Are you faint?" he asked. His eyes narrowed and lines drew themselves across his forehead in genuine concern. She felt so safe in his presence. Serena almost fell over laughing, but forced herself to smile instead.

"I think I really should be going." She stood and then placed her hands over her face to prevent herself from looking at him again.

"What? What are you doing? Are you sure you aren't feeling any discomfort?" Vincent stood and reached for her. She pulled away and then peeked from beneath her fingers. Vincent found her behavior inconsistent.

"If you don't mind me asking, are you under psychiatric care?" Serena only giggled and shook her head. Then she laughed as she thought about Cathalina. Technically she was, and she laughed again. He had no idea.

Regrouping and pulling herself together, she managed to calm her giggles and bring out an air of professionalism. The sensations between her legs were making her vulva quiver, and she squeezed them tightly, sending sensations through her clit that immediately creamed her thongs. She tried to will the wetness not to stain the back of her skirt or run down her legs. *I have to get out of here.*

"Mr. Ratigan, I am indeed indebted to you. You have really been kind. But it is time that I go. I have been out later than I anticipated, and I do have some obligations at home that need to be tended to." Stumbling a bit, she gathered her strength and walked toward his door.

"Well, if you ever need an ear or a helping hand, you know where to find me," Vincent called after her. He didn't feel like asking her to stay again or chasing after her. He just wanted to watch as the fine specimen of a woman sauntered away from him, and as much as he enjoyed the view, he was concerned for her driving to wherever she was destined. He hoped he would see her again and spend more time with her. She was the most refreshing thing to happen to him since he started his life over.

"What am I thinking? What if this woman is some crazy nut?" He snickered to himself as the door closed behind him, leaving him feeling a bit rejected. "That's the last thing I need in my life right now, sexy or not. I have too many of my own issues to deal with right now." He sighed under his breath as he prepared to go back and continue his evening walk. He tried to get Serena out of his mind for the rest of the evening, but he just couldn't. He was drawn to her vulnerability, her seemingly innocent disposition. And his night was filled with thoughts and dreams of her.

9

Elizabeth got into her car and drove down the highway in Atlanta's rush hour traffic. She felt hot and bothered, but couldn't help enjoying being in the sexual mecca of this day and age. Yeah, her type could really thrive here, where there were more undercover, down-low brothers than anywhere else in the United States. The play she was starring in was in its final week, and she was getting antsy to have it completed.

She pressed the CD button on her car stereo and relaxed as Jill Scott's smooth grooves relaxed every tense bone in her body. Just as she pulled into a small pizza joint, her cell phone rang and she saw that it was Serena.

"Hey, sweets, how are you feeling these days?" The question was truly rhetorical, because Elizabeth knew the side effects of the initiation. She herself had a rough time dealing with it and she hoped that Serena was well. Her black widow was always perched proudly in the crevice of her bosom, nestled discretely beneath her cleavage. It was a tattoo mark she had grown to appreciate over time.

"Liz, it's so good to hear your voice." Serena breathed

slowly, trying to calm herself, trying to be and sound rational. "How are things going for you in Atlanta?"

"I'm good. The play is almost over, and I miss you guys. Things have been pretty quiet since your induction into the team."

I wouldn't say quiet, Serena thought. *I would say things have been nothing less than psycho.*

"How have you been feeling? Is everything all right?" Liz asked, sensing a bit of hesitation in Serena's voice.

"Well, to tell the truth, I have been feeling sort of queasy," Serena told her, not wanting to divulge too much information. Liz was cool and everyone loved her, but Serena was afraid to tell anyone what she was experiencing. Maybe it was just a side effect that would pass if she gave it time.

Elizabeth looked toward the entrance to the pizzeria. She was starving, but something told her to stop and listen to Serena. She could almost feel an eerie sensation come over her, and her chest pumped twice as if her skin was ripping from her body. She sensed that Serena was in trouble. The thought came to her as though it was not even her own thought.

"Sweetheart, have you been getting enough rest? You have only been indoctrinated for a week. You need time to get used to the process, the venom. There is more to the bite than just doing it. You need to give yourself time to heal."

Serena tried to calm the stimulus that was causing her heart to race and her blood vessels to fill. The word heal hit a nerve with her. She hadn't healed. She had gotten worse with time, and she was getting tired.

"I guess I haven't slept much except for the day after the ceremony, but I've felt good, and today was my last workday for the week."

"Good, so what are you doing now?"

"I am lying down in my bedroom. I'm about to take a nap. Jason is here with me. I'm safe. I just really wanted to say hello," Serena lied, but she didn't realize that the communal connection they had would send waves of uncertainty through the phone, letting her peer know that she was shaking uncontrollably as she curled into the fetal position on her bed, and juices of unknown desires ran down her legs and saturated the sheets. She thought of Vincent and felt guilty.

Elizabeth could feel that there was more that she wasn't saying. But she, too, had been guilty of allowing things to just happen. Even once she found out that killing was not making her feel better, she still did it, not wanting to disappoint Cathalina. She was guilty of not being honest with Serena now as she reached out to her.

"OK, Serena. Well it's good to hear from you. I will be back in Miami next week. The play is wrapping up, and I am happy that I am not far away from home. Serena's soft chuckle sent surges of painful regret through Elizabeth's heart. She knew she should do something, but felt compelled by obligation to Cathalina.

"Hey, Serena, I gotta get back, so let me go get something to eat and I will touch base with you again soon." Liz rushed off the phone as though it was contagious, and threw it on the seat as soon as the last words of dismissal were out of her mouth.

"What am I doing?" Liz asked herself, speaking to her car as though she would get a response. But the only response she received was the throbbing ache in her heart and the guilt that stabbed at her soul.

She picked up her cell phone and dialed Cathalina's cell phone number. She needed to let Cathalina know what was going on right away. It rang, but the voicemail picked up so she sent a page with their special code requesting that

Cathalina return her call. Then Liz tried Cathalina's home number, and as a last resort she tried her office.

"Dr. Shekhar."

"Working so late?"

"More like thinking and planning." She chuckled. Cathalina wasn't sure if she should regret what she shared with Cleo or not. She needed to focus on what had happened to Lara. She couldn't believe that she was dead. How was she going to explain to Elizabeth and Serena that Lara was gone? She wasn't even sure how Cleo was handling Lara's death since she hadn't taken Cleo's calls lately, despite the fact that Cleo was blowing up the phone. The last time Cathalina had spoken with Serena, she sounded as though she was in a daze.

"Is everything on schedule, Cathalina?" Elizabeth placed the phone closer to her ear and tried to listen to her recruiter with more than just her ears. She sensed a form of distress. She couldn't place her hands on it, but it was weird that Cathalina sounded so out of sorts.

"Yes, dear, all is well. But tell me, how is your show winding down?"

"It's coming to a close nicely, I am happy to say. I am tired of it now. I miss home." her voice trailed off, but the true intent of her call had not left her mind. "Cathalina, I spoke with Serena a moment ago. Is she adjusting well to the Brazilian wandering spider's bite?"

"Why do you ask that?" Cathalina was now alert. Elizabeth had struck the nerve to one of her concerns.

"She seemed not altogether there. I sensed that she might be torn somewhat, deciding, not adjusting well. I cannot really tell, but something is going on."

"We should be meeting up tomorrow as a group. The only person missing will be you. But we will fill you in later," Cathalina informed Liz, ready to quickly get off the phone and go find Serena. "Thanks for the call, Liz. You are wonderful and I miss you."

"I'll be home next week. I am anxious to see how Serena has acclimated herself as our newest member." They both silently acknowledged the same wish, and then disconnected the call.

Elizabeth felt a strange connection to Serena. Maybe she identified with Serena. When she met Cathalina, she wanted to change her life, to belong, to not feel like an outcast. To find love. And though she felt she had those things now in the dysfunction of the sisterly bond they had, she felt alone. Maybe Serena understood. Maybe that's why she felt a connection with her and not Cathalina? Maybe that's why she called. She wasn't sure, but she knew she had to get back home. She didn't get out of her car, nor did she ever get her meal. She had become transfixed on the emotional pull from Serena. She was always very calm and in control, but so much more aggressive than the other ladies, maybe because of her testosterone level.

She drove back to the Hyatt where the cast for her play stayed, and rushed to her room. She needed to alleviate the pressure of what was building in her. The adrenaline, the confusion, the sick rush from what they did, caused her to become excited, even when she didn't want to be. She couldn't get her erection down.

When she walked into the lush double suite, she heard singing coming from the opposite end of the room. Her roommate was in the shower. She always loved to hear her sing the show tunes as though in a rehearsal every time she took a shower. She also knew that Francesca had a crush on her. Liz was the leading lady and Francesca was her understudy. She sat on her half of the room, trying to will her huge penis to quell itself, but the images that Serena was sending to her were violent and hungry. They sent surges of electrical energy through her and she needed to quiet down. She didn't want Francesca to come outside and see her like this. A twelve-inch dick on a beautiful Asian woman would be hard to hide.

She lay back on her bed and tried to masturbate the pain away, tried to seduce herself into letting go.

She heard the shower cut off and Francesca stepped out. She looked at the flagpole her erection was putting up and grabbed for the sheet to cover her embarrassment. This was her insecurity, feeling like she wasn't a real woman. Having this part of her was a source of her shame, causing her to be unable to have a relationship with a man or a woman. She just wished she could be normal.

"Liz, I didn't know you were here." Francesca told her after composing herself from her initial surprise. Liz never returned to the room that early, so she was taken aback some.

"Sorry if I startled you, Fran. I just came in and I'm feeling a bit tired," she lied, feigning fatigue as she yawned, stretched her hands above her head, and turned on her side. Liz fought with the desires that forced themselves on her and thought about Serena. Maybe she could talk to Serena. Maybe she would be the one to understand her.

"Hey, what's wrong?" Francesca came and sat at the edge of the bed, reached out for her leg, and gently caressed it. "You look like you've seen a ghost. All the blood has left your face," she said, stretching her long, frail body alongside Elizabeth in sisterly concern.

They had chatted like this numerous nights, and it was no big deal. But the image of Francesca's damp skin and wet, black, Shirley Temple locks were wrecking Liz's cool. Francesca smiled innocently and her big, blue eyes sparkled as she anticipated what Elizabeth would talk to her about tonight. Their time together was winding down and she knew she would miss the gorgeous Asian beauty. She wished that she didn't feel so distant from her and wanted on so many nights to hold her. But Elizabeth always kept her at arm's length. While the rest of the cast frolicked erotically together and mixed and mingled, Francesca had no stories or memories to share with the group as they gossiped about hot nights spent making it hotter.

"Please." Elizabeth barely uttered on a ragged breath. "Please, don't do that." She sighed, placing her hand on top of Francesca's hands to stop the fluid, gentle movement of them up and down her thigh.

"I'm sorry." Francesca blushed. Feeling rejected, she began easing herself up to go.

"Francesca, it's just that . . ."

"I know. You don't like girls. I feel so stupid." She exhaled and raised herself on her elbows to remove herself before she lost any more of her pride. As she did so, the towel that was casually wrapped around her bosom loosened and Francesca's beautiful cantaloupes bounced joyously at their release. She reached to cover them, but Elizabeth touched her hands, stopping her. She shuddered from the ripples of desire that found their way through her body, and if she had made any progress on quelling her hardened penis, she was duly exposed now. She couldn't hide it anymore.

"You are so beautiful," Elizabeth said as a husky, sensual sigh came from deep inside her throat. She inched her way closer to the woman whose naked body screamed for her. The towel barely covered Francesca's thighs as it fell and revealed the closely trimmed, hairy mound of the Eden she hid between her legs.

Francesca smiled a pleasing smile. Her eyes danced with curiosity and willingness. Hope filled her as her breaths became raspy and short, and her chest heaved up and down in anticipation.

"You think so? I mean, I didn't know you . . ." and before she could finish the sentence, Elizabeth closed the gap between them, her left hand reaching up to Francesca's face and pulling her down toward the bed, and her right hand finding her waist as she pulled her to meet her desires, turning on her back and allowing Francesca's body to slowly slide on top of hers.

Suddenly there was a gasp and a shudder. Francesca jumped to her feet and her eyes bulged from her body.

"What the hell is going on here?" she asked. "What are you?"

"I tried to tell you, but . . ."

"What do you mean you tried to tell me? Am I that difficult to talk to?"

"No, it's nothing like that all. I have always had this problem and . . ."

"Problem! You call that a problem? You are a chick with a dick. That's not a problem. That's an atrocity!" Francesca exclaimed frantically. She paced back and forth for a moment, and then ran to the bathroom to find her clothes.

"You are the one who wanted to get laid, and now I'm an atrocity? You don't like dick? You don't want it?" Liz yelled, walking over to the other half of the hotel suite to where Francesca was, hoping to get her to calm down.

"Of course I like dick, I just didn't think . . . I mean I wanted to be with you."

"Well, this is me. And if you like dick, well then I've got one. So what's the problem?" Elizabeth yelled. As she got closer, Francesca closed the bathroom door.

"That's just not normal. That is not normal. It's huge," she screamed. "I will scream rape if you come in here, I swear."

A wave of shame and embarrassment swelled within Elizabeth. She knew this would happen. She had hoped that since Francesca was insistent on coming on to her that she would find it a delightful surprise. But she was wrong. Sad tears welled in her eyes as she stood outside the shut bathroom door hearing Francesca panicking on the inside. Her erect penis grew limp and hung down her clean-shaven, sexy, feminine legs. Her vagina throbbed with desire.

"Well if all you wanted was a pussy, I've got one of those too, you confused bitch." Elizabeth yelled, her anger getting the best of her, and then she stormed away.

"Get away from me, you fucking freak. Get away!" Liz heard the frantic screams emanating from the closed bathroom door. She walked over and began packing her things. She had to get out of there. Francesca was no doubt going to tell everyone in the cast what she was.

Suddenly, she heard the door to the bathroom open so violently that it shook the room, and Francesca came storming out.

"OK then, I'm game." Francesca pouted, her breasts perking to the occasion as she slowly slipped her fingers in between the tartness of her legs. Her pubic hair glistened with moisture as she rubbed furiously at her hot spot, and then reaching for Elizabeth's hand, she pulled her close. Elizabeth was mesmerized by the transformation, so she followed Francesca's lead, allowing her to replace her hand with Elizabeth's fingers. For a moment Elizabeth closed her eyes. Captivated by the wetness of her, the erotic sounds of sensuality she emitted from the pit of her abdomen caused her shaft to rise again.

Francesca moved into her, filling the electrified space with hungry desire. Draping Elizabeth behind the nape of her neck with her hand, she forcefully pulled her toward her. She stuck her tongue inside her mouth and allowed their lips to do a tantalizing, eager dance.

Francesca's mind was filled with all the fantasies and freaky longings she had ever dared to imagine, and she squeezed her legs tight, almost cutting off the circulation of

Elizabeth's hand when the juices for her desires dripped shamelessly down her legs. With each thought of Elizabeth ramming her dick up every crevice of her body, she felt spasms like electrical bolts shocking her head back, causing her spine to arch and her hips to gyrate. She pressed herself into Elizabeth for deeper penetration. Just as she reached for Elizabeth's male piece, Elizabeth stiffened with tension and moved her hand away.

"What are you doing?" Francesca yelled. "Why the fuck are you stopping?" Elizabeth just looked at her, and using both hands, held her at a distance so she could quell her desires.

"I am sorry, Francesca."

"Sorry? What do you mean sorry?" Francesca wrestled her hands free of Elizabeth's grasp. "On top of being a freak, now you're a tease too?" She was stunned and hurt, but Elizabeth was shocked. She never would have guessed that this woman had this violent nature in her. She turned her face away, awed, her body succumbing to the pressure and the heartache of being so verbally smashed.

Then suddenly she felt a lightening fast sting on the side of her face. It happened so fast that she didn't know what had hit her. Elizabeth placed her hand to her cheek and felt the burning, like fire had scorched her. As soon as she turned to look at Francesca, Wham! Another slap, causing the rouge color on each cheek to match.

"How you like that for leading me on?"

"You are fucking nuts," Elizabeth seethed from between her teeth. She couldn't believe what this woman was doing. Had she lost her mind over a piece of ass? Was it the rejection? Damn!

She had barely recovered from the shock of being slapped twice, once on each cheek when she heard the screeching owl of a siren and the waving banter of a mad-woman rushing her. She ducked just in time and fell backward onto the bed, her suitcase coming undone and her clothes flying in every direction. Francesca went tumbling into the wall and smashed her face.

"Now look what you did," she yelled at the top of her lungs and attacked Elizabeth again. Elizabeth placed her hands over her head to stop the hit she knew was coming, and yelped when she felt her back snap, moving her knees defensively into her abdomen defensively. She almost laughed at the absurdity of it all. Was she really being assaulted for saying no to a woman? But the thought didn't stay there long. She had to protect herself from Francesca, and she knew how the story would go once it was all over, but as of that moment, it was all over anyway.

"Don't do this, Francesca. You know that what you are doing is irrational, and it makes no sense at all."

"Now you are patronizing me?" Francesca balled her fists into pink knuckles and prepared to swing, but Elizabeth slowly crawled off the bed and stood on the opposite side of it to give them distance.

"We don't have to go where you are taking this. We can sit and talk this out." She laughed in her mind as she said the words. Francesca was obviously not in a talking mood, and there was going to be no way out but through her.

"Oh, so now you want to talk? What happened to all that deep logical communication I was dropping on you earlier?" she snickered.

"I just don't want to argue with you. You have been a good friend up until this point. I think we can work this out and go our separate ways without this getting any nastier than it already has."

"Well, you see that's where I think you are wrong. Things are already nasty, and it's about to get worse. I mean, who the hell do you think you are? Coming on to me, teasing me, and then getting on your high horse about not finishing what you started," she exclaimed in shock as though the mere thought of not getting her freak on was the worst thing that could ever happen to her.

"We are both adults here, and I think you are being ridiculously unreasonable. What do you want to do? Rape me?" Liz asked this as a rhetorical question, but the crazed look in Francesca's eyes and the way she was heaving, her balled fists turning pink and her knuckles turning white from the bones rubbing against the skin, Liz knew that was exactly what was on the woman's mind. Liz shook her straight, black hair and her slanted Asian eyes squinted tighter. She was beginning to get furious. Who the fuck did this bitch think she was dealing with? Her anger pained her so much that she could feel the fanged legs of the black widow gyrate against her bosom, and its red underbelly mark burned scarlet to match the fury that had now built in her.

"Listen, things are about to get way out of hand." Liz used her hands to exaggerate just how out of hand things would get by stretching them as wide as her arms would go. "You are not going to like it if you really piss me off, and I am trying like crazy to be understanding. You are gonna make me fuck you up," she warned. The pure stirring of Elizabeth's passion was spreading her anger like venom, spreading like wildfire through her system.

Francesca didn't wait to lunge again. She hurled herself at Elizabeth and started to punch her. Elizabeth blocked her face with her hands, and used her fingernails to squeeze into the woman's jugular and temple. Her fingernails held onto Fran's neck, choking her until her fingers punctured Fran's throat. She felt the energy of this woman's spirit, and she drew on her fear, played on her emotions. Elizabeth was out of control and knew it. She reached to the tray where Francesca was eating and grabbed the steak knife and plunged it deep into Francesca's jugular. She knew she should have to stopped, but it was too late.

The screech that echoed from Francesca's lips almost made Elizabeth freeze in the very spot she lay on the floor. She removed her hands from over her eyes and saw that foam had gathered at the corners of this once beautiful woman's mouth. Fran's eyes had fallen back inside her head and she couldn't make any sound.

Liz pulled her hands away, but it was too late. Francesca fell to the floor and began convulsing. Elizabeth didn't wait. She got herself together, grabbed her things, and ran out the door. The play was scheduled to end next week when she was to return to her family and friends, but the play ended at the exact moment that Elizabeth raced to take the Amtrak train from Atlanta back to Miami.

10

"Don't go, Liz," Francesca pleaded weakly from foamed lips and a bruised face, neck, and temples. She couldn't hear and she couldn't see. She felt paralyzed. "Please come back." Fran felt a tear escape and fall down the side of her face. She pulled her body to the door of the luxury Hyatt and kicked at it with all her strength. But her strength was gone and she could not muster enough energy to kick hard enough. Then she tried to laugh. Blood oozed from her throat and out of her mouth.

Someone heard the commotion and called onlookers to her door. She heard the persistent knock at her room door as she quickly lost consciousness to the world of the living. Her head was aching and she felt numb all over. But that was nothing compared to the severe cramping she felt in her abdomen. She could barely breathe. She couldn't answer the door.

"Elizabeth, Francesca. Is anyone in there?" one focused voice asked, amidst a pandemonium of voices outside the door. She tried to answer, but the words were only in her head. She couldn't speak, and she was losing her grip on reality.

"Somebody answer this damn door now or we're coming in," a man's voice she vaguely recognized yelled. It was her stage manager, but because her mind was having a hard time, and taking leave of cognizant thought, she couldn't remember who that voice belonged to.

The banging went on insistently until hotel security was called and the door was programmed to unlock. The cast of the traveling off-Broadway play rushed into the room to see a naked Francesca curled in the doorway.

"Oh God, is she alive?" Frauline asked, terrified by the foaming puke that oozed from the corners of the violated woman's mouth. But she couldn't help thinking how great it would be to finally be in a position to play the understudy to Elizabeth, whose position she truly coveted.

"Get the police. Call an ambulance," the stage manager yelled frantically, and hotel management put a call through to the emergency dispatch. Everyone looked on, horrified at the scene unfolding before them, and gawked in awe at the ambulance crew as they whisked the stupefied Francesca away.

Francesca was pronounced dead upon arrival to the hospital.

"So what have we got?" Homicide Detective Minto asked as she approached her male peers, who all stood in awe of her professional status and her uncanny beauty.

"We can't find her roommate, the star of the show. Seems like a clear-cut case to me. They had a cat fight, the other girl used the steak knife, stabbed her, and took off." Detective Kendal fidgeted with his hat and fumbled to find his words, awed by Minto's mysterious eyes. She was something special, and she was the only woman on the special investigation homicide unit. She was young and busted her ass, and she didn't play.

"Got all the evidence?" Detective Minto asked, her eyes

slowly lingering on each of the three men, passed by them nonchalantly as she sought out the answers to her questions.

Detective Tyme handed her all the information that they had been privy to.

"We put out a search for the roommate; we're waiting to hear back now," Detective Perkins chimed in. He smiled broadly when Minto nodded her approval before she walked away.

"Hey, man, I think she's into you." Kendal chuckled, giving Perkins a high five and a playful shove.

"You must be drinking, man. She ain't into nothing but her job. That's her man, and she probably wants to keep it that way," Perkins stated, pushing Kendal back and wishing with all his heart that the smile she gave him was more than just an appreciation for the information he provided.

All three men looked after her as she sashayed her round, perky bottom away, wearing the hell out of some Guess, fitted, bell-bottom jeans, spiked cowboy boots, and a white dress shirt with a necktie. She had an eclectic style about her that was unique and all her own. She wore her hair short in African kinky knots that resembled little, round, knitted rolls of yarn. She was black and beautiful.

The men looked on and drooled until she reached the corridor and was about to turn, but she didn't. She turned back and walked full speed back toward them. Something told her to go check on this woman, a natural instinct she had always had about people, but she didn't know quite what was propelling her this time. Must just be a hunch.

The three men, almost in shock at her abrupt about face, stood there transfixed to their positions, watching the graceful, six-foot-one-inch woman strut toward them in her boots that gave her at least an added two-inch boost.

"Let's go." Her directions were a concise and direct order.

"Where are we going?" Perkins jogged to catch up with her as she sped past them.

"Where is her room?" she asked, spinning around on Perkins, stopping him in his tracks, and almost causing a back-to-back collision when Kendal and Tyme stopped just short of running into the backs of each other.

"You are standing in front of her room," Perkins told her and pointed at room 912 with almost shaky hands. He couldn't believe it. The woman had practically followed a trail like a bloodhound, stopping exactly where the trail ended, and acting as though she didn't even know it.

She turned to look where the detective's finger led and made a quick turn to pursue it. The men turned to look at each other. The detectives were in pretty good shape, but none of them would even try to take down Minto. Tyme was about five feet, nine inches and had been in the army as a maintenance sergeant before leaving and becoming a police officer. He was built thick and broad at the shoulders and average looking. Perkins was tall and stood eye to eye with Minto. But he knew that with her boots off she would be a good three inches shorter than him. He smiled at the thought and turned to look at Kendal, who was the only light-skinned one among them. He was shy, but smart, quick on his feet, easy to work with, and was the youngest of them all.

But looking at Minto made them all feel awkward. She was lithe and strong. Her muscles rippled like a fitness body builder and her skin was as smooth as a baby's bottom. They all felt that she could take them if push came to shove, and they gave her the respect she warranted.

Her reputation preceded her. She went straight from high school into the police academy, even though she was accepted at Harvard, Yale, New York University, and Rochester Institute of Technology, not to mention Spelman and all the top black universities that were dropping full scholarships at her feet or the athletic offers she had for track, basketball, swimming, and gymnastics. The woman's stats were mind-blowing. She went to the police academy and blew everyone out of the water—men and women alike. The FBI, CIA, and all government posts recruited her based on her impressive IQ tests alone. She could have walked right into the top ranking team in any department she wanted and be paid more than the commissioner of police. But she wanted to stay in her community and help her people. She was tired of hearing about people who accomplished great things, then ran away and called themselves anything but black. She wasn't having it. She was going to stay in Atlanta and clean up her home.

Just as Minto was about to turn the doorknob, she suddenly buckled over, slowly bending to the floor with a pained look on her face.

"Oh my gosh." Detective Minto panicked and felt a weird aching in her abdomen. She was suddenly trembling as though she could feel what Francesca had felt, now that she stood at the door of the room where she was pronounced dead. She stood by the door with the detectives in tow and allowed her premonition to pass. She wasn't sure if she was having a legitimate premonition since they stopped nine years before. Her therapist told her only something traumatic could trigger it. But this was her job. She was used to horror. Why now?

"What is it? Are you OK?" Perkins asked as Minto quickly got up and walked out the door. As Minto cleared the doorway, her feet gave way and she fell right into Perkins's waiting arms. He led her to a nearby bench to sit down.

"Get her some water, Tyme!" he ordered and the detective was off to fulfill this duty while Kendal took his handkerchief and patted down the perspiration that had beaded on Minto's forehead.

The woman doesn't even wear makeup, he marveled to

himself as he looked at the white fabric in his hand that would have come back stained with colors of rouge had she been the average woman.

Her eyes slowly opened to expose beautiful, deep brown eyes that seemed to sparkle when the lights hit them. Her chills suddenly disappeared as she eased herself up from Perkins's lap. She was up on her feet and smiling thankfully at Perkins. His heart skipped a beat and then began racing as he watched her eyes curl into tight slits, and then open again when her smile disappeared and she began to speak.

"We have a lot of work to do. We need to call in the forensic team and the coroner's office to find out what the autopsy will show." She stood and acknowledged Tyme, who was just returning with the glass of water.

"Thank you," she told him, taking it and emptying the glass in a few short gulps. "There is something very odd about this. Don't ask, I just know. We have to find the Elizabeth lady. We need to get some answers." Minto handed the glass back to Tyme and walked away, again displaying her ass, bouncing with joy as she departed.

Dyania Minto looked behind her and suddenly felt tired, the weird urges that had followed her throughout her entire life had returned with a vengeance. She thought her doctor told her they were under control, and for years they seemed to have been. But for the past few months, they had been returning steadily and becoming increasingly more powerful. She needed to call home, call her guardians. They owed her some answers.

She looked favorably at Perkins who was still in the middle of his telephone conversation. From the moment she told them what needed to be done, he was on the phone spewing orders and getting the job done. She liked him. She gave a light nod of approval and walked away.

"Have a good weekend, guys. We will pick this up on Monday. A sistah needs to get some sleep." She winked playfully and was gone so quickly that they had to blink twice to appreciate the exit.

Liz was ecstatic to be back in her North Miami home. She looked over her Collins Avenue condo balcony, closed her eyes, and imagined the ocean water washing over her and cleansing her. She still couldn't believe what had happened, or that she had allowed herself to get caught up in an incident that could be detrimental to her identity. She had to let the others know. She had worked so hard to protect who she was, and now look at what had happened. She had to run off the set of a show she had worked so hard to be a part of, and all because of some crazy woman. All her life she had wanted to become an actress, and she had become well-acclaimed within her own right. Now she had lost it all.

"Hello, Cathalina," Elizabeth answered, waiting for the third ring so that the caller ID could register the person on the other end. She breathed a sigh of relief since her psychiatrist and friend was exactly who she needed to speak with.

"Hello, my dear. I just received your message. Sorry I didn't get it earlier." Cathalina had received Liz's message the night before, and had wondered what was going on, but she was a bit tied up with Cleopatra and could not get away. She tried to keep the personal counseling of each member private and only shared what was necessary among her sisters.

"You're back early; I thought you wouldn't be back until next week." Even though Elizabeth sounded like her normal, calm, and tranquil self, Cathalina sensed something very wrong simmering below the surface.

"Well, things are not good, Cathalina. I think I may have gotten myself into trouble."

"What kind of trouble, Liz? You were away working. What would make you return from your job a week before it concluded? Does it have anything to do with us?" The phone went deadly quiet, and Cathalina felt her heart begin to pound against her chest as she sat in her Coral Gables office and stared out over Biscayne Bay. She placed her hand on her chest in a subconscious attempt to hold her heart in.

"No, Cathalina, it has everything to do with me. But . . ." her voice trailed off and Cathalina could hear her swallow hard. "But it will affect us," she finished, lowering her eyes as though Cathalina could see her pain and the anger that she rarely allowed to surface.

"Liz, come on, baby, talk to me." Cathalina sighed deeply, her mind working a hundred miles per minute, wondering what the hell was going on.

"Psych!" Liz yelled, "I got ya!" She laughed exuberantly.

"What the fuck you mean, psych? Liz, this is not a joke and I am damn sure not playing with you. Tell me what the hell is going on," Cathalina demanded.

"Nothing is going on, Cathalina. You gotta chill and relax a little. You are too uptight," Elizabeth counseled.

"What exactly do you mean by that?" Cathalina asked, being careful not to show too much anger. She had to remember that the women still depended on her for counsel. They were still so much like children needing to be told they are loved.

"Listen to me. I'm not trying to disrespect you, Cathalina, but you need to relax. Go to the spa, take a break, and take care of yourself. I feel mad vibes coming from you, a crazy, sexual energy that seems to be fighting its way to be unleashed." Liz did feel the passion that Cathalina was emanating. She couldn't quite put her finger on it, but she felt that Cathalina couldn't handle any bad news right now. Maybe nothing was wrong anyway. Maybe Francesca was fine and just jonesing for a good fuck and that was it. But something told her she was wrong.

"All right, I feel you, sweetheart. But this is not the time for jokes or games, Elizabeth. We have business to take care of. Actually, we should meet. Some things have happened that you need to be updated on." Cathalina's gut instinct told her that there was something Liz was hiding, but she didn't want to have her friend's homecoming be a sad one. She had come and gone as they needed her, taking breaks in between shows and making last minute travels to arrive back at her home by morning. She should be rewarded for that.

"How about we meet for a late breakfast? I'll drive up to see you," Cathalina told her. "Hey, what about that nice breakfast nook on the beach on Collins Avenue? Is it still there?" Cathalina asked excitedly.

"I think it's still there. Gosh, we haven't been there since, since . . ."

"Since I began initiating you more than a year and a half ago. We've been friends a long time."

"Yeah," Elizabeth acknowledged, allowing herself to drift back to the past when she had felt really lost and alone.

"They served the best prosciutto and salmon slices with toast and juice."

"The special."

They both giggled.

"Yeah, let's meet there. I can't wait to see you, sister. I have missed you."

"OK, you're on." Elizabeth laughed.

"Last one to The Nook is a dead spider!" Cathalina giggled and hung up the phone.

"Oh, no you didn't just hang up on me. I live right around the corner, woman," Elizabeth said to the beeping dial tone and hung up. The phone immediately rang back.

"I do know you live around the corner, but your slow ass takes forever to get dressed and go someplace, especially when you think you have the advantage," Cathalina bellowed through the phone lines.

"How the hell did you know I was thinking that?"

"Because I know you, heffa. Now get dressed. I'm out."

11

Serena tossed and turned herself into frenzied, sexual tension, and her dreams could not let the image of Vincent Ratigan go. He held her emotionally captive and she could not understand why. Her dreams ran rampant and got progressively more stimulating from night-to-night. She would dream about his voice, his bald head, and his sexy lips burying into her snatch, and she would erupt in multiple orgasms, finding herself calling his name every morning when she awoke.

"I must really be losing my mind," she said to herself one morning. Soon I'll have to check myself into a psych ward for being delusional." She laid her head back on the pillow and snuggled into her sheets to get comfortable, but as soon as she closed her eyes, the images tore at her mind again.

She would imagine little Latoya's mangled body, and visualize him raping and killing child after child. She did not know and couldn't comprehend what to do with all those feelings, all those emotions.

"Jassssssssoooooon!" she screamed, jolted from her

sleep drenched in sweat. She was naked, chest heaving, and confused.

"Serena, what's wrong?" He was at her feet with lowered eyes, holding on to her bedside awaiting her bidding or punishment. He never knew which would come to him each time she called.

"Jason, Jason, oh Jason." Her tears streamed down her face and she felt violated all over again. She was that same little girl having sexual interactions without her consent or full knowledge of what was happening. She hated the feeling of being out of control.

"Jason." His name echoed from her lips in short, raspy whimpers and when she reached her arms out to him, he crawled on the bed toward her. He wasn't sure what was going on, and feared for her life as well as his own.

"I am here, Serena. I am here with you, love." The consolation came sincerely and she panted sadly in his arms.

"I am sorry, Jason. I am sorry for everything."

"No need to think of that now. It's in the past. Everything is going to be OK." Though he spoke the words, he knew things would not be OK. He wished he could snap his fingers and make everything right again. Go back to the day he first met her and make every thing right.

Elizabeth woke up throbbing and couldn't understand why she was suddenly immersed in urges she never had before. She had sprung awake screaming every night, with no one to hold her hand, sending her into spasms of overwhelming desire and chaotic thoughts. Her already guilty conscience was not allowing her much sleep, and the added effects of demanding sexual desires were not helping her at all.

She heard the phone ringing. She took a look at the clock and saw that it was three in the morning. She cringed with worry and frustration as to who would be calling at three AM on a Saturday morning. She turned on her back and closed her eyes, ignoring the annoying sound of the telephone.

A few minutes went by and the phone started ringing again, refusing to be ignored. She tossed and turned, pretending that the ringing instrument was just a figment of her imagination. The caller stopped momentarily. Elizabeth smiled a sigh of relief and attempted to return to her slumber, but the caller would not give up. Elizabeth jumped to her feet and snatched the phone from its cradle.

"It's three in the morning. What do you want?" she demanded without knowing who it was. She had not even bothered to turn on the lights. She just wanted to be left alone.

"Liz, you bitch you. Why didn't you tell me that you were back in town?" a drunken, slurred voice asked.

"Cleo? Is that you? What are you talking about? It's three in the morning! I have been back only one week and we are meeting today at Sex Cell, so what's the big deal?" Liz was annoyed at the disrespect that Cleo was showing her, but the fact that Cleopatra was drinking, and was obviously dismayed caused Liz to soften her voice.

"Have you been drinking Cleo?" Elizabeth asked, hearing the woman's sobs in the background.

Cleo was aggressive and confused most times. She always had a need to hunt and destroy, but unlike the others, she had truly embraced this lifestyle. It was more than retribution to her, more than making things right. It was who she was and these women were her family. She tried not to think of how her father had prostituted her and her siblings to his friends beginning when she was just seven years old. He would force her to watch his male friends penetrate her ten-year-old sister as tears ran down her face. Bloody screams were just a turn on to these men. Her oldest sister was violated in every orifice she possessed, and her brothers were raped over and over again by these men, as well as forced to have sex with each other. She was allowed to lick and suck and touch her father as he fingered her vagina and performed oral sex on her.

One day Cleo walked in on her oldest sister, who was eleven years old at the time, and her youngest brother, who was eight, having sex. Her brother's face was between her sister's legs, and her sister was using what looked like their mother's dildo to violate her brother's anus. He was bleeding and whimpering, and the more he whimpered, the more violent her sister became. Cleo ran to the garage, got a bottle of kerosene oil, and threw it on the both of them. Her father stopped her as she was about to light the match and burn them both. She was scared and terrified by the ruthlessness of her family.

It destroyed her when her oldest sister got tired of the whole thing and bit the dick clean off of one of her daddy's friends. Her father was so angry that he got his revolver and blew her head off. Then he threatened the same treatment to any of them who dared to do something like that again.

Poor Cleo was terrified and peed herself as she watched the man bleed to death. Her father took the man, her two older brothers, and now her only sister to the backyard at three AM to bury him. The pedophile and her sister were buried together. Their mother dared not fuss or ask too many questions, not that she was capable of doing so anyway. Her father had Cleo's mother drugged up and turning tricks on the street corners to put food on the table while he ate, drank, and fucked the life out of the rest of the family.

As Cleo cried, she remembered the years of torture. By the time she was nine, she had endured three years of watching her mother shoot up drugs into her arms and do whatever her husband told her to do. For three years, she had watched her brothers and sisters as they began to enjoy the abuse and started acting up in school. No one cared about ghetto children living in the worst drug-infested areas of Tallahassee. Not even the police would venture there after dark.

So at the tender age of nine, Cleo took her father's gun and put them all out of their misery. She was found dirtied and disoriented in their backyard, trying to dig a grave for the rest of her demented family members. She hadn't slept in days, nor had she eaten. She had defecated and pissed on herself for days, so the waste was caked to her body. She had gone temporarily insane and was admitted to a psychiatric hospital until she was nineteen. And then Cleo was released into a world she had no idea about. She found her way to Miami with the only talent she had.

"Don't worry about me. I'm fine," Cleo answered after she got her tears under control. "I have just been missing you is all. I'm really excited that you're home."

"Thanks, Cleo. I know you were holding down the fort for all of us. How have you been?"

"Drama, girl. You know these men are no good. If it wasn't for their money and their dicks, I would get rid of them all." She snickered. Elizabeth smiled with a light chuckle so Cleo would know she understood where she was coming from.

"You know it's not *all* like that now, don't you, Cleo? I mean, not all men are bad, just like not all women are good."

"Are you trying to insinuate something, woman?" The sudden intensity of Cleo's anger flashed through the phone lines and stung Liz.

"I am not trying to say anything, my friend." Elizabeth backed down softly. She knew that this was a touchy subject for Cleo. They all knew each other's stories to some extent. Only Cathalina knew them all in detail, and there was a certain level of confidentiality among them. "I'm just saying that women are sometimes just as worthless as men, like the ones at Serena's ceremony. There are good and bad in each sex of the human race. That's what makes eradicating one or the other sex so damned hard, otherwise, I would be out there with you on a beheading hunt. You know that, don't you, sister?" Elizabeth tamed her voice and used their friendship to bring Cleo down from her defensive stance.

Again Elizabeth heard sobs from Cleo, and her heart ached for this woman whom she had known now for a full six years. Liz worked at Sex Cell for a long time before she met Cathalina and began seeing her. Cathalina was Cleo's prized commodity, and she wouldn't let any of her workers or patrons near her. Cleo and Cathalina met and became friends ten years ago, so their friendship had survived and seen much, and it was clear that Cathalina was partial to Cleopatra's feelings.

"Cleo, baby girl, I will see you soon, OK? Save a nice big hug for your little Nina, OK?" Liz's giggle was contagious and Cleopatra began to laugh. Cleo had always loved when the submissives came to see Elizabeth back in the day when she worked for her. They loved her diverse sexuality. Cleo began calling her Nina, because on the street Nina was the nickname for a nine-millimeter gun. And just like a gun, Cleo said that having sex with Liz was a dangerous and deeply erotic thing. She always got her man or gal, and if she wanted to, she could have them walk out without their wallets.

"See, I knew I could make you laugh."

"Yeah, Nina, you were da bomb. Always was and always will be," Cleo told her as she drifted off into her own thoughts. Elizabeth was special and Cleo hoped she knew how much she meant to her.

"So how about we get some sleep? I will see you soon." Liz smiled her way through the call. She had to go lie down. Her dick was as hard as a rock and she needed to jerk off.

"OK, Nina. Goodnight." Elizabeth blew Cleo a kiss and hung up the phone.

When Elizabeth got off the phone she headed to her bathroom. She spread her legs and stood over the toilet seat with her throbbing sex in her hand. She picked up the porn magazine that was hidden in the center of the magazine rack and placed it on the toilet bowl, turning the page as she gently massaged her shaft. Her moans came slowly as she imagined how good it would have been to place herself inside Francesca's pleasure center. Gaining momentum, she imagined withdrawing herself as Francesca took her twelve-inch weapon all the way down her throat without even gagging. Her pants came in rapid spurts and her breasts heaved, perspiration beading on her forehead as she prepared to orgasm.

"Humm, yes. That's it, girl, right there." She spoke to the imaginary bobbing head that took her love stick into her trachea and shoved herself in and out of her hands as though the soft moistness of a woman's lips propelled her building desire. "Don't stop, don't stop." Her raspy voice begged the naked woman in her mind to take her in deeper. "Yes, Yesssssss, Yessss!" she breathed, as her ejaculation squirted into the toilet bowl, blending with the water and making it a creamy, murky color where her cum fell.

Drained from the experience, she pulled herself together and sighed deeply. It had been a while since she had been intimate with someone for her own pleasure, a while since someone had accepted her for who she was and allowed themselves to taste the advantage that being with her would present, especially if that person was a man. But things had not gone in her favor. The only physical contact she could recall lately was when she was punishing a perpetrator, but that was not fun. It was work. *Well, sometimes it was fun*, she thought to herself as she took a washcloth out and wiped herself.

Slipping into a silky, black gown, she pulled out an elastic strap belt that was about the size of a thigh gun holster. She put on her crotch-less panties, because those were the only kind of underwear that could make her feel like a woman and allow her penis to hang. She took her now flaccid member and allowed it to hang against her soft, inner thigh, and then she took the strap and bound her penis against her legs so that when she was dressed like a lady, all that could be imagined between her legs would be a vagina. The only problem was that it hurt like crazy if she got excited, so that was why she masturbated first.

Wrapping herself into her black, silky negligee, she slid herself under the covers and closed her eyes.

"I cannot believe it's almost morning," she mumbled as she turned to her lamp on the nightstand and turned it off.

Elizabeth had nightmares about Francesca that night. She didn't know exactly why her body began to tremble and perspiration involuntarily formed on her body, making the bed sheets feel as though she was underwater and couldn't breathe, but she knew something was wrong. She sensed it. She couldn't understand why the nightgown that made her feel sexy only hours before had transformed into a death garb.

"Oh my gosh, oh my gosh," she squealed to herself. "Something has happened." She ran to the phone and began dialing Cathalina's number. But then she stopped. "No, I am being paranoid. I can handle this." She consoled herself. "I cannot keep running to Cathalina every time I think something is wrong. Every time I get myself into some crazy situation, she has to get me out of it. Nothing is wrong. NOTHING is wrong," she stated firmly, and then placed the phone back on its base.

She began laughing; laughing so loudly that she could hear herself echoing across the early morning dew. She walked to her balcony and looked out across Collins Avenue to the rising sun coming over the horizon of the ocean.

"God, you are so amazing, so powerful, and so awesome in all your glory. Just look at you. Go on with your bad self!" she praised, and then raised her hands to the heavens and began to cry.

12

Cleopatra hung up the phone and turned around to face the mound of molding, fetid bodies piled behind her. She had been collecting them for a week, ever since Cathalina allowed her to taste the sweet succulence of her nectar once more. She didn't understand why she had gone out on her own, why she was uncontrollably propelled to destroy, but she felt better than she had since before Serena came into the picture.

She choked and began vomiting again as the smell gained in intensity. She had to do something. This was her workplace, her business. A dungeon, yes, but the fact that she had brought the decaying bodies to the underbelly of her home, dug deep on the underside about three levels beneath the main floor where the rooms and her girls worked their feminine and devious magic with their bodies for money, was a risky move. She took the bodies to the level where she kept her pets—her crocodiles that she knew didn't judge her and would enjoy the appetizing, rotten, semi-decaying pieces of flesh. She could have concealed her reckless acts a long time ago, but she refused to allow the crocs to partake of her kill this time. She wanted to see the bodies decay, their jawbones becoming decomposed and slimy with the teeth structures exposed, eyes sunken, and bodies wrapped, warped, broken, and dismantled. It was obvious that something strong and powerful had gotten to these people. She looked at the bloody, gross mass of body parts on mismatched and half-eaten bodies. Her stomach churned with disgust and hunger as she again began to regurgitate the day's meals.

"Madam, madam," Natalia called frantically from the second floor. Cleo knew she needed to meet her quickly before she got any closer and smelled the stench. Natalia knew that no one was allowed past the main floor without specific clearance, but she just couldn't help it. She understood that she was special to Cleo; therefore, she felt she could break some of the rules.

"What is it, Natalia?" Cleo suddenly appeared at the second landing to the curving stone stairs that looked like a dragon's lair. The walls were unfinished and rocky, and cobwebs and mold made the place realistically spooky, to say the least. Natalia wrinkled her nose like a rabbit's and moved it around awkwardly. She didn't want her mistress to see her so openly put off by a scent. One of the lessons Cleopatra always taught was that smells came in all varieties, and that the customers were also varied. If they couldn't control their noses, then they wouldn't be able to control their pockets.

"Madam, Joanna and Fatima are at it again."

"What is it this time?" Cleo asked in a surprisingly cool and calm voice that scared Natalia. Cleo would normally burst forward yelling, and spring into action.

"Oh, it's the usual, madam. A man."

"Really? What is so special about this man?"

"Money, mistress, and this is the same man that they have fought over for months. He is always saying the same thing about how he gets away with murder."

"Murder?" she pondered mischievously. "I wonder what the pull is to him?" she asked herself, dazed, and almost gliding her two-hundred-pound body up the spiraling, dungeon stairs.

Natalia lingered behind her, curiosity pulling at her to go check where the foul smell was coming from. She eyed Cleopatra as she made her exit.

What could smell so horrible? Natalia wondered, pinching her nose to stop the odor from forcing itself upon her. She looked behind her again and heard the upper level door close, and then she began creeping down. Not seeing the slight trail of blood on the stairs, she slipped.

"Shit!" she exclaimed as she tried to regain her balance. "What the hell does she do down here all the time?" she asked herself aloud.

As Natalia made her way down the stairs, Cleo stealthily crept back through the door that led down the spiral staircase to her private dungeon. She watched Natalia cough and gag as she neared the stench of the week-old, dead bodies. It was very dark and she could not see what was causing the smell, but she knew there was something rancid down there. She was taken aback as her feet neared the landing and touched something soft. She squealed and looked cautiously behind her to see if anyone had heard her.

Cleo watched the woman who had become her most trusted whore, her money-making coochie. She wanted to see what she would do, how much more she could trust her. She swung her big, bodacious body behind a stair when Natalia turned around, then peeked her head back out as the woman stood still, not knowing what to do. Then Natalia began ascending the stairs backward.

Cleopatra speedily crept back out of the stairway and walked a little way down the hall, then turned back and made her way forward, bumping into Natalia as she was making her way from Cleo's secret place.

"Madam, did you see them?"

"No. Actually, I had something else to take care of, so I sent Hercules to settle the dispute."

"Hercules? Why did you do that? He would kill somebody!" Horror plastered itself on Natalia's face as she thought of her friends.

"Well, you know my rules, Natalia," Cleopatra said, drawing her name out in an Italian accent. She loved the way the woman's name sounded coming off her tongue. "I don't want fighting over money or dicks. We can get both easily, and we are all above it. We are family," she told her calmly. Then she glided by Natalia and opened the door to her special place of solitude.

Natalia gasped. She was starting to become concerned that she didn't know just how much this woman was capable of. Her instincts told her to beware.

"But, ma'am, they were two of your best girls. Did you tell Hercules to take it easy?"

"How dare you question me? Would you care to be in their place?" Cleo asked, red burning in her eyes, the scales on her back rising, and her shoulders stretching. She was already stressed. She felt sexual urges and desires she wasn't even sure were hers. She also felt that Cathalina was ignoring her since she had re-sampled the goods, and now her slaves and her workers were overstepping their boundaries. Even from Natalia, she was not having it today.

"I didn't mean to say anything wrong, Madam. I was just concerned." Natalia lowered her eyes apologetically and stepped to the woman to receive whatever wrath she wished to bestow upon her. But Cleo just turned and walked away from her. She didn't want to hurt Natalia. She just wanted her to know and remember her place at all times.

"I am expecting the gang. Let them down here when they

arrive. Tell Hercules to bring the man my girls are so infatuated with. I want to see just how murderous he is, and what he is packing in his pants to drive my sisters wild." She snickered at the thought, but felt herself building moisture between her thighs. Now she knew something was wrong. She never got excited over the thought of a man.

Natalia smiled quickly at the thought of seeing Elizabeth and Cathalina. She had heard so much about them both. These ladies were legends. They were so cool and suave. *The gang!* she thought. Now this should be interesting. And then there was all that talk about Serena, who had stepped in with Cathalina. She hoped she would be there too. Her stomach knotted with excitement. She rushed off with butterflies tingling in her stomach and her mind racing.

Cathalina knew that this day would be hard. She knew that after what she had shared with Cleo at the Ft. Lauderdale airfield, that Cleo would expect more. It could never be just about the moment with her.

"Serena, baby, are you ready, girl?" Cathalina asked as she kissed the woman on her forehead. She relaxed in the back of the black car she decided on for transportation to Sex Cell.

"I'm doing fine, Cath. I just keep having these dreams and headaches. It hurts," she confessed. "Sometimes I want them to stop. Sometimes it's as if my mind is bombarded with things I have done in my past, and from a life I know I have not lived. Yet it feels so real."

Cathalina snuggled closer to Serena and placed her arm around the woman's shoulder. She then gently touched her temple, urging her head to find a resting place in the crevice of her chest. She felt her heart beat as Serena recounted the dreams, the fantasies, and the spider's anger, not to mention the visions. She knew there would be some side effects, a consequence to Serena being inducted with the Brazilian wandering spider. That spider was the most deadly, and they had no idea how it would interact with her system. Cathalina had searched for someone like Serena to be their leader. She would be their counsel. She didn't want to take the risk of having the Brazilian wandering venom in her system. It was too risky, but she also felt unworthy. Cathalina was excited and scared all at once at the prospects for the future, but for now she just listened.

"It's going to be all right, honey. I know this is all new, but it's so exciting. You are the Spider Queen. Now we will meet for the first time as a family. Today we will understand how we are tied together as a unit. Today we will map out our journey and you will become stronger and more powerful as you learn your way around the team." Cathalina smiled widely, thinking of all that she had worked for to get to this day, this moment. The side effects were an extra benefit. "You will become," she stopped herself to make a correction, "No, you *are* our leader, our queen bee, and we are at your disposal for anything you need us to do within the ranks of our association." Cathalina's voice was soft, motherly, comforting, and totally in control. She needed Serena to adapt to these skills quickly, and to adapt to her new body. She never meant to hurt anyone; she thought she was giving them all an opportunity to exact vengeance on those who deserved it. Now, she wasn't so sure.

Serena curled her legs under her and snuggled closer into Cathalina, listening to her map out her destiny.

"How long before we get to Liz?"

"We are close now. She will be waiting outside for us, and then we will head to Cleo's. She is expecting us." Her voice dipped a few octaves at the thought of Cleopatra waiting for them. She didn't want Serena to become too aware of what was between her and Cleo. She wanted Serena, and she needed her to love and depend on her as a partner. But she knew that no matter what, Cleo would be a problem.

"Make a left here." Cathalina provided instructions for the limo driver to exit off on Collins Avenue and to enter the approaching estates. "This is it. Have the guards buzz us in," she told him.

As they pulled up to Elizabeth's condo, they saw the creamy olive complexion of the delicate Asian woman with her full, round face smiling brightly at them. Her even, white teeth shone with joy as her eyes became almost fully closed when she smiled. Her straight, long, black hair fluttered in the slight breeze, which also coiled her long, flowing, white, linen dress between her legs, curving it around her body.

Cathalina exited the vehicle and dashed toward Elizabeth.

"Woman, what a sight for sore eyes you are. You are even more beautiful today than the day I met you," Cathalina complimented, spinning her around to admire how well she put herself together, and then hugged her again. "No one would ever be able to tell that you are packing a twelve-inch weapon between those gorgeous legs." They laughed heartily and pulled away from each other with a smile.

"I missed you, Cathalina. I felt like I was missing a part of myself being away from home." Sadness came over her as she thought back to Francesca. An eerie feeling enveloped her and she cringed. *Oh gosh, I hope she is OK*, she thought.

Noticing the change is Elizabeth's face, Cathalina became concerned.

"Is everything all right?" she asked, searching Liz's eyes for the answer. Perking up, Liz put on a great big poker face and nodded her head.

"So can I see our new initiate? I want to see how she has bonded with her soulmate," Liz commented and walked toward the other side of the limo where the driver stood with the door open, waiting for her to enter. Elizabeth noticed the man was on the phone and he slipped it in his pocket when he saw them coming. She didn't like it.

Cathalina slipped in on the left side where she had exited, sliding back in next to Serena, who was now sandwiched between Elizabeth and Cathalina. The driver began to yell and scream at someone on the phone.

"Hey, could you keep it down?" Elizabeth banged on the partitioned window. He seemed flustered. Elizabeth turned on the intercom in the luxurious limousine and listened in as the man threatened his family.

As the women settled into the comfort of the seat, ready to make the forty-five minute trip from North Miami Beach to Miami, where Cleo's spot was, they shared an electrified sensation that brought them to sudden alertness. Each woman sat up and grabbed the arm of the other so that they were huddled together and interlocked. It drew their attention away from the driver.

"Oh God, did you feel that?" Cathalina asked as excitement filled her. The sensuality she felt was beyond anything she had ever experienced. It was like having ten people massage, caress, and gently kiss her body all over, rolling her in soft rose petals and bubbling champagne that was as smooth as butter, wrapping her in a cocoon of love and delight as passionate urges throbbed between her thighs and dripped down her legs. She felt as though light was around her, the life after death kind of light with angelic serenades. The split second of transmission held her captive, causing her to emit a sound that was so profound, she was speechless.

"Yes. What was that?" Elizabeth turned and looked at Serena. She didn't say anything, but the startled, horrific look on her face elicited fear within them.

"It's all right. She is probably just having another reaction." Cathalina soothed, making an attempt to calm the anxiety rising within them.

"Yeah, but Cathalina, did you feel that? Maybe it's the excitement from hearing the driver on the phone. Hearing him angry." Elizabeth was hard-pressed to believe that Serena was making them feel this incredible. But the look on Serena's face didn't say she felt incredible. She looked to be in pain.

Another sensation jolted them back to the smooth leather upholstering that covered the seat. While they sat affixed to the seat, they felt another sensation, a thought.

"What was that?"

"What was what, Cath? I didn't feel that."

"No, not a feeling. Did you say something?"

"I didn't say a word. I thought you said it?"

"But Serena hasn't moved. She didn't say anything." Cathalina was sure. But the voice did sound familiar to hers, though muffled and filled with rage.

"That's it. We are all paranoid and hallucinating. This has to stop." Elizabeth said. She'd had enough drama over the past week to last her a lifetime, and she didn't want to be freaking out among family.

Suddenly, Serena's back arched and her head fell so far back that Cathalina and Elizabeth grabbed her simultaneously to prevent damage to her neck. As they wrapped their arms around her back, they looked at her and saw that her face became distorted with pain, yet she still had not made a sound.

"I think you are overreacting, Serena," Cathalina responded, not realizing that the words were not spoken to her, but sent telepathically.

"I agree with Serena," Elizabeth responded. "She is right. Why should he get away with it? That poor child must be traumatized."

"But he has not done anything wrong," Cathalina argued, thinking that she just really needed to get over to Sex Cell so that they could figure out what was going on and where to go from there. Things were developing so fast and seemed to be spinning out of Cathalina's control, but she knew this would happen. She was no longer the one guiding the group's action. Something within Serena was.

He has not done anything yet, Serena transmitted back. *But I can feel it. I know he will hurt them.* After another violent convulsion, Serena doubled over in the back of the limo, regurgitating the mountain of food she had consumed earlier that morning.

"My gosh, Serena, what did you eat?" Cathalina asked as she and Elizabeth released the hold on Serena to cover their noses and mouths. The smell that was permeating through the limo was making them feel sick.

This man has been beating his wife senseless for the past four years. He has a few lovers, but that has not satisfied him. He is tired of his wife and children getting in his way. He feels trapped and wants out.

Cathalina and Elizabeth looked at each other, and then toward the front of the car where there was a transparent, soundproof, glass partition. They could see the driver, but he could not see them. He could sense that there was something going on, a commotion, but it was not his concern. He had more important things on his mind, and didn't realize they were listening to his conversation through the intercom.

"But how do you know this?" Cathalina asked, terrified and fascinated by the shared knowledge they were experiencing.

"What if you are wrong?" Elizabeth asked out loud. They were trying to be reasonable, but the sensation that Serena was sending them was not one of collaboration, but action.

Anger rose within them as the driver screamed into the phone, unaware of the eavesdroppers.

"I am going to cut your fucking neck off!" he bellowed over phone.

They cringed, listening to the vocabulary, the horrible words he used to talk to what was obviously his wife. He seemed to become angrier with the minutes.

"We should do something about this man," Serena decided.

"No, I don't think we should do this. Not here. Not in broad daylight."

"I am not asking your permission, Cath," Serena bellowed, words cascading from her lips for the first time since they were all inside the car.

"I am not being disobedient, Serena. I just think we should be strategic." The reasoning coming from Cathalina was hard to deny, and Serena's respect and admiration for her caused her anxiety to quell and she relaxed.

"We can do this another way. We know who he is now, and where he lives. Let's just get to our destination and take care of this later."

But he intends to burn his home down tonight and cover it up so it looks like an accident to collect the insurance money. Two years ago, he took out life insurance on his entire family. This man will hurt his family before the day is out.

Serena couldn't seem to get those thoughts to leave from her mind. The children looked to be the same age she was when her father decided he wanted more from her.

"It will be OK, Serena. Please, trust me. I have not steered you wrong yet."

Serena turned slowly and looked at Cathalina. She wasn't happy, but she decided to let it go.

* * *

"Hurry, let them in," Cleo bellowed when she saw the limo pull up to the beautifully established looking day spa. The outside façade prevented any suspicion about what went on under the three-tiered dungeon specializing in torture and bondage. Natalia put on her best professional smile and walked briskly through the front door and into the posh waiting area where unsuspecting clients awaited their manicures and pedicures, reading and listening to smooth jazz.

Cathalina hugged Serena close to her and Elizabeth ran behind them. There were a few suspicious stares at the women who arrived and were ushered in behind the closed doors leading to the spa quarters. They received a few undesirable stares from those who thought they had skipped the waiting area and were receiving preferential treatment, but the most that happened were a few crossed eyes and the hissing of teeth.

"What happened to you guys?" Cleo questioned, looking Cathalina up and down with a nonverbal I-told-you-so while she waited for a response. Cleo waved Natalia away with the flip of her wrist and the woman knew what to do.

"It's a long story, Cleo. Can we get away from here and go into The Cave to have this discussion, please?" Cathalina snapped. She was in no mood for Cleo's barking, ignorant ways.

"This is not the time to get all high and mighty on me, Cath." Cleo spat. "I am the head bitch in this place." She clenched her fists and stormed off. "What? Aren't you coming?" she turned to look at the stunned faces behind her. She didn't see the piercing look that Serena gave her, or the stance that Elizabeth took. Her anger was all she saw and felt at that moment, and she didn't care what any of them thought, especially Serena.

"I would keep walking and cut that temper down if I were you, Cleo. This is not the time to act butch. You don't know what's going on, and you are going to put yourself in harm's way if you don't chill," Cathalina warned calmly, then smiled, hoping that Cleo would pick up the hint. She felt Serena's temperature rise and her body shudder. She knew Cleo was about to put herself in immediate danger.

"Whatever!" Cleo stammered as she walked off, leading the way to their specially established place at The Cave. Once they were all behind closed doors, Cleo pressed the hidden button on the wall and the huge, steel door slowly pulled shut behind them.

"Cleo, listen, things have changed. There have been some advanced reactions to the spider initiation on Serena that we didn't know about. You need to be . . ."

"I don't need to be or do anything, Cathalina. That's what you all don't seem to understand. I am so tired of everyone running around talking about Serena this or Serena that. Who the fuck is Serena?"

"Cleo, please calm down." Elizabeth begged. She was on telepathic communication with Serena, and was now bound by her commands since they had pledged to follow whoever was initiated with the Brazilian wandering spider. Serena had passed the initiation. She had survived, and was the first to have done so in the years that they had been trying to find a leader to guide them. Since Elizabeth joined, at least three women had died in the quest to accept the Brazilian spider. But Serena was strong, and she was now pulling their strings and forcing them to do her bidding just by her sheer will.

"Why the hell are you two acting all scared of this bitch all of a sudden? She has never even been fucked and is so naïve it's not even funny. We are the elders here, not her. We are the leaders here. We tell her what to do!" The minute the words came out of Cleo's mouth, Serena walked up to her and slapped her hard.

"Please, Cleo," Elizabeth begged.

But it was too late. Cleo was not having Serena slap her and not do anything about it. She balled up her fist and punched Serena in her face. They began to fight. Cathalina and Elizabeth tried to pull them apart, and even though Cleo was considerably stronger than Serena, she was not having an easy time either. They were all surprised that Serena could hold her own. Once they were finally able to pull them apart, Elizabeth and Cathalina stood between them, keeping them at some distance from each other.

"Cleo. Please calm down. Stop it. You are being unreasonable. You are our guardian and have provided us with a safe haven." Cathalina used her calming techniques to stroke Cleo's ego, but Cleo could not be calmed. Cleo was upset that Cathalina took Serena's side as though they had not been friends and lovers way before Serena was even a thought.

"Fuck you, Cathalina. Fuck all of you. I don't need this shit and I can do what we have been doing all by myself and even better. . . ."

"Cleo, it's not even fair for you to say something like that. We are all in this together. Family."

"Really, Cathalina? We are family? Family like the one I am coming from I don't need, and that bitch Serena is acting like she is the shit around here."

Serena started to lunge at her when Cathalina turned to her.

"Serena, we have all been hurt. She was a victim in this, too, just like the rest of us," Cathalina said as she jerked back the tears that threatened to invade her eyes.

"Life could be so much better," Serena said, turning her attention to Elizabeth and Cathalina, who stood by her side. "Look at us. We are accomplished, educated, successful, beautiful women with careers and assets that make us the envy of many women in everyday life. But what kind of life is this that we are living? Look at what I am becoming.

The hatred and rage in me is eating me up and consuming me to the point that I can no longer think about anything but destroying the very idea of the bastards who do things like this to people like us. I am having nightmares, imagining things."

"It's not just you Serena, we have all gone astray and away from what we thought was right, or just. I have been having my share of troubles and I am scared too," Cathalina reasoned.

"Whatever." Cleo turned her back. "I am not going to cry and feel sorry for myself. Shit happens. That's life. We deal with it or die. What you guys scared and crying about?"

"There are predators out there destroying our innocence, taking away our rights and our choices by compromising us. You know this, Cleo. Why do you have to be an ass all the time?" Serena asked.

"I am not afraid of you, Serena. You need me, not the other way around." Cleo found the courage to retaliate. "Listen to you. You are weak and foolish. You think that life out there is good, that somehow, if this had not happened to us we would have been living this fairy tale life with love, husbands, and children and shit? You have definitely lost your fucking mind."

Serena closed her eyes and began to talk to Cleo and tell her all that had been happening. Cathalina was shocked and turned to Elizabeth, who now had tears in her eyes.

"Now she knows," Serena said, and fell unconscious to the hard, stone floor. Cathalina began to wail in a way that she had not cried in years. She felt her anger bubble to the point of not knowing what to do. She stood up and began banging on the walls so hard her nails broke, and her knuckles were scraped and bled. She couldn't stop the agonizing torture that she had suppressed and that had been released through Serena's words, her thoughts, her grief.

"Oh God, Elizabeth, what have we done? What have we

become?" she asked in her despair, pain dripping through her pores as she became drenched with sweat. "We have become monsters. I hate these no good pieces of crap who did this to us, to me. Oh God, why did you let this happen? Why? Why? Why?" she screamed, wailing, getting angrier, and becoming more resolved to go out and finish what she started.

"Cath, it's not our fault. It's not our fault," was all Elizabeth could say as she reached for Cleopatra to make peace with her. She remembered back to when she was ten, learning and understanding how different she was, finding out that people thought she was a freak. Saying, "It's not my fault," was the only thing that kept her sane.

"That's right, Liz, this is not my fault, and I refuse to let them get away with it. They made me like this, and I will move heaven and earth until they pay," Cathalina said with a new determination in her voice.

13

As soon as Cleo sent Natalia away, she took the opportunity to sneak around the dungeon while Cleo was distracted. She knew Cleo's secret hiding places and all the passwords to get through. She sensed that Cleo had some idea that she had access to her private domain, yet she did nothing about it. She pressed the password into the keypad hidden behind what looked to be overgrown, wild ivy that had spread onto the back of the building, and a door appeared in the seamless wall. Natalia entered the third level and stepped over what sounded like crackling bones. She smelled and that same stench from earlier, when Cleo caught her snooping.

She held her breath and her nose at the same time and cringed with repulsion at what she had stumbled onto. She didn't stay long. She had to get back to the other women before she missed anything. She had heard so much about them from Cleo that she felt she was among the luminaries.

She didn't take the back entrance out. Instead she stepped over the dead, decomposing body parts and walked along the edges of the pond where Cleo kept her "pets," then she rushed to the spiraling staircase where she was almost caught by Cleopatra earlier, and made a discreet exit. She looked around and headed to the only place she knew Cleo could have taken the others. When she rounded the bend she overheard Cleo yelling at the others, asking them what had happened and yelling at them for their recklessness. She hid until they walked into The Cave, and then she snuck in behind them. They were so engrossed in their conversation that they didn't realize that had been followed.

Natalia could barely keep herself still when she overheard the women's conversation. She snuck out and decided to take the rest of the day off. With all the commotion and everything else, no one noticed that she was missing for the rest of the day.

Natalia swerved through traffic like a madwoman in her little Mini Cooper. The small vehicle slithered and pushed its way through traffic so fluidly that Natalia felt like she was flying. She had to slow down so that the state troopers didn't pull her over. This was all too weird and good to be true.

As soon as she pulled up to the great gates, she pulled the small car to the side and hid it as best she could among the huge trees and overrun ivy plants surrounding the premises, and then she took off her shoes. Since she was wearing short shorts and an above-the-navel cropped T-shirt, she was dressed perfectly for what she needed to do. Natalia's adrenaline pulsed through her as she slowly scaled the walls of the twelve-foot gates guarding the semi-mansion. She reached the other side safely, with only a few bruises on her knees, legs, thighs, and arms. She noticed that her tan shirt was stained as she tried to brush herself free of debris.

She crept to the huge windows and tried to peer in, but the frosted, opaque glass gave her little leeway to be nosey, so she decided on the next best thing. If the rumors were true, then she could definitely work her new plans.

She walked up to the huge, wrought-iron gates and studied the doorknocker that looked as if it were alive. The huge iron spider, delicately crafted and etched and edged in all the right places made her skin crawl. The eight-eyed creature stared at her with thick talons that appeared to move with each knock. On the fourth knock she waited patiently for an invitation to enter. It seemed to be taking forever.

Jason looked through the windows and stared back at the beautiful, petite stranger who was peering back at him. His heart raced in shock, as there had not been an unannounced visitor to that house in years. He was not sure what to do, but he ached for company and his loneliness got the better of him.

Jason ran to the door that led to his private hallway. He had grown accustomed to not wearing much around the house, but for the first time since tragedy befell him in association with his acquaintance with Serena, he would finally be given the chance to feel free, like a man, admired by a woman who didn't know his plight. His need to see someone outside of Serena and her crew, his curiosity as to why this woman was there, and his need for company propelled him forward. He found a white, button-down, collared shirt with breast pockets and put that on. Releasing his locks so that they fell to his shoulders, he reached for some khakis; he had not worn any in more than two years. His thoughts raced as his mind's eye went over the casual and messy look of the beautiful lady with bright green eyes and flowing, straight brown hair. He rushed back to the front door, hoping and praying that he had not been gone too long and that the reprieve to his solitude was still there.

Relieved to still see the woman standing outside, he opened the door as slowly and casually as possible, so as not to appear anxious.

"Good afternoon. Can I help you?" he asked, his voice almost cracking as the open door and sunlight streamed down and illuminated more of the beauty that stood before him.

"Hi, I'm Natalia." She extended her delicate, manicured hand to him and waited for him to take it. *Yes*, she thought to herself excitedly. *The rumors are true so far. She lives with a man. Wonder if he is really a eunuch?* She smiled brightly at him as her excitement grew. *So far, so good. Now I just have to get inside.*

Jason, still uncertain as to whether it was a good idea to let this woman into the house, looked at her extended hand suspiciously and then returned his gaze to her eyes with a crooked smile. He knew that in light of all the things that had happened recently, Serena would not be herself when she came home, and there would be no telling what the results would be if she found out he had female company in her house while she was out.

"How did you get in here?" he asked with amusement lacing his voice. He knew it must have been hard to get over the gates, and it was quite a walk to the front door. "You look like it took you quite some effort." He smirked.

Jason had not felt like this in years. Speaking of his own free will caused a part of his mind to release. He could be the man he used to be around this woman.

"Are you Jason?" Natalia asked, wiping the smile from his face as fast as one might blink an eye, totally shattering his moment of freedom in thinking there was a stranger who did not know him. He hung his head and slowly began closing the door. "No, please don't do that. I have news of Serena." Seeing that she had caught his attention again, she pushed on. "May I come in, please? I promise I am harmless." Her smile brought the sunshine back to his heart, but the mention of Serena's name made him nervously clench and unclench his fists.

"Yes, please. I'm sorry. Come in." The door was again pulled open and Natalia slipped in.

"Wow, this is gorgeous. It must be so great living in a place like this. I have heard so much about Serena's home," Natalia gushed. As though it was some strange kind of living shrine, Natalia jabbered on and on as she spun around in circles with her head looking up toward the high, cathedral ceilings.

"Would you like to tell me what you came here for? It must be important if Serena sent you." Jason interrupted her admiration of the house he had grown so accustomed to and endured so much pain in. He could no longer see or appreciate the beauty that was contained throughout the mansion.

"No. I mean, it's not what you think." She closed her eyes, placed her hand to her throat, and coughed. "May I have something to drink, please?" she asked, stalling for time and wanting a few more moments to look around at the exquisite luxury surrounding her. She had never seen anything quite like it. Besides, she had no clue how she would get information out of Jason or get him out of the way so she could really look around. *Damn, he is off-the-scale gorgeous*, she thought as she watched him leave her.

Reluctantly, Jason left the room to fetch her something to drink. He was almost afraid to turn his back to her, but he realized that the sooner he got her what she wanted, the sooner she would leave. Luckily for him, Serena was picked up in a limo with Cathalina, so he knew something big was going down. She wouldn't be home at her normal time, so he could relax a bit. As he poured a glass of apple juice for Natalia, he decided that he too felt a bit parched and poured a glass for himself. Returning with two full glasses

Denise Campbell

in his hands, he extended one to Natalia and motioned for her to sit on the small, plush, velour chair in a far corner of the room.

"OK, so now you need to tell me why you're here," Jason stated as soon as Natalia sat down. Now that he was aware that she knew his mistress, there was no reason to be coy. She was not here by mistake. She was here for a purpose.

"I work with Cleo," Natalia began slowly, wanting to capture every reaction that he might have to her words. His face was stoic at the mention of Cleo's name, and she wasn't sure if he knew of whom she spoke. "She always hangs out with Serena and Cathalina and she owns the place called Sex Cell." She began speaking fast. "I was there today. They came in all messed up, and I overheard something weird, then Serena turned into this weird thing . . ." The words began rushing out of Natalia's mouth so fast that Jason could barely understand her.

"Please slow down. What are you talking about, and what do you want from me? There is nothing I can do about all this, and if I were you, I would stay out of it," he warned, but he sensed that Natalia had something else in mind. Unfortunately, Jason could hardly concentrate on what she was telling him, because he was being distracted by her beauty and the fact that he was actually sitting down fully-clothed, having a conversation with someone other than Serena.

"One moment, please." He excused himself and made his way back to his private quarters. Grabbing a fresh, white washcloth, he doused it in warm water and made his way back to where he left Natalia.

Thinking quickly as Jason made his exit, Natalia rummaged through her pockets to see if she had any emergency medication left. She found a couple of dime-sized packages of Roofies and barbiturates. Cleo always provided her girls with the top-of-the-line drugs for clients since some of their fantasies were to be raped or taken advantage of during role-play. They liked to keep it as realistic as possible. Thinking quickly, she wasn't sure if she should put the drugs in his drink. But since the barbiturates she had were in a capsule that she could empty into his drink without detection, she decided to place it in his drink to detain and distract Jason, allowing her to prolong her stay. If she could get solid proof, pictures, something, anything of what she had heard and seen that night, she could sell it to the tabloids and stop selling her body for sex. Natalia's mother would roll over and die in Alabama if they knew what she was doing for a living. They thought she was an up-and-coming model, and at twenty-nine years old, she was running out of time to find a good career. Her excuses for keeping her mother from visiting her would not last much longer, and then she'd have to show her who she really was.

Jason returned with the washcloth and gently reached out to erase the dirt from her face. She jerked back a little, not sure what his motives were, but then she smiled and allowed him to wipe the dirt from her.

"There," he said. "Now you're as good as new." He chuckled, sincere joy rumbling up from inside him. Then he picked up the drugged juice, and in three big gulps finished it. "I am sorry to rush you . . ." he began again.

"Natalia. That's my name."

"Natalia. It's nice to have your company, but I didn't expect you, and that's unusual around here. So could you please tell me again how it is that you ended up here, and if Serena sent you? I understand what you said, but Cathalina and the others are all big girls, and from where I am standing, they take pretty good care of themselves."

"Yes, you are right, but don't you find all of this strange? I mean, if I didn't see it with my own eyes, I would have sworn it didn't really happen."

"I think that you might have had a bit of a hallucination. The story you recounted does sound very strange, more like something out of a science fiction movie. But I don't know anything about any of what you have said. Actually, I feel somewhat relieved. I thought you were going to tell me something serious."

Natalia gasped at the blatant insult to her intelligence.

"Are you saying that I am making all this up? You must be really crazy!" she spat. "Are you that whipped, dumb, deaf, and blind not to see what's going on around you? These people are a small cult group. They do weird, stupid stuff and are defying natural human law. They are talking about killing people, and as far as I know, Cleo has already done so, and that's a fact. And now you tell me that I have made the whole thing up?"

She knew he had to be lying. He had to know something. He couldn't just be living in this place with the one that they now called the Spider Queen, and be ignorant of the facts.

Natalia didn't have to fight with him much longer, though, because the barbiturates began to take effect. She softened her voice and began role-playing as if she was at work.

"You are truly a beautiful vision, and I would love to help you, but this is very dangerous, and I don't think you know what you're getting yourself into," Jason reasoned, looking at Natalia with tears forming in his eyes, his true pain and emotions showing themselves. "But it's so good to have you here. Thanks for coming."

"It's OK, Jason. I have heard a lot about you, and you are as stunning as I could have ever imagined." She sighed and inched closer to him on the small vanity chair.

"What would you want me to do?" he asked, his inhibitions beginning to give way.

"You don't have to do anything, Jason. Just allow me to

go look around. That's all. No one would ever know I was here," she cooed, allowing her sultry voice to soothe him as he began to inhale the smell of her hair. The drug continued sedating Jason, and soon he wouldn't be able to stop her one way or another. He relaxed as the drugs took a hold of his system. He began to caress Natalia's face.

"So smooth and soft," he uttered so low that she almost didn't hear him.

"Why don't you sit back and relax, and let me just look around a bit? I promise I won't be long and I'll be right back to sit and chat with you."

Jason nodded in agreement. He liked the sound of her voice. There was a slight semblance of a Southern accent, but it was not very pronounced.

Natalia inched her way from beneath Jason's amorous attempts and began her search. She knew she was on to something, and she was not going to let this opportunity slip away.

14

Dyania got up three days after Francesca's death and decided to go over her notes regarding what happened to the woman prior to her getting to the hospital. Everything was listed, including the cast members' names and addresses. The show still had a week to go, and there was still one person missing—the star, Elizabeth Chung.

"Elizabeth!" Dyania ran the word slowly over her tongue. "—the name Elizabeth." She jumped to her feet in her small office space in the corner of her bedroom and grabbed the phone.

"Yes, Tyme, I want you to go into the computer systems and let me know what else the original reports have to say about Elizabeth Chung of Miami."

"Is this another lead? Did you find out something?" Tyme asked excitedly. He knew that her request could only mean that she was on to something, and it didn't miss him that she called him and not one of the other detectives.

"Really, Tyme, you're over-thinking this and asking way too many questions. Please just do as I ask. When I know more, I'll be sure to clue you in." Dyania told him and hung up the phone.

Feeling somewhat idiotic at the sound of the dial tone, Tyme dismissed the idea that her calling him over the others meant any more than what she needed to have him do.

My number was probably the first she could get a hold of, he thought in silent reprimand to himself as he grabbed his jacket and rushed off to the police station. "Maybe I will just give this to Perkins to do, since he is so gung ho about her." Tyme's jealousy reared its head, but deep down he knew that they all liked this woman. Shoot, the whole freaking Fifty-sixth Precinct liked her, and that may have even included some of the female officers. He snickered as he turned the ignition in the car and drove off.

Dyania went back to the pile of the reports on her full sized bed and rummaged through them uncontrollably. Where was Elizabeth and why did she disappear the day of Francesca's death? She grabbed her notebook and wrote down a few scribbled notes regarding the case and what she had so far.

Frustrated, she threw the papers back on the ruffled, unmade bed and rushed to her closet where she found a pair of wrinkled, flare bottom jeans, thong sandals, and a tank top. She quickly got dressed and then rushed through the door with her thoughts racing a thousand miles per minute. "I have to get out of here."

She stopped suddenly, a thought crossing her mind, so simple she couldn't believe she hadn't thought of it sooner. She retraced her steps back to the telephone and dialed directory assistance.

"City and state, please?" the automated voice asked.

"Miami, Florida."

"Please hold while we connect you to the operator." Dyania tapped her feet and wrenched her fingers as she waited for a live operator to pick up the call.

"Is this business or residential?" Finally, the operator was connected.

"Residential."

"Name of your party?" Before answering, Dyania grabbed the papers with the correct spelling of Elizabeth's name. She was so nervous she wanted to make sure she got this right.

"Elizabeth Chung. That's C-h-u-n-g."

"Thank you, one moment please." Dyania felt like she was being pressed down by ten tons of steel. She couldn't wait for the woman to release her findings.

"Ma'am, I am sorry. I did find an Elizabeth Chung, but the information is private and unlisted. Is there anything else I can get for you?"

"No, thanks for your time," she told her and hung up the phone. She was so excited that she couldn't keep still. "That's just fine, Ms. Operator Lady. I will just go to the office and demand the number be released from there." She grabbed her keys and the papers and walked out the door smiling.

Cathalina didn't know what to do with herself once they all left Sex Cell. Cleo was pissed, Elizabeth looked confused and out of character, and Serena was exhausted. She wasn't sure what was happening to them, what would happen to them from here on out, but she was scared and felt as though she was totally out of control. She was not the one behind the wheel anymore, and that would have been fine, except the person behind the wheel didn't yet know how to drive, and that only added fuel to the fire.

She knew the kind of place she was coming to; a seedy nightclub frequented by seedy patrons.

"Hey there, pretty lady. Want some company?" a rusty, drunken voice from behind her asked. She didn't turn to look around. The music was so loud anyway that she decided she wouldn't even respond.

"Don't you hear a gentleman speaking to you?" the voice

spoke again, this time in her ear, the man pressing into her back. She could feel his penis nudging into her spine.

"Listen, you are drunk, and I just want to be alone with my thoughts. Please go away." Her voice was nice and calm, but loud enough for the man to hear since he was getting up close and personal with her. She was hoping he didn't cause any trouble. She turned to look at the bartender and called him over. "May I have another bloody mary, please?" Her smile melted him and he felt as though she smiled only for him.

"Why, of course you can. Anything for the only real lady in the house tonight." The bartender complimented her and she nodded a thank-you and looked away. She thought the drunk was gone and so she turned to look at the dance floor, where men and women made carnal acquaintances and found love, sex, marriage, and divorce all in one night, walking away strangers when it was all over.

"So, you think you are too good for me? You can talk to the hunky bartender, but you can't smile at me?" the tall, huskily built man asked. He looked liked he could have been a football player in his glory days, stretching up to about six foot five with a neck size of about eighteen inches and broad, thick shoulders. Except now, his belly hung so far below his waist that it appeared as if his backside was on his front side. His pants hung below the crack of what should have been his posterior, and he had more breasts than the average woman. Cathalina looked at him and laughed.

"You are serious?" she asked, not really wanting to get into anything, but seeming to have found herself in something anyway.

"What do you mean, am I serious? Why all you bitches feel like you get some smarts, and wear nice clothes, and process your hair that you can't talk to a good, upstanding man like me no more?" He leaned into her, his breath reeking with liquor and something else that she could not rec-ognize, and then it hit her. He smelled as though he had his face in between someone's legs only moments before and the blend of stench made her want to puke. He reached his hand to the bar, and the combination of the odor of his underarm, his overall poor hygiene, and the fact that his fingers were obviously at some point scratching his behind, made her gag.

"Listen, I'm sure you are a very nice man, but I am going through some things right now. I want to disappear and be left alone. Can a lady ask an upstanding man for her space?" she pleaded, trying to use the false, good guy attitude this man was attempting to reason with, but his true intentions soon came to light.

"Oh, now you want to play nice? It's a little too late, don't you think?"

"Is this jerk bothering you?" the deep, resounding voice of the bartender asked. Even with all the loud music, his voice came thundering through.

"Actually, no, but thank you," she said to the bartender, and then returned her attention to her suitor as the bar-tender walked away, unwilling to provide service to the other drinkers. "Where were we? Yes, I remember. You wanted us to go to the bathroom and do the horizontal dance like everyone else here, right?" She smiled, her voice soothingly intoxicating as she spoke. Her lashes fluttered as her deep, dark skin radiated from her smile. Caught off guard, the man didn't know what to say.

"Ah, yeah, let's go to the john and do what everybody else is doing," he agreed, grabbing her hand and pulling her to the location which he seemed to have had memorized. "I knew I had you pegged right—the goody-two-shoe type pretending you don't want to get jabbed with some real beef," he mumbled.

Had it not been for Cathalina's hypersensitive hearing at

that point, she would not have heard a word the man said, but she remained quiet, her anger building inside her, her thoughts tearing through her brain and making her head hurt. Sure, she knew better. Sure, she was supposed to be the calculated, precise, and ordered one. She was the one in control and steering the ship. But things had changed, and she knew it was only a matter of time before the volcano blew. Something was going to happen, and they might have to go underground again the way they did before when it was just her and Cleo.

All she had wanted was to be alone. She figured in a crowd of this many people she could disappear and get a drink without being harassed. But this wasn't the first jerk to come on to her so aggressively. Frankly she had lost count, but she was tired of it, and someone was going to get the backlash of her frustrations.

The man pushed past the line of other men waiting to go into the bathroom. Some held their crotches to prevent themselves from pissing their pants, and others held onto the next whore willing to give it up at a moment's notice. The man pulling Cathalina seemed to have garnered some bathroom respect, because no one grumbled or complained as he pressed forward, passed them, and brought Cathalina into a toilet stall. She could hear moans and see legs held high at unnatural angles. The man ripped the top of her dress, buttons flew, and she yelped.

"That's right. I like screamers." He looked at her in what appeared to be an attempt at goo-goo eyes, and she heaved, bringing up nothing but dry air since she had not had anything to eat since the day before. This day was supposed to be a celebration of the joining of the four women with dinner and wine. But instead, there turned out to be chaos among the crew.

"Oh, so you like that?" Cathalina asked sheepishly. She knew his type, the criminal-minded. It was about power, rape, and abuse. This was not about sex or love or anything else. He wanted to have control over someone, and she was going to let him think he was in control up until she had him where she wanted him.

"Did I tell you to talk? Bend over so I can get a good look at that ass," the redneck slob demanded. He revolted Cathalina, but she was the one in control of this little drama, and it was going to go her way or no way at all.

"But, daddy, I just need to taste that dick of yours. Can I smell it? Just for a second, please? Can I just look at it?" she whined while slowly inching her way to her knees. The bathroom guests, enacting their own dramas began to pay attention to them, and to her submissive behavior.

"Damn, usually he brings them in kicking and screaming," one man moaned from a neighboring stall.

"Yeah," his partner, another male with a higher-pitched voice, agreed. "She must be crazy or nuts, because that dick got diseases that haven't been named yet," he uttered between sighs of pleasure as his head banged against the toilet stall.

"She really gonna do him on purpose?" one woman whispered in the ear of her partner for the night.

"Looks like he hit the jackpot. Oh, damn, you feel good, baby." He squeezed himself into her and pressed her back against the mirror, almost cracking it.

"Yes! This is what I am talking about," the fat, white man who felt like king of the toilet stalls that night, yelled. He was getting it willingly, a history-making event for him. Feeling extremely dominant, his forceful nature prevailed and he yanked Cathalina's long hair back. She squinted her eyes and tried not to look at him as her anger swelled. She didn't let the hold on her hair stop her because she had one purpose and goal in mind—to show these disgusting dregs of society what a real woman was made of.

She lifted the twenty-five pounds of lard above his waist

and found his belt, which barely held his pants up above his knees. She didn't let the pungent and foul odor that greeted her stop her either. She was so angry that her black face had turned blue at just the thought of being placed in this position, of people like him always placing women like her in this position without their permission. He leaned back and allowed his hands to linger and roam over her ass and back, slipping his fingers down her underwear and allowing them to slide down the crevice of her behind, seeking out her womanhood. She clenched and squeezed her legs shut, and received a heavy slap upside her head.

"Open up those legs, bitch," he demanded. Whatever she was going to do, she was going to have to move fast. She had nothing to lose now. This situation was out of control, but, then again, so was the rest of her life.

"Fuck it," she uttered under her breath and reached for his penis, which seemed to have disappeared among the layers of fat that made up his thighs. She had to bury her head under his stomach and between his legs to get there, and she feared suffocation. She sought out his member with her hands, and as she heard him moan, she knew she had found it. She quickly pressed her face forward, moaning sounds of disgust that passed as desire. She took his penis in her mouth, ignoring the crusted blisters that she felt as he went in, ignoring the sores that felt as though puss was oozing from them as she pressed him into her mouth.

His body began to move and gyrate in her face. She almost gagged a few times, feeling him inch his way in and out of her mouth. She knew she was contracting some form of STD from this man, but at that moment, even concern for her own safety was gone. Her thoughts wandered to when her right to be a mother was taken from her, to the women she counseled every day, and to the perpetuation of this sickness that no one ever seemed to want to talk about and no one wanted to acknowledge. Instead, women were forced to hide away like vermin.

"Enough!" Her scream came as she garnered all the strength she could find, directing all of her rage, disgust, loathing, devastation, and anguish to one central focal point—her teeth. In what seemed to be a split second, she pressed her vicious, oral tools as firmly and as tightly together and she could. Her bite was administered with such forceful passion that she felt his blood vessels and the skin on his male member sever from the man's body, and his penis was released into her mouth. She stood, feeling the blood run down the sides of her mouth, her teeth still snarling like an attacking animal. The man who stood before her like a giant fell to the floor and exploded into screams so horrific and terrifying that they could be heard outside on the dance floor, and above the thundering music.

He held his penis-less crotch, his eyes closed tightly shut as he yelped, shrieking, rolling on the floor and writhing in unimaginable pain that only became intensified at the sight of his blood gushing all over the bathroom stall from the rupture of a major artery. The audience in the bathroom was shocked and petrified at the sight of such fury. Astonishment and disbelief gripped them. Disgust filled them as the stench of the man shitting on himself, along with the blood, all mingled together within the close proximity of the bathroom.

"She is out of her freaking mind," one man observed as he quickly buttoned his pants and the woman he was with ran out behind him in horror. Cathalina stood up, allowing her stained dress to drop back below her waist and down to her ankles.

"You are nothing. You are a worthless vulture who preys on the weak and the young. You should die." She seethed as she held his detached penis in her hand. She reached for the man's face, which was still scrunched up in an expression of pain. He moved as though he was experiencing a seizure, so she found it difficult to get a hold of the man's head and keep it still. She wrestled with his agonizing body for a few moments, but the anger that fueled her gave her indescribable strength. Finally, she opened his mouth and stuffed his penis down his throat, causing him to gag.

"Now, doesn't that taste good? Hmm, yummy!" she mocked. "Take that rancid, decrepit, useless piece of slab you call a dick and go to hell." Her voice was soft and calm.

She stood there emotionless, watching as the man's mutilated body jerked and convulsed since he was no longer able to breathe. Shock and fright traumatized him and she didn't move until his eyes rolled back into his head and all she could see was the white of his eyeballs.

She pulled the front of her dress together to prevent any more of her breasts from being exposed and walked out as if nothing had happened. When she walked through the small club house, news had gotten around. The place became still and she had a path cleared in the center for her to exit. There were murmurs and whispers, and for some reason she smiled when she stepped into the fresh dew of the wee hours of another Florida morning. She could swear she heard cheers.

He was glad when she called. He hadn't heard from her since the last time she came by unexpectedly. She had been tired and worn and he could tell she had a lot of things on her mind. That had been her third visit and she was so stunning he couldn't take his eyes off of her. She wore an off-white linen skirt that flirted around her ankles, and an off-the-shoulder top that showed off a wonderfully and intricately designed spider. He had never seen anything like it. It was beautiful. He remembered how she flinched and backed away when he tried to touch it, as though he was about to hurt her. He couldn't believe that a tattoo artist was able to capture such details. It was stunning, and in some strange way, that too, was a sensuously erotic allure.

They had spoken briefly and she claimed she was in the neighborhood and wanted to thank him for his help the first day they met. That was three meetings ago and her excuse was still the same. She wanted to thank him. The last time he almost lost control and tried to kiss her. He stopped short, but he could feel her wanting him, daring him.

"I must be losing my mind." He chuckled lightly to himself. He didn't want to get close to anyone at this time. He had been out of prison and living a free life, somewhat privately for the past three years. No one had bothered him and he stayed clear of temptation. How was he supposed to court a woman who worked for the court system? And as a judge, nonetheless? She could snap her fingers and make his life a living hell.

"What am I doing?" he asked himself again. "Why am I nervously, anxiously waiting for this woman?" He walked to the refrigerator, took out a jug of freshly made iced tea, and poured himself a large glass over five cubes of ice. The air conditioner was blasting, but he felt a surge of heat that he couldn't explain.

He clasped his hands and put them toward his face, taking a deep, heavy breath. He was waiting for her now, as she said she was on her way. When he first met her, he thought she was crazy. Now he wasn't sure if she was nuts or he was. He had become so drawn to her—the way she walked, talked, smelled. He couldn't get past it. He was a fiend for her like she was a drug. He liked her and he could tell she liked him as well.

When Serena awoke from her semi-comatose state, she was alone in the secret meeting room. Cathalina, Cleo, and

Elizabeth were all gone, and she sensed that they were all off dealing with the revelations of the evening. It didn't go quite as planned, but they all needed their space.

She went through the wardrobe that Cleo kept stocked with the latest styles and fashions in a variety of sizes for her girls. She found a short sundress that was a soft pink color and slipped it on with a pair of pink sandals to match. She threw her ripped clothing from earlier into the trash and decided to call a cab.

She wasn't sure why she had called Vincent. She knew what he was and who he was, that he was the very epitome of what she was fighting—the evil they were all wrestling with. Yet, time after time, she found herself at his doorstep. The last time she thought for sure she would pass out if he kissed her. She didn't know if she had the strength to keep resisting him. Her thoughts and her deferred desires were her worst enemy. She would feel like ripping him apart, but at the same time, she felt like parting her legs so he could rip into her. She was a web of confusion and emotional contradiction.

"You made it." Vincent greeted her at the door when the taxi pulled up. She leaned in to pay the cab and he felt his heart race at the long sleekness of her legs. When she turned around, her auburn reddish hair bounced as if in some secret celebratory joy. Her hazel eyes sparkled and again Vincent was forced to breathe deeply.

"Yes, I suppose I just needed to see a friendly face." *Finally, a sincere reason. At least she couldn't say she was in the neighborhood this time. She actually called first*, he thought ecstatically.

"I was thinking of you. I am happy you called." The smile on his face deepened his dimpled cheeks. Taking her hand, he led her through the house toward the back. She seemed to have become fond of his back porch swing, which was shaded by giant weeping willows and swayed by the gentle, cool breezes. She followed without reluctance.

"Had a little dispute with my friends. Didn't quite see eye-to-eye on some issues." She sat on the plush cushion that seemed to invite her bottom from the first time she sat in it. She closed her eyes and for a flicker of a moment she saw Jason's face and felt a bit of guilt. It startled her, but she brushed off the image and the guilt and smiled at Vincent as he handed her a fresh glass of iced tea and sat down beside her. He smiled and she nodded a grateful thank you. She looked out across his backyard at the healthy trees and beautifully manicured lawn in an attempt not to stare at his strapping biceps, which seemed to bulge and flex with every move he made. The black, fitted shirt he wore tapered into his chiseled waist and boasted his eight pack. His thick thighs contracted in khaki pants that draped comfortably over his loafers. His smile took her breath away, and she could almost feel him inside her. She dreamed about him so much.

"Do you want to talk about it?"

She laughed.

"Seems you have become my new therapist," she said. She thought about Cathalina and where that venture had led her. "Looks like therapists come in all types of packages these days—prizes, surprises, and consolation gifts," she remarked sarcastically, thinking of how she went to Cathalina for help and where it got her. Now look at whose shoulder she chose to cry on; the same type of man she thought was the scum of society. A predator. Maybe people can change. Maybe he did. She allowed her thoughts to wander as she quietly sipped her iced tea.

"And which one of those am I?" He looked at her with slightly arched, questioning eyebrows that made his dark eyes dance with curiosity.

"I'm not sure yet. But you'll be the first to know when I have figured it out," she reassured him.

"I will hold you to that." He leaned in slightly closer to her and allowed their forearms to brush. "So you were saying about your friends?" He changed the subject and simultaneously took a gentle, loose hold of her hand as they rested between them on the swing. She took a deep breath and began to recount the evening as vaguely as possible.

"I just don't know if I'm going to be able to go though with some plans that we made," she told him.

"What plans?"

"Can't say right now." She felt a tingling sensation on the shoulder that bore the spider and giggled when she felt the twitch between her thighs. She couldn't decide what her body wanted her to do as she felt the grip on her hand tighten.

"But you are being very vague, and it's making it difficult to do my job as your psychiatrist," he joked.

"Don't laugh. It's not funny." Shoving him playfully with her forearm, she turned to look at him and found herself face-to-face with his trembling lips and his captivating eyes. She couldn't pull away as she felt the space between them slowly close, and then the moment of truth came when he pressed his lips to hers. She began to shake as the tremors of desire seized her. In that passionate moment, on one hand she was bombarded with images of innocent screams and tortured young bodies that were dismantled and discarded by this man, and in the same moment, her body longed for him.

The glass fell from her shaky hands and they found their way around his neck. In one quick swoop he had his hands under her and he cradled her like a baby, lowering her to the hardwood floors that were the foundation of the porch. Their kiss became passionately intense and erotic. His hands found her thighs and explored them, raising her short sundress and causing her to feel what she had only ever imagined. Powerful sensuality that had caused havoc on all of her senses now captivated her.

Vincent lowered himself on top of her and she felt his potent need rise between his legs, forcefully and dominantly pressing against her inner thighs. She spread her legs apart, her body begging him to fulfill all the visions that had tormented her for so many weeks and nights since becoming indoctrinated.

For the first time, she felt like a woman in the arms of a willing man; a man she wanted just as badly as he wanted her. He pressed his lips into her neck, her shoulders, and her chest, kissing trails of soft, tender wanting everywhere there was free space. Using his teeth and tongue, he gently and sensitively removed the fabric that kept their bodies from touching. Becoming somewhat possessed, Serena felt as though she was a fly on the wall of her own experience, and she allowed her body to become enthralled by the touch of a man who could really fulfill her in a way she had never felt. She allowed her legs to fall apart, sending electrical surges up and down her inner thighs and forcing her to arch her spine. Pressing her breasts into his chest, she stirred a burning need in him and caused deep, guttural moans and groans to erupt from his lips.

"I want you," he uttered softly in her ear. "I need you, Serena."

She moaned, not knowing what to say or how to feel. She was caught up, and the desires were so overwhelming and intense that she was only able to sigh deeply, heaving into his hard chest. He took that as a sign of permission and quickly released his belt buckle. Releasing his desire from its restraints, he used his knee to part her legs. Slowly, he began moving into her, pressing his body close so that there was no space or even air between them. He grunted deeply, feeling the tip of him press into the silky softness of her underwear, seeking to move it over and away from her Garden of Eden. The moistness of her panties made him urgent, and without using his hands, he was able to use his heat-seeker to move the restrictive garment. A cavernous, unified mating call was sent from one to the other as the tip of him sampled her soft succulence.

She flinched and he paused to look at her. Her eyes were squeezed shut, but her hips gyrated sensuously against his groin, urging him to continue. Gently, slowly, moving in rhythmic patterns like a fluid waterfall, he began to penetrate her. He wasn't hitting her hymen yet, but the pressure of his dick awoke in her pleasures and pains she could not fathom.

Her movements drove him crazy. What she was doing to him almost made him lose all reason and press himself deeply into her to satisfy the cravings they were both experiencing. But that look on her face told him she was innocent. He knew what her body was saying, and he knew that this might not be the right time.

Damn, I cannot even get through the entrance, he thought to himself, believing it impossible to have that kind of resistance at her age.

In any case, he liked her and didn't want to rush her, so he began kissing her softly again, trailing her nipples through the fabric of her dress, and going down to her belly button, pulling and yanking lightly as he neared her mound. He eased his body down, allowing his face to rest between the crevices of her thighs, and inhaled the essence of her womanhood. He rested his head there as he caressed her forearms and thighs. Serena didn't say anything. She was grateful he decided to stop, though she was left with an unfulfilled desire. For the first time in her life, she felt that she could care for a man, maybe find freedom in him. Maybe what she needed was just someone to talk to, someone to listen to her without any ulterior motives of their own. Someone to love her in a healthy way.

15

Natalia returned to Sex Cell after her exploration of Serena's home. She left totally intrigued, fascinated, and overwhelmed by what she found. As she sat in her room preparing for the next shift, she held on tightly to the trinket she found. Tears slowly began to flow down her cheeks.

"This just could not be possible. It cannot be possible," she repeated over and over again as if trying to deny what she knew to be true. She couldn't control the immense anger and injustice she felt at knowing that Serena was alive. The thought crossed her mind to call up her father's people—the members of the Klan and their descendants, who formed a pact to impart justice on those responsible for her father's gruesome death. They thought that child had just faded away and become a bum, but here she was, right under Natalia's nose, and being praised as some kind of queen.

Natalia thought of all the times she felt jealous, abandoned, and not loved as much as Serena. She thought about how her mother and relatives would talk about the black trash that her father had embraced. Sure she was his whore, but so what? Serena's mother got to live in his mansion, eat the good food, and have her bastard sent to the best schools. Natalia was the one with the beautiful, long hair that only a pure white person had. She was the one with green eyes and rosy, freckled skin. She was the one who was white and should have had all the advantages.

Natalia remembered the pangs of hunger and beatings of despair that were bestowed upon her just because her mother was pissed at her father and couldn't get what she wanted.

Natalia couldn't believe what she held in her hands after all these years. She had immediately gathered her things and ran straight out of Serena's house when she found the special object. The pendant with the emblem on it could only be owned by someone from her own family. Natalia was petrified to learn that Serena was her half sister, the black bastard everyone had made a big deal about.

Natalia retrieved the small box of personal items that she kept with her when she traveled. She took the box and walked back to her twin-sized bed. Wiping away the tears that clouded her vision, she curled her feet under her bottom and took a deep breath. She opened the box and rummaged through some trinkets and stones she felt had helped guide her to safety. As the path cleared at the bottom of the box, she was finally able to see the gold emblem tucked securely in one corner and hidden from plain sight.

She took it out with trembling hands and slowly brought it side-by-side with the trinket she found in Serena's unlocked footlocker. As Natalia brought the two pieces closer together, their striking resemblance to each other was uncanny. When placed together, they fit like two matching puzzle pieces, displaying the crest of her father's family, founding members of the Ku Klux Klan. The crest contained a Confederate flag with the letters KKK in the center. Serena's piece added a noose hanging from an upside down tree with blood dropping down onto the flag. Some of the police who had arrived at the scene of her father's murder were members of the Klan and had secretly handed the one piece to her mother, who later gave it to Natalia. The crest was the heart of their family and was only to be handed down through the bloodline. There was no way Natalia could have known there was another piece matching hers.

"Oh my gosh." She spoke out loud and looked to the ceiling to will the tears from coming again. "Serena Kowtow. It's her. She really is my sister." Suddenly Natalia was startled by a heavy knock on her door. She knew that only one person knocked with such persistence and insolence.

"Come in," she invited, quickly shuffling about and putting away her things before Cleo saw them. She couldn't allow Cleo to know who she really was.

"Natalia, I waited and searched for you all night until two AM. Where were you? You missed a few appointments and I lost a lot of money."

Natalia wasn't able to put everything away fast enough, and tried to sweep the emblem under the covers and out of Cleo's line of vision.

"I am sorry, Madam. I had an emergency and I had to run out."

"What kind of emergency can you have without leaving a note? You have no family here. Are you seeing someone?"

Relieved for the way out, Natalia began to laugh.

"I am sorry I didn't tell you before, Cleo. It's just that it's new and I wasn't sure he really liked me."

"Is that where you were coming from, Natalia?" Cleo asked, drawing nearer to the girl's frail looking form curled on the bed. "Is that where you were and why are your face and arms look bruised as if you were in a cat fight, and your legs are stained with green moss?"

Natalia tried to think fast to get out of being caught with her pants down.

"Well, ah . . ."

"What are you hiding, Natalia? This is simply not your style." Curiosity flowed on Cleo's face, causing her eyes to squint and pierce the girl's already torn and hurting heart. Cleo swayed her big, Betty Boop body over to the small bed and used her hips to scoot Natalia over so she could sit down beside her. Natalia tried to remove the objects from beneath the sheets before Cleo sat down, but she was unsuccessful.

"What the . . ."

"I am sorry, Cleo. Let me get that." Natalia tried to remove the crest pieces quickly, but again was unsuccessful. Cleo reached under Natalia's behind and pulled up the gold pieces of metal, each dangling from a piece of fragile string that was old, worn, and looked like it could fall apart at any moment.

"These are beautiful," Cleo observed at first glance. Then the reflection of the emblem hit her eyes for the first time. She saw the raised markings and reached to caress them with her right hand. She held the two parts together and joined them to read the engravings. And then the meaning of the markings registered in her mind. Cleo's eyes sought out Natalia's. Natalia could see the questions in Cleo's eyes that she wanted answers to, and she was almost certain that she no longer had a job, but she would have to blame that on Serena as well. All of the ill will that had befallen her over the years she had blamed on the Negro bastard that had the home she should have had. And now she had discovered that the bastard was alive.

"They're not mine. I found them."

"Found them? Where? These are solid gold and worth a lot of money. They're from the old days, and date back to the original KKK members. To get one of these you must have blood lineage connecting you to a founder of the KKK or at least something close to that. I am not sure, but these don't just drop off of trees."

"I . . . I stole . . ."

"Natalia, don't lie to me. You are shaking like a leaf and your eyes are red." Natalia was at a loss for words. Her emotions had betrayed her and she couldn't hide the truth of the value of the emblem. "I am so sorry, Cleo. I am so sorry." She began to wail, covering her face within the palms of her trembling hands.

"God, are you? You mean to tell me?" Cleo couldn't wrap her brain around the thoughts. She sat quietly for a moment and stared at the medallion. "It's broken in two." The words came out slowly, like an observation, as her mind scrambled to try and understand what it all meant. She watched some television, and because of her exploits, she read the newspapers, and from time to time learned something other than how she had helped to raise the death tolls.

Natalia swallowed hard and brought her hands down to her thighs. Her mascara had run so badly that her face seemed to be stained black. She took in deep breaths and decided that she would not hide from who she was. Wasn't that what she wanted after all? To be recognized as her father's firstborn? The privileged one? The one to carry the bloodline and the history of her father's passions? How ashamed would they be of her now, were she to continue to pretend she was not who she was?

"Cleo, half of the emblem belongs to me," she confessed as steadily as she could. She would be a woman and stand and take the consequences of who she was. Today she would put aside her fear of Cleo and be a white woman who had power in her blood.

Cleo's face turned red. She didn't exactly know what Natalia meant, but whatever it was, had to be powerful. She wanted to know more.

"What does all of this mean, Natalia?"

Natalia just hung her head as tears came.

"What does it mean that half of it belongs to you? Its worth a lot of money? Is it really all gold?"

"Yes, it's gold. But I just got the other part of it."

"How? Why is only one of them yours?" Cleo liked the look of the trinket. Thoughts crossed her mind to take it, but she wanted more information.

"In the event of the passing of a true Klan member, the medallion must be separated and shared between the two eldest children of that member's bloodline. It's the way they kept the emblem secret and hidden for so many generations." Cleo was fascinated by the knowledge that Natalia was sharing with her. She had never heard anything like it before in her life.

"May I have those back?" Natalia asked, reaching across the short distance to Cleo's hands.

"Not until you tell me who the second half of this belongs to, and how you have them both. How you stole it."

"I cannot do that. It would be a betrayal."

"Betrayal? You are worried about betraying someone other than me?" Cleo asked in mock surprise in the face of the girl's insolence.

"You know better, Cleo." Her confidence in what Cleo held in her hands grew. "You know who I am now and there is no need to play those games. You understand that I cannot disclose any more information to you."

"I could threaten you with beatings and pains so insurmountable that you wouldn't care, and then kill you. But that wouldn't give me the information I need. I will return these to you and walk away if you tell me who the other half belongs to." The curiosity in Cleo was desperate for this knowledge and in that moment she is willing to do anything to get it.

Tears again welled in Natalia's eyes and she turned away.

How could she tell Cleo that a member of her close, trusted group of friends carried the lineage of one of the most hated and feared groups in United States history? Suddenly, she began to smile and decided to step outside of her emotions in a practical, more devious way. Cleo could become her confidant and even an accomplice. It was perfect. She would finally get the revenge she wanted and she would use Cleo's anger and hatred toward Serena to do it.

"OK then," Natalia agreed, turning to face Cleo, whose eyes lit up like a child's face on Christmas day. "I'll tell you everything."

16

Dyania rushed from the police precinct armed with Elizabeth's life history and the information from the files in Miami. Earlier when she sat in her small cubicle engrossed in her research, Detectives Tyme, Perkins, and Kendall sat back with stale coffee watching helplessly as a woman did the kind of work that would make a grown man cry.

Dyania had been pissed when she arrived at the station hours after she had entrusted the research to Tyme, only to find that he had griped about the project instead of actually doing it. She was not surprised when he turned his head in shame as she walked in. Seeing him squirm under her heavy gaze made the others laugh heartily. He was so ashamed, that before she got up to leave, he ran to the restroom in order not to be subjugated by her sneer again.

Rushing back home to her small apartment, Dyania could not be more excited. She had to get packing. She couldn't believe all the unsolved deaths and strange occurrences being logged into the south Florida police computer systems. She had come across these unsolved crimes as she searched the Florida system for any prior crimes that Elizabeth Chung may have committed, and her keen investigative mind would not let her rest until she found some answers. *Why wasn't anyone curious about the whole thing?* she wondered. There seemed to be no questions asked, no aggressive research done, nor any thorough investigations performed. She was appalled at the mediocrity of the police force. She was so tired of it all.

Dyania didn't have much to pack, as she was a tomboy. She threw jeans and sneakers into her heavy hiking backpack and grabbed her police badge, gun, and a special necklace with a pendant that was given to her as a gift from her parents when she was old enough to inherit it. She had never figured out the meaning of the pendant, but she treasured it as the most personal thing left to her from her parents. She went through her things and took her journal, which she stuck to the far back of her bag where it was almost hidden. It was as though she was being propelled to Miami, as if there was more to going there than just following up on an investigation. Her instincts told her that there was something there that could explain some of the disturbing gaps of not only this case, but her life. Or maybe she just needed a change of scenery.

Dyania did not waste any time after catching the first flight out of Atlanta into Miami. She called up the Miami-Dade Police Department and asked to be forwarded to the Sunny Isles Beach Precinct on Collins Avenue. According to the location of the paperwork filed by Detective Taylor on the suspicious double suicide in North Miami Beach, this was the precinct she needed to be in contact with. She tapped her foot outside of Miami International Airport, waiting for the line to be picked up.

"You have reached Detective Isaac Taylor, Sunny Isles Beach Precinct. If this is an emergency, hang up and dial 911. If you would like to leave a message for Detective Taylor, then do so after the beep." The recording weighed on her patience; she didn't have time to wait for him. When the beep came on she was abrupt and to the point.

"Detective Taylor, I am Special Homicide Detective Minto from Atlanta. Contact the station immediately upon receiving this message. I am getting into a cab and heading to your department. Clear your calendar. We have work to do."

She hung up the phone and hailed the next taxi that came around the corner.

She hopped into the backseat and gave the address to the driver. She grabbed her pendant, which was shaped like a spider, and held it tight.

"I must be working too hard," she whispered and closed her eyes as she reclined back into her seat. *I think I need to retire, find something less rigorous to make a career of.* Suddenly, she thought of her parents and sadness overwhelmed her. She always had visions of them in the likeness of pictures she saw before they died. She had many dreams of them guiding her and supporting her.

"Don't go," her mother said in a voice she didn't recognize. She was too young when they died. But she knew it was her mother. She jumped, startled by the vision.

"I need to call my therapist." She leaned her head back in the taxi and closed her eyes, waiting to arrive at her destination.

"Everythin' es A-OK?" the Latino cab driver asked in broken English.

"Yes, I am fine. Thanks. Just a little thirsty," she told him and gently placed the pendant back inside her shirt, tucking it securely away from prying eyes. It seemed like forever before they arrived on Collins Avenue, where there was as much traffic as at the airport. She shook her leg anxiously as the taxi pulled up to what seemed like a very upscale shopping complex. She paid him and got out. She felt the fresh breeze from the ocean hit her face and she reached for her sunglasses to block the glare of the late afternoon sun. Turning around to get her bearings, she was immediately greeted by a sign announcing the police station, and she walked inside.

"Yes, can I help you?" the officer at the front desk greeted her.

"Yes. Is Detective Taylor in?"

"He just stepped out. Is there something I can help you with?"

"Where did he go?"

"Excuse me?"

"Ma'am, I think the question was pretty clear." Dyania's voice was stern and agitated. She was beginning to lose patience with this paper pusher who was acting as if she was Taylor's bulldog.

"Listen, this is a police department and there is no time to play guessing games with people who have nothing to do with their time other than harass people on their jobs." The woman behind the desk sneered at Detective Minto.

"Listen, Officer . . ." she reached over to read the name on her tag, "Lopez, shithead, I have no time for your games," she seethed. This woman was wearing on her patience. Her anger flared and she reached inside her purse to pull out her badge and ID for the woman, who panicked and screamed for help.

Soon there were officers upon Dyania, vehemently pulling her arms behind her back. Her nostrils flared ferociously and an adrenaline rush kicked her anger up a notch.

"Let me go, you idiots, before I have all your asses canned." And in one swift, smooth motion she freed herself and simultaneously sent the two men staggering back away from her. "I am Special Homicide Detective Minto. I was about to show this sorry excuse of an officer my credentials when she started screaming like a banshee." They all looked at her and then at each other, embarrassed and seriously concerned for their jobs. The moment she said her name, they were aware of who she was. She was a luminary, a hero, a legend among them. They were thrown off by her narrow, tall frame, and her youthful, hip look, which gave off the impression of a hip-hop girl from the streets.

"You are not the way we expected you to look."

"And what way is that you . . ." She paused as she struggled to find words to describe how she detested the treatment she received and their lack of professionalism. She suddenly realized why they had not followed up with the investigations for the unsolved cases.

At that moment, Dyania could not comprehend the emotional stampede that overcame her. Her head began to hurt and shake. Her eyes flared and almost squinted to slits as if the light was bothering them. She balled her hands into fists and her lower lip trembled. She fought off the urge to punch the living daylights out of the three officers who had only made her entrance into North Miami more difficult than it had to be.

She turned to look at the woman, who took one look at Dyania's face and began to back up into the wall behind her. Her face was stricken with fear and she began to perspire. Dyania's face turned beet red and so did the whites around her pupils.

"Listen, I only want to know where Detective Taylor is. I don't have time for this. I am tired, I had a long day, and I really would like to get some work done before I hit the sack, if that's OK with you."

In that instant, there was a tap on her shoulder and she turned abruptly, her anger now focused on the person who had dared to interrupt her. But she was suddenly calmed and her fists relaxed.

Dyania's heart was beating so fast that she had to will it to slow down so she could breathe. She put on her poker face as the officer who tapped her shoulder introduced himself.

"I am Detective Isaac Taylor. Is there something I can help you with?" He extended his hand in a warm greeting and Dyania relaxed. Still no smile on her face, she took his outstretched hand and shook it.

"Special Homicide Detective Minto from Atlanta."

"I see. I just checked in on my voicemail and got your message.

I checked the system and saw that you have a series of deaths that were left unsolved."

"That's right. And I believe some strong leads are here in your jurisdiction."

"Yes. Let's go this way," he told her, taking her by the forearm and trying to lead her toward the back of the station to his desk. Dyania did not take lightly to that. She planted herself where she was.

"Would you be so kind as to release me?" She smiled sarcastically as her eyes pierced his. Taylor stopped and stepped back a few feet away from her.

"I'm sorry. My apologies."

Dyania placed her hands before her and prompted him to lead the way.

"After you." She smiled and they began to walk.

Arriving at his desk, Taylor explained to her the double suicide that was so strange that they had no other way of listing it. It almost seemed as though the two people agreed to die that way.

"Well, have you ever come across a case or a few cases where somewhere along the line a Elizabeth Chung was in the vicinity, got off with insufficient evidence, or was considered a suspect but it was never followed up on?"

"Why do you ask?"

"Seems like there are a lot of unsolved murders in this area or the Miami area in general. Missing persons reports of grown men, in most cases with background information proving they were serial killers, pedophiles, or brought up on abuse cases. Always something along those lines. Haven't you ever found that suspicious?"

"No, not really. You and I are in the same business. Things like this happen all the time."

"Does that make it right?"

"Not exactly, but whoever is doing it, sure is helping to make my job easier. Less paperwork." He laughed jokingly but noticed that Dyania had no trace of a smile on her face.

"Why are you so serious?"

"Don't you think this is serious business?"

"Absolutely, but there is only so much we can do. You take it to heart and it will give you a heart attack."

"It's my job and I take it seriously. You should try it some time."

"Hey, wait a minute here. I am trying to help you. I am good at my job and do my best, why are you chastising me?"

"I am only going by your words, Detective Taylor."

"OK, then tell me, I don't understand why you are here. Why all the interest in unsolved crimes in Miami?" Taylor asked, a bit perturbed. He didn't like the idea of some detective from another state stepping on his turf, gorgeous or not. And he was not going to give her the pleasure of letting her know that he knew who she was. As far as he was concerned, she was just another cop trying to show him up.

"I want to know if there was anything that you have done, seen, or investigated that was connected in any way to an Elizabeth Chung."

"Not that I can recall. But why are you so interested in her anyway?" he quizzed.

"It's classified." She stood to leave

"What do you mean classified? You come all the way here, put the fear of God into the department officers, demand information, and now it's classified? Bullshit!"

"Then we work together."

"Good, I want in. I have some information that might help us. It's a long shot, but I want to be a part of this. Are you game?"

She stopped and turned to face him. His eyes searched hers with an irresistible plea. Dyania thought about it. She was a guest here. She didn't know Florida. He knew the place and could make her job a whole lot easier.

"OK, tell me what you know. I'm game."

"You're in!" he exclaimed.

Dyania smiled for the first time at his childlike enthusiasm for the job. She sensed that he was protective about his work and was not trying to impress her. She found that refreshing and felt she would enjoy working with him.

"Where are you staying?"

"Don't know."

"You stay with me. I have a large place; more than enough room. I am never there and the refrigerator is full."

"Well, I only need someplace to rest my head for a couple hours and shower. I don't want to be harassed."

"OK, that sounds good. I don't want you to get any ideas either," he joked. She looked at him and they laughed.

"Great. Let's go."

As they walked out, the officers who first met her when she came in backed away and cleared the exit for her.

"So, what's the information you think can help us?" she asked as she got into his red 2005 Jaguar XK series. She paused to admire the expensive luxury car and its premium import leather interior. "Nice ride," she commented.

"Thanks. I borrowed it," he told her, putting the car in gear. She looked at him in disbelief. "OK, it's mine," he admitted.

"How can you afford such a car on a detective salary?"

"I invest my money. I am free, single, and disengaged, and I try to put a little something away from time to time."

"Smart."

"But don't tell anyone. Women around here seem to only be interested in the kind of car a man drives. I worked long, hard hours and made sacrifices for the few luxuries I allow myself. Like this."

"I understand," Dyania said, turning to look behind her into the backseat. She nodded her head in appreciation. She didn't have to be offended or feel insulted by what he said. She knew who she was and what she had. It was nothing to her.

She went back to business. "Now, the information you promised?"

"Her name is Cathalina Shekhar. She was the psychiatrist treating one of the suicide/homicide victims. I know it's a long shot, but I just feel she is connected somehow. She actually showed up at the scene."

"Well, what are we waiting for?"

"There is one more thing. It's rumored that a woman fitting her description bit off a man's penis and choked him to death with it in downtown Miami the other night. I was about to check into it when I got your message." Dyania started to laugh. "What's so funny?"

"It just sounds ridiculous." She chuckled.

"Well, there is a dead man with a severed penis stuck in his mouth. Bet he doesn't find it funny," Taylor grumbled defensively.

Cathalina could barely hold herself together once she left the nightclub. She felt high from all the cigarette smoke, drugs, and alcohol being served up in the place, not to mention the extreme funk of everyone bumping and grinding the night away. She could smell the stench of death, blood, and sickness on her. She couldn't stand still anymore. She reached for the wall of the building to hold herself up. The world was spinning so fast that she couldn't stand up straight. She leaned over and began to puke. She was heaving so badly that she began to see blood coming from her mouth. She wasn't sure if it was the dead man's blood or hers. Her eyes were bloodshot and tired. She felt like crying, but couldn't bring up any tears.

She staggered to a raggedy looking vehicle and tried the door. It was opened. She got into the car and threw herself in the driver's seat. Then she suddenly found her tears. They came first in small sobs, then full blown bawling.

"Well, that's the way the cookie crumbles." she banged her head on the steering wheel. "I tried. I did everything. Why am I here? Why this? Why now?" She heard the questions leave her lips and then she began to laugh, her mind beginning to protect itself by bringing about her alter ego, the part of her that was strong, fearless, and determined. She sniffled and searched the interior for some tissue, but all she came up with was a McDonald's napkin. She sneezed into it and wiped her nose.

"I am not going through that feel-sorry-for-myself crap again. Been there, done that. This is a different time, a new me. Cleo will know what to do." She smiled. She found the key, left in the ignition by the careless patron to the bar. She turned it and headed for Sex Cell.

17

Serena was glowing. She couldn't have been happier with the time she spent with Vincent. She felt so good waking up with him the next day. She knew he could have gone all the way, but stopped, that convinced her he was a changed man. Whatever he had done, she wanted to forget it and move on. She felt tired of the hate and pain that had consumed her all her life. She allowed herself to curl into a ball of female vulnerability and rest her head on his broad, thick shoulders as he drove.

"I am glad you allowed me to take you home, Serena. I would have been worried sick allowing you to take a taxi home by yourself." He leaned over and gently pressed his lips up against Serena's forehead, and her smile broadened.

"Well, you make it impossible to fight you. You are just too persistent and I am too tired." Serena smiled up at him. "Besides, why wouldn't I want a hunk like you escorting me home?" When Vincent looked at her, she was smiling mischievously.

"What's that look on your face?"

"Nothing, I am just, well, happy," she confessed jovially and tightened her hold on his ample biceps.

"I never thought that after everything I have been through in my life, I would be able to meet someone as special as you, Serena. Thanks so much for giving me a second chance at life." Vincent's words pierced her heart; she never told him that she knew about him and his crimes, or that she was destined to kill him according to the code of the organization of women she vowed to be loyal to. For a brief moment, she flinched nervously, hoping he had no idea of her original intentions. She wanted this chance to find love. She was tired. For her, this was a glimmer of hope in her otherwise loveless future with a eunuch as her companion. She didn't want to let this new possibility go. So she relaxed and listened to Vincent tell her how special she was. The words were like music to her ears.

Vincent smiled at her silence and continued to drive. He knew there was something more to her, a secret he could not quite put his finger on. In prison, he learned one important rule—never show your hand and keep a poker face at all times. But he, too, didn't want to chase away this opportunity. He would see it through to wherever it would lead them.

Cleo and Natalia sat outside Serena's home anxiously. Cleo couldn't wait to get rid of Serena. Finally she had her chance to be done with her. She was so nervous that she couldn't sit still. They had waited hours. Natalia wanted to confront Serena immediately, so she would be vindicated as the true daughter and recipient of the legacy of her father. Neither had to wait much longer, though. They watched the strange, black Maxima pull up in front of her semi-mansion home. They gasped at the sight of Serena stepping out of the car with a man.

"I thought you said she was pure," Natalia chastised.

"Well, if she wasn't before, she's a liar, and if she was, I guess she's not anymore." Cleo snickered. She could not believe her eyes, but then it occurred to her. Cathalina's precious Serena was a whore. Now she could get Cathalina back with this news about Serena, and she couldn't wait. Her heart began to palpitate just at the thought of having Cathalina all to herself again, like in the old days. Cleo squeezed Natalia's hand as Serena pressed the code into her security gate and got back into the car with Vincent. They entered the compound and the gates closed behind them.

"Why didn't we go in?" Natalia whined.

"Because, you idiot, they will know that we are following them. When I get my hands on her, I want her to shit her pants," Cleo seethed venomously. Natalia smiled at how vehement Cleo was toward Serena. She hit the jackpot with this one. She couldn't believe how easy this was going to be with Madam Cleo at her side. She watched as the gates slammed shut, and Cleo drove away.

"Why are we leaving now after hours of waiting? This is bullshit." Natalia was pissed off. She was tired and nervous and eager to get everything over with. And Cleo was backing down like a yellow belly.

"Slow and easy wins the race, Natalia, dear. Slow and easy." She caressed Natalia's legs gently and smiled arrogantly.

"I don't know what the fuck that's supposed to mean. I have waited my entire life for this moment. You promised you would help, and now you are spewing some philosophy shit."

"You need to calm your fast little ass down, Natalia. If we do things the way you want, we might screw the whole thing up and then you would really be angry. Do you want to be caught and go to prison for murder?" Cleo turned briefly toward Natalia to see if she was making herself clear.

"I've been doing this a long time, and I'm not about to mess it all up now because you feel you want to rush into things."

The women sat silently for a moment as if thinking about it.

"So what do you plan to do?" Natalia conceded.

"I plan to mess her up so badly that she won't even remember her damn name." Cleo smiled. She was going to make this hurt, and she was not going to stop until there was no more breath left in Serena's body.

For a brief moment, Serena sensed that something was not right as Vincent walked with her to her door. She turned to look back toward the gated entrance and cringed.

"What's wrong?" Vincent asked, taking her hand in his and caressing her forearm.

"Yes, I just thought for a moment . . ." Then she looked up at him. "Forget it. It was nothing." She smiled coyly and began to open the door. As usual, Jason was there waiting for her to come home, dressed in his loincloth and ready to do Serena's bidding. The shock of seeing a man with Serena brought such horror to him that his impulse was to attack Vincent. Like a bulldog on watch, Jason flew at Vincent's throat and had him pinned to the wall. But Vincent was a big guy, and was much bigger than Jason pound for pound. He slammed Jason to the ground and began to pound away at his face.

"Stop this!" Serena demanded, her voice a fervent echo throughout the vast house. The two men did not relent. Jason was fighting for his life. He had served her now for years, and without her, he was nothing and he had nothing. He sacrificed his manhood to be with her.

Serena went to the staircase, pressed the button to the hidden wall, and retrieved her cat-o'-nine tails. She marched down the stairway and snapped it two times to get Jason's attention. Vincent looked up and received a punch in the face and then a knee to the groin. He rolled over on his back in excruciating pain and Jason jumped to his feet and began kicking him in his abdomen and torso.

"Who the fuck are you?" he asked as his feet made contact after contact with Vincent's body. Vincent's moans and groans were painful and Serena cracked the whip several times, but Jason was defiant and she had to lash out at him, tearing the whip into his skin to get him to even flinch. It took two more lashes onto his torso and legs before Jason stopped. His heavy breathing did not subside as he turned to look at Serena. His nostrils flared with anger and his eyes burned with determination.

"Why did you do this?" His voice was so deep and low that Serena almost didn't hear a word he said.

"Who are you to question what I do in my own house?" She took a move toward him.

"You are my woman."

"Your woman? What can you do for your woman? Can you fend for me, provide shelter, or fuck the shit out of me when I need it?" she screamed as she proceeded to face him.

"I gave you everything. I gave it to you the way you wanted it and I showed you love with the ultimate kind of sacrifice," Jason retorted, stepping into her face.

"Back up your disgusting, no-good, stink breath. Out of my face," she demanded, appalled by his questioning and the stance he was taking.

"Oh, so now my breath stinks?" His pride was stung deeply.

"I hate you. I have no respect for you. You are a stool for me to step on and a pot for me to piss on. You are not a man. You are garbage, something to be used and put out when I am done. Now BE GONE!" She dismissed him, and as soon as the words escaped her mouth, he slapped her so hard across her face that she turned almost as red as the color of her hair. She reached her hand up to snap the whip again, but her hands were restrained by him.

"You no longer have permission to use me, Serena. I am not your slave. I gave myself to you as a gift of love and you took me for granted, and now I see your true feelings for me. You no longer have permission to hurt me." His eyes were burning fire, and just when he rose his hand to hit her again, Vincent came up behind him, fighting to protect Serena from another assault, but this time Vincent's strength and muscles were no match to Jason's passionate anger.

"Don't you know never to fuck with a man who has nothing to lose and nothing left to live for?" he asked as he spun on Vincent and delivered another kick to his groin, flipped him over, and twisted his arm behind his back, crushing his fingers.

"Serena, do something," Vincent yelled.

"She can do nothing. I have been living with her day in and day out. I know all her secrets and what buttons to push to make them work. She cannot do shit in a situation like this. But I will show you what I can do." Jason was yelling at the top of his lungs, and Serena sent her whip out again. But Jason grabbed it, pulling her to him as he sat on Vincent's back, bending his arm into unnatural positions. As Serena neared the burning furnace of anger that fueled Jason's rage, she began to sob. She had never seen him like this before. His soft, gentle hands when he touched her, his passionate kisses and caresses, his words of love and devotion to her were all she knew of Jason.

"You are so damn naïve, Serena. Did you really think that was the way I was, harmless and stupid? I did that for you." He breathed into her face as she closed her eyes to prepare for his next assault. "You started this, now finish it," he demanded, releasing Vincent's hands so he could use his fingers to plunge them inside of Serena's vagina. "Don't you like that?" he asked, still sitting on Vincent, who managed to turn around to see what the madman was talking about. "Oh, so you want to see the woman you are about to fuck? This is it, she, whatever the fuck that is." Jason pointed and stood up so that Vincent could get a better look. But he did not release Serena from his choke hold. "See what she did to me? She cut my fucking dick off just so she wouldn't have a moment of weakness and say yes, just to keep her precious virginity." Jason removed his loincloth and stood naked as the day he was born before Vincent. It was the last straw for him. His mind could not take Serena with another man on top of everything else he had to endure.

Vincent's eyes popped from his head at the sight of a black Greek god with no penis. *They would love him in prison*, he thought. Vincent was a killer, and he had done some horrible things in his life, but he had never seen anything like this. He felt sorry for Serena and sorry for Jason. What was this world coming to? There was a time he could stomach such horror, but he was trying to move on from that. He wanted a chance to live.

Jason dropped Serena's weak form to the ground and walked away, spitting at the sight of her. Vincent reached out for her, and held her, whispering all the while that he was sorry. He couldn't completely comprehend the situation or understand her sadness, but now he knew where her sadness lived. He lifted her into his arms and walked right back out the door. He put her in the passenger seat and reclined it, then jumped into the driver's seat and sped away. When he got to the gate he realized that he didn't know the code. He looked to the semi-conscious Serena, who whispered to him.

"Spider," she said, and closed her eyes. Vincent opened the gate and took Serena back to his home.

Jason stood at the door and watched Serena ride out of his life. He was filled with angry confusion and was not certain what was to become of him. He laughed eerily as he looked down at his naked body.

"What life is out there for the likes of me? I have lived here for years with nothing of my own—no bank account, no contact with family or friends. I don't even own the clothes on my back." He laughed again as the cold reality hit him. He went to the staircase and pushed the button to the secret doors, releasing the chains from their hiding place. He went to the middle of the living room and began restraining himself the way Serena would when she was ready to have her way with him. Only this time, he didn't just bind his hands and legs. He took one of the chained links and harnessed it around his neck. Holding the remote control in his outstretched hands, he pushed the button so hard that when the chains began to pull, his neck was snapped, killing him instantly.

18

Cathalina groggily pushed herself up on her elbows to see what was going on around her. She felt the restraints holding her down and fell back into the small, uncomfortable bed. She shook her head wearily and tried to force her eyes open. She lay still, attempting to adjust her eyes to the bright light, but one of her eyes was swollen shut and she became afraid. Her body felt sour and aching, her face felt swollen, and her mouth tasted like dried-up, stale blood.

"What's going on here?" she asked more to herself than to anyone else. The words came out muffled. She couldn't see, and was frightened when she received an answer.

"You are in the hospital, Dr. Shekhar." The voice was feminine, soft, soothing. "I have been waiting for you to wake up for some time now," the female said again. Cathalina squinted one eye and tried to look again. She wasn't sure who was talking to her, and she couldn't understand why this woman had been waiting for her to wake up.

"What happened to me?" Cathalina asked, feeling around her body and finding the wires attached to her to monitor her heart rate, and intravenous needles to administer medication.

"You were in a car accident two days ago. Do you remember anything about it?"

"I don't know what you are talking about. I don't remember being in an accident." Her one eye adjusted to the lights and she batted her eyelash until she was able to look upon the face of the tall, beautiful, dark-skinned woman before her. Her slenderness added a harmless disposition, but Cathalina knew she was more than she appeared to be. She chuckled at the thought. After all, she specialized in picking out special people.

"It was pretty bad. You are lucky you survived it." Dyania moved closer to Cathalina and touched her hand softly. "Are you in pain? Would you like me to get the doctor?" she asked. She felt a strange connection to Cathalina. She admired any woman who would stand up for herself, who refused to be victimized.

"Do you remember being in a nightclub two nights ago?" Dyania asked. Dyania looked at Cathalina, calmly assessing her as she pulled her chair closer so she could sit next to her, so Cathalina wouldn't have to strain her voice. "It seemed you had a very busy day before you ended up here." Dyania fixed Cathalina's bed sheet and smiled warmly at her. She felt so much more at ease and comfortable having now made contact with Cathalina. When she and Taylor were called to the accident scene two days ago, she suddenly felt that she had arrived at the right place. She hoped this woman would recover so she could get some answers.

"Is my doctor here?" Cathalina asked shakily, tears forming in her throat.

"Your Palm Pilot gave all the information needed to the ambulance team who picked you up. We also knew you were a donor just in case the situation turned tragic," Dyania told her.

"Who are you?" she finally managed to ask.

There was a soft knock on the door before it was cracked opened.

"Is she awake?" Taylor asked before entering and gently closing the door behind him. "I see she's up and talking." He smiled as he, too, pulled a chair to the opposite side of Cathalina's bed, and then gently patted her hand as he took it into his. Cathalina looked at Dyania quizzically.

"Cathalina, this is Detective Isaac Taylor, and I am with a special homicide unit. I'm Detective Minto, but you can call me Dyania." She smiled again, disarming Cathalina.

"I don't understand." Cathalina closed her eye and swallowed hard. She willed her thoughts and her heartbeat to be still and found the control to pull off a facade of confidence even in the face of such eminent danger.

"Do you remember me, Cathalina?" Taylor asked, forcing Cathalina to turn her head, bringing her attention to him. She shook her head slightly saying no, but she was fully conscious of who he was. "We met briefly. One of your clients, Lara Lopez, was involved in what seemed like a double homicide/suicide. You identified her for me. Do you remember?" he asked again. He stretched to look into her one opened eye, but then gave up as she strained to see and tried to gain focus.

"Don't worry about it now, Cath. Your doctor will be in to check on you soon and we'll know how bad the damage is. We can talk later. We were just checking in on you as we have been doing for the past couple days," Dyania told her as she brushed a strand of hair from her forehead.

"Thank you," Cathalina said as she tried to muster a smile and wondered why she had called her by her nickname. "Has anyone been here to visit me?" Cathalina asked. She wanted to know if Cleo or the other girls knew what had happened to her, but just at that moment her physician walked in.

"Cathalina, haven't I always told you to take care of yourself?" he asked with a chuckle. "Doctors do make the worst patients, you know?" he commented to Dyania and Taylor.

"So I have heard," Dyania responded. She was in great spirits.

"How are you feeling, darling?" he asked as he took a small pen light and flickered it across her eye, then pressed gently on the swollen one.

"Horrible."

"So I would imagine," he told her as he checked her vitals on the machine and made notes on her chart. "But it seems you will live, and live well, my dear." He turned to address her guests. "I have to give her some pain medication and some tranquilizers. I need to be alone with her now."

"Oh, no problem, Doctor." Taylor got up and placed his chair back in its original place. Dyania smiled again at Cathalina.

"I will see you tomorrow." Cathalina nodded and closed her aching eye. Taylor and Dyania turned to leave and closed the door behind them after taking one more look in on her.

"So what do you think?"

"I think it's great that she is going to be OK. Once she is well enough, I would like to have a psychological evaluation done on her." Dyania walked toward the exit of the hospital, followed by Taylor.

"Now that's ironic." Taylor snickered.

"What is?"

"A psychological evaluation done on a psychiatrist." He laughed heartily.

"Now you know that's just plain mean, Isaac. Mean!" She laughed, unable to resist the humor of it all.

"In all honesty, though, I think you might have a point. What kind of psychological state can someone be in to bite off a man's penis and then stuff it down his throat while watching him die? That's just deranged." Taylor reflected on the information that came in to them at about the same time they were called to the scene of Cathalina's accident. Just the thought of it had him pausing to grab and check his own manhood as discreetly as he could. Watching him made Dyania laugh again. The image of him vicariously experiencing another man's pain tickled her pink. She knew it wasn't funny, but she couldn't hold back from watching Isaac squirm.

"Exactly," Dyania said in between bubbles of giggles. "According to some of the eyewitnesses, this man had raped so many women in that same bathroom that it was only a matter of time before he grabbed the wrong one. According to the coroner, this man stunk and had lesions on the exterior of his manhood. She must have seen all that," Dyania reasoned, and Isaac just continued to distort his face at the thought. It wasn't the blood and gore that bothered him. He was used to that. It was the idea of another man losing what made him a man. It hurt him to the core.

"I understand what you mean, though. A sane person seeing lacerations on someone's genitals wouldn't venture there, fearing for her own life. Maybe something triggered her anger; maybe she went temporarily insane, like Lorena Bobbitt." He chuckled again, unable to contain the mirth of the whole situation.

"Come on, let me buy you a cup of coffee and you can help me go over some of the information I came up on the Atlanta case." She pushed her arm casually through his and began walking.

"Where are we going, Detective Minto?" Isaac stopped in his tracks and turned to look at her.

"What do you mean? I just told you." Seeing that her

good mood was being turned by his question, Isaac decided to save himself. He liked her this way, laughing and in good spirits. He didn't want to see the woman who walked into his department two days ago anytime soon.

"No, that's not what I mean. I meant that you are a guest here. You shouldn't be buying me coffee. Let's see. What time is it?" He paused to look at his watch. "It's only eleven thirty. That's breakfast." The smile that crept up on Dyania's face prodded him to keep going. "How about I make it for you?" He paused to study her reaction. When the smile remained, he continued. "At my place." He shrugged his shoulders nonchalantly to shake off just how much it would mean to him.

"Well . . ."

"I mean, if you don't want to, we can go somewhere else. There's a diner just around the corner," he added before she could respond.

"If that's what you want," she told him as she began walking again. "I guess you don't need to know what I was going to say then." She turned to look at him with a smirk on her face. Her full, luscious lips curled into a smile and her eyes twinkled in the glare of the morning sun.

"If you were going to say no, then you don't have to tell me what you were going to say." Taylor jogged the few feet to catch up to her as she picked up pace again, putting her arm back through his. "But if you were going to say yes, let me kick myself right now for putting my foot in my mouth, throw myself at the mercy of the court, and ask you to ignore my male ego and let me make you breakfast," he bargained. Letting him off the hook, Dyania stifled another giggle.

"Well, lead the way back to your place?"

"Yes!" Taylor exclaimed as he did the happy shuffle and took her hand gently. "Right this way."

* * *

Elizabeth tried to reach Cathalina for two days and couldn't, then she tried Serena and Cleo. She was not able to reach anyone except Cleo. She was becoming frantic as her senses were going into overload. Her body was always on fire, and now she was locked into Serena's every thought. She wasn't sure if she was just straight paranoid and losing her mind, or if Serena and Cathalina had really gone AWOL.

"Oh God, please, not now. Not now," she whispered into the telephone as it rang.

"Sex Cell. May I help you?" the pleasant receptionist asked.

"Cleo, please?" Liz requested, trying hard to steady the telephone receiver. She waited while the woman put her on hold, but she couldn't hold much longer. She couldn't contain her nerves. Her hands were shaking so hard that she was banging the receiver against her ear. She pressed the speaker phone button and put the headset back into its cradle. She hadn't eaten or slept since two days ago before the meeting when everything went dreadfully wrong. Every moment since then had been painfully eroticized with passionate nightmares, and she wasn't sure if she was dreaming or awake most of the time, or whether she was getting transmissions or losing her noodles. She was tired, hungry, her nerves were fried, and she was frustrated. She needed to talk to somebody. She realized that Cleo had yet to come to the phone. She hung up and pressed the redial button.

"Sex Cell."

"Listen to me. Get Cleo's big, fat ass on the phone now before I reach through it and ring your damn neck." She didn't have to say it twice.

"Hold, please."

"Who is this and what the fuck do you want?" Cleo was her natural, same ol' nasty self. She was only cordial to Cathalina and didn't take nicely to anyone else unless there was something in it for her.

"Cleo, it's me. Something is wrong."

"Liz? Liz, are you OK? You sound like shit."

"How pleasant of you, Cleo. Thanks," Elizabeth said, trying to sound normal, letting Cleo's insults roll off her back like they used to. But this time, she couldn't help taking it personally. After all, it was the truth. "Something is wrong, Cleo. I can feel it. Serena has gone AWOL and I cannot reach Cathalina." The moment Cleo heard Cathalina's name, Liz gained her full attention.

"What do you mean you haven't been able to reach Cathalina? Did you try her at home? The office?" Cleo asked, dread beginning to spread throughout her body.

"Of course, I did all that. I wouldn't bother to call you if there were some other way to reach her," Elizabeth hissed.

"What are you supposed to mean by that?" Cleo asked defensively.

"Listen, forget it. Our girls are missing and that's the main concern. You can grill me later, but right now, I am freaking out, Cleo. I cannot stop shaking. I feel like a drug addict going through withdrawal and I don't know if it's something that I am doing or if I am picking up something from Serena and Cathalina. I bled this morning when I went to the bathroom and I am aching as though I got run over by a truck. Yet, I feel like I could run a hundred miles right now from the adrenaline rush I am having. I feel sick." Tears began flowing down her face as she spoke. Her eyes were so misty that she could no longer see and her voice was all choked up.

"Calm down, Liz. Where are you now? Are you home?" She could no longer decipher Elizabeth's words, so Cleo assumed that was a yes when she heard the gurgled sounds come from Liz's mouth. "I am on my way. Stay there," Cleo told her and hung up the phone. As soon as Liz hung up the phone, it rang again. She wanted to pick it up, but couldn't. She was in no shape. Her voice was gone and her hands were trembling uncontrollably. She couldn't do anything. Then the voicemail picked up.

"Hello, Elizabeth. My name is Detective Minto. I would like to speak to you regarding a Francesca Trivilani. You can reach me at this number . . ." Elizabeth's mind blanked out for a second and she didn't hear the number after the woman mentioned Francesca. She knew it. She was right. Francesca was dead and now they were coming after her. Heaven help her. "I would like to hear from you at your earliest convenience," Liz heard the detective say. "By the way, it seems you are a patient of Dr. Cathalina Shekhar. She was in a very bad accident and is in the critical care unit at Larkin Community Hospital in South Miami. Hope to see you there."

When the phone went dead, she was stumped. At first, she couldn't find her breath and she was struggling to find her voice. She didn't know when it happened or how she found the strength or got the energy, but she knew she heard a loud wail, like a hundred screaming mothers in the throes of childbirth. When she realized the sound was coming out of her mouth, she began wailing in shock and terror, and the tears flowed freely until they withered into sobs as she curled into the fetal position on her bed. The thoughts came in spurts. What was she going to do without Cathalina? She was their voice, their strength, she was their counsel. Who was going to rescue her? She couldn't leave Cathalina alone in the hospital. Yet, if she went, she would be arrested for sure. How would she survive?

She wasn't sure how much time had passed while she laid on the floor, but she began to notice a loud thud at the door. She was jolted from her semi-conscious state; half asleep, and looked at the clock. It was four in the afternoon when she called Cleo and it was now six thirty. She pulled herself from her bed and moved shakily to the door. She wasn't sure who it was now, and she was attempting to be cautious. Her brain was fried and she couldn't take another attack. She needed someone to talk to.

She lifted the brass peephole to verify who it was, and for a brief moment, she felt relief. It was Cleo. Cleo charged into the apartment and was filled with disgust. Apparently, for the past couple of days, Elizabeth did not find the need to shower or change her clothes. She reeked and she was falling apart. She was in emotional shambles.

"Oh, baby." Cleo found the love she had always held for Liz. "I am so sorry. Look at what she did to you. Look at what she did to you."

"What who did to me, Cleo?" Liz asked, shuddering from an internal draft.

"Serena, your so-called Spider Queen. Where is she now when you need her?"

"Don't blame her, Cleopatra. We started all this long before she came into the picture. If anything, we should think about what we did to her, what we brought her into, and did to her life," Liz said, fatigue consuming her as she began to slide to the floor.

"Here, let's get to the bed." Cleo swooped her up in her arms in one motion and carried Liz, looking at her with the love of a mother. She had groomed and raised Elizabeth from a teenager. When she discovered what she was, she gave her a home. Of course it wasn't the best of homes or the best of jobs, but it was what she had to offer. Then she allowed Liz to leave to pursue her dreams as an actress. Cleo's heart was sad at the thought of Liz falling apart the way she was now.

"Would you like some water? Have you had anything to eat?" Cleo looked around, picked up a few things from the floor, and placed them in a pile. Elizabeth was immaculate. For anything to be out of place for her was unusual. She had apparently been breaking things because there were broken glasses on the floor in the kitchen and water stains on the walls.

"Cleo, what am I going to do? I am in trouble."

"Don't worry, sweetie. We are going to find Cath."

"No, it's not that." Elizabeth coughed, her eyes burning and red from her tears.

"I don't understand. You are not in this alone." Cleo placed her hand around Elizabeth's shoulders for comfort. The smell of Elizabeth made her get up and walk to the bathroom to run a bath. She walked into the living room, where the drapes were drawn and the lights were dark, making it almost look like night outside. Cleo pulled open the drapes and balcony doors so the cool, ocean breeze could circulate inside the North Miami apartment.

Cleo walked back to the bedroom where Elizabeth was laid out, and began undressing her. She chuckled.

"I remember when I found you," Cleo said. "You were almost as vulnerable as you are now." She stopped to turn off the water faucet and poured some bath oils and Epsom salt in the tub. She gathered Elizabeth's vanilla and lavender candles and lit them, aromatizing the room, and then she dimmed the lights and placed Liz gently in the tub.

"I am really in trouble this time, Cleo, and nobody can help me."

"Hush now, child. I am going to put on a pot of tea, clean up the rest of this place, and get to the bottom of this." As she cleaned, Cleo noticed that the voicemail light was blinking.

She probably hasn't checked her messages yet, she thought, and directed herself to the nightstand where Elizabeth kept her phone. She pressed the button and listened to the various messages from colleagues, her agent, and friends. When the message from Dyania played, Cleo almost gagged.

"Oh no." It hit her hard. She now understood. Elizabeth was in trouble and they had connected her to Cathalina. They were all in trouble. Cleo finished cleaning up as best as she could, took Liz out of the bath, and got her comfortable in bed. Liz had fallen asleep before she was even able to drink her hot tea. "That's all you needed, baby girl. That's all you needed," Cleo said as she walked to the balcony. "Now, what am I going to do about Cathalina?"

Dyania went over all the information that Taylor had to offer. She couldn't understand where the connection was between Elizabeth and Cathalina beside the patient-doctor relationship. She shared with him the information on what had happened in Atlanta, at the risk of sounding ridiculous.

"Amazing," was all he could say as he cleared their breakfast plates and placed them in the kitchen sink.

"She was Francesca's roommate and the only one from the cast missing after her death. She was not being charged with the murder yet, but it's the only lead." Dyania moaned a sigh of confusion. She knew there was something more, but she just didn't know what it was.

"So, what's next?"

"I am not sure. Let's think about it." Taylor's mind was on overdrive.

"And then we have a case that seems totally unrelated. Your Lara Lopez, a patient of the good doctor. How the hell does all this relate?" Dyania stood and paced the kitchen floor. The drip of the water as Taylor washed the dishes helped her gain a mental flow.

"Do you think there's a connection between all these cases?" Taylor wiped his hands and walked over to her, stopping her by holding onto her forearms at arm's length.

"It's quite a quagmire. I mean, think about it," she told him, pulling away and continuing her pacing from the kitchen sink to the table. "What are the odds that Dr.

Cathalina Shekhar got into a car accident in a vehicle she stole, following a moment of insanity when she bit off a man's penis and killed him with it? And this same Dr. Shekhar also just so happened to have been the attending psychiatrist to your Lara Lopez, who ended up dead in a suicide/homicide situation. And finally, our Dr. Shekhar is the doctor of none other than missing-in-action Elizabeth Chung." Dyania spewed her words off so fast that she had to catch her breath when she was finished.

"Damn, I didn't even process it that way." Taylor sat down as the incredible burden of evidence laid on him like a ton of bricks.

"It's all just too . . . gosh, I don't know." Dyania sat across from him, flung her hands on the table, and dropped her head to meet them, gently banging it as if to force out more thoughts to make sense of it all. "I don't know why, but I am feeling it's all connected. Something is just not adding up," she finally said, piercing his eyes with hers. His mouth had dropped open at her revelations, and all he could do was stare back at the youthful face of this investigative wiz.

19

Cleo decided to leave and allow Elizabeth to get some sleep. She needed to know what the situation was with Cathalina and to figure out their next move. She left Elizabeth's condo and got into the Mini Cooper she had borrowed from Natalia. As she plopped into the driver's seat, she reached for her cell phone and dialed directory assistance.

"Larkin Community Hospital," she stated into the automated voice activated service. She didn't wait for the number to be repeated before hanging up and dialing the number that was given to her. She was finally able to finagle her way through the automated system at the hospital until she received a live person who gave her the room number and location of Dr. Cathalina Shekhar. She drove as fast as she could without being detected by a state trooper. She made her way through Coral Way Village, past the University of Miami and onto to SW Sixty-second Street where the hospital was located. She found the parking lot and headed into the hospital lobby.

When she arrived at Cathalina's door, she stood breathless as she hesitated to enter the room of her most trusted confidante and the love of her life. She choked up as she looked through the small window opening on the door and saw Cathalina laid out. Her face was scarred and healing from the stitches they had given her, and her legs were in casts. She stifled her tears and swallowed hard. Slowly turning the knob, Cleo put a smile on her face as she entered the room.

"Hey there, gorgeous," Cleo said as Cathalina turned to look at her. Cleo concentrated on keeping a smile on her face. She didn't want to give away just how horrible Cathalina looked—the scars, the swollen eye, the stitches. But to her, Cathalina was still the most beautiful woman she had ever seen.

"Sweetheart!" Cathalina mustered as much joy as she could. She didn't think anyone would find her. No one knew she was there.

"How did you find me?" she asked and then coughed. Her throat was dry and she reached for the glass of water next to her bed. Cleo rushed over to her aid and placed the straw in her mouth.

"There was a message from a Detective Minto on Liz's machine that you had been in an accident and were in the hospital."

"Minto?" Cath's mind raced to make sense of how the female detective who had sat at her bedside had found out that she knew Liz. Then it hit her. "My Palm Pilot."

"Do you think they are going to find out? I mean, we have done a lot of stuff over the past ten years. What will happen if . . ."

"Shuuu!" Cathalina mustered as much strength as possible to put her finger on Cleo's full, thick lips. "I need to do something right now. You have to get to my office. Sooner or later someone is going to get there and start rummaging through my records. Delete all the files marked Man Killer on them. They are coded, but it won't be hard with the police technology they have on hand to decipher them." She smiled when Cleo's mouth dropped open.

"You kept files?"

"Don't be silly, woman. You are an entrepreneur. You have files for your organization, don't you?" She took Cleo's nod as a yes.

"But . . ."

"Let me finish, Cleo, please. I am tired, and I cannot keep talking much longer. My throat is dry and I might pass out soon. Besides, it's only a matter of time before they bug my room, if they hadn't done so already." Cleo kept silent and listened as Cathalina continued. "Once you have gone through my computer files, I need you to go to my combination locker. The password is Man Killer. Open it and shred everything in there. I have copies, don't worry. They are hidden in a safe place. If anything happens to me, the information will be destroyed."

"Where?"

"That's not important now. Do as I say, Cleo. I have evidence on us—about people and things and situations—that would expose details about what we have done that no one would ever figure out on their own. You understand, don't you?" Again, all Cleo could do was nod her head. She knew that if the cops got their hands on Cathalina's files alone, they would be closing unsolved deaths spanning a decade.

"How do I get back in touch with you?" Cleo asked. She could not stop the tears now. The information and responsibility that was being placed on her, without Cathalina beside her, was overwhelming.

Cleo pressed her lips tenderly against Cathalina's with as much passion as she could muster without hurting her. She caressed her face and kissed her forehead.

"I love you, Cath," Cleo told her, resting her cheek against Cathalina's moist ones.

"I love you, too, Cleo," Cathalina responded, squeezing Cleo's hand with all the strength she could muster. "Now, do it."

"Do what?" Cleo jerked her face away from Cathalina's with horror in her eyes.

"You remember. What we used to talk about years ago, just in case, when it was just us two." Cleo's tears turned to wails and sobs as she sniffled and reached for a napkin to blow her nose.

"That was a joke. We never intended . . ."

"Desperate times call for desperate measures."

"But this is not it." Cleo was adamant about not listening to Cathalina's sickly ranting. She coughed on a sob and used the back of her hand to wipe her tears away.

"This is it, Cleo. You promised me you would do this for me, and I made you the same promise. Were you lying?"

"No, but, Cath, it's going to work out. We can fix this."

"This is the way to fix this. It will close the ranks." Cleo dropped her head back to Cathalina's shoulders and grabbed Cathalina's head, lifting her slightly from the bed, hugging and rocking her.

"No, oh no, oh no, I love you so much, Cathalina. You are the love of my life. You have given my pitiful existence meaning and placed me on a journey. You took away my pain and allowed me to see a bigger picture. You loved me. How am I supposed to live without you?" she asked. But she knew that Cathalina would not answer because Cleo had done what her dear friend had asked. The reality of their situation was obvious. "Cathalina Shekhar, I will never forget you."

Cleo gathered herself and placed Cathalina's broken

neck back in its place on the bed. Cathalina's eyes were already closed, and her face was peaceful as Cleo hugged her friend. She leaned in and kissed Cath softly on the lips one last time, lingering there to carve the feel of her lips into her mind. Then she pulled away and walked swiftly out the door.

20

Serena turned blissfully in the comfort of Vincent's king-sized bed. She smiled as she woke from her sweet dream.

"Hey there, sleepy head." Vincent kissed her forehead as he presented her with a breakfast tray of fruits and orange juice. "Hope you're hungry."

"Famished." Serena laughed. "Do you have pancakes? Eggs?"

"Of course I do. Would you like to get dressed and come sit with me in the kitchen? We can talk as I cook," he offered.

"Sure, I would love that."

"Great. Take your time and get yourself together. Come and join me when you're ready." Vincent kissed her gently on the back of her hand, reached closer, and brushed his lips against hers, then eased from the bed, took the tray, and exited the bedroom.

Serena sat up in the bed and surveyed herself. She wasn't wearing the sundress she had on the day before. Vincent had changed her and had her dressed in one of his over-sized dress shirts. At first, she was alarmed that he had changed her, but then her alarm turned to embarrassment. He had seen her home and what she did to Jason. What would he think of her? What could be worse than that? Then her thoughts turned to Jason. Her feelings were jumbled, but she didn't blame him for his reaction. It was all her fault.

She looked around and noticed that there was a master bathroom adjacent to the bed. She gathered herself and slid from the bed. Once in the bathroom, she saw that things were immaculately set aside for her. A new toothbrush, towels, and soap were all neatly folded on a shelf with a rose lying next to them. She smiled and felt a tinge of awkwardness.

"Are you comfortable? Is everything to your liking?" Vincent yelled from the foot of the stairs.

"Yes, I'm fine. Thank you."

"Girl, you sure are fine," he mumbled as he walked back to the kitchen to start the lady's request.

"Excuse me? Did you say something?" she yelled back as he headed away.

"Oh nothing. Just missing you already, that's all." He smiled and continued on his way. As soon as he began to beat the eggs and set the table, Serena glided down the stairs to meet him.

"I didn't realize you were so immaculate. Your home is beautiful."

"Thank you. It feels like a home now with someone as regal as you in it. It's never felt this good." He winked at her and made her shy away. She couldn't stop thinking of her home. The thought of Jason gave her a twinge of guilt in her abdomen. She wondered how he was, and how things would be from here on out. Things were forever changed.

"Did I say something wrong?" he asked when she didn't respond to his comments.

"No, it's just that, well, everything is so weird. This is not how I envisioned spending the night in a man's bed for the first time in my life," she told him shyly. The admission took Vincent off guard and he stopped cooking to talk to her.

"Are you serious? You have never spent the night in a man's bed?" He was filled with shock and honor.

"Yes, I have done a lot of other things," she swallowed hard, remembering all the foreplay, finger play, and tongue play she had participated in, "but I have never had sexual intercourse with a man." Vincent grew an immediate erection at the thought. All this time he was out there raping babies, killing, being a criminal. He was regretful of his past and hoped Serena wouldn't panic and leave if and when she found out one day. He didn't know what he had done to deserve the gift now standing before him, but he never wanted to go back.

"Come on, let's eat." He gently pulled himself away from her and moved back to the kitchen table, placing a plate of eggs, Sizzlelean, and pancakes in front of her. Picking up a piece of the meat that was cut like bacon pieces, but much thicker and less fatty, she looked at it as she turned it around in her hands.

"What's this?" she asked, bringing it to her nose to take a sniff.

"It's called Sizzlelean. It's better than bacon because its cured beef and turkey. It's much healthier," he told her.

"It smells really good." She smiled and took a big bite. "And it tastes really good as well," she told him. "I cannot believe I have never heard of this."

"Well, usually everyone is in the same mindset. If you don't look for something different, you won't find something different," he told her as he dug into his eggs and poured maple syrup onto his pancakes. They ate silently until Serena broke it with a cough.

"Here, drink some juice. Probably eating too fast."

"Yes, this is the best meal I have had in a long time. Thank you."

Serena?"

"Yes what is it?"

"Can I ask you something? If you don't want to talk about it, it's OK. We all have our secrets, things we don't readily share."

"No you can ask. I will try to answer the best I can."

"At your place, when the guy there was attacking you, you, you . . ." She tensed and he could sense her discomfort. "I don't want to make you uncomfortable."

"It's not that. I just didn't expect anything like that to happen."

"I don't understand. You live with a man, he said you cut off his genitals, he tried to kill you. What happened?" The concern in his voice made Serena want to confide in him, but she just couldn't find the words in that moment. She wasn't prepared to tell the man she was falling in love with that she was a criminal pretending to be something good. Not even knowing Vincent's past made it any easier.

"It's fine. You don't have to talk about it. But whenever you're ready, if you ever need someone to talk to, I'm here." His offering brought tears to her eyes. He changed the subject. "So, what's on your agenda today?"

In that moment, Serena's cell phone started ringing.

"I think that's my phone. Where is my pocketbook?" she asked Vincent.

"Here, let me get it for you." He walked down the three short steps to the living area from the kitchen dining area and retrieved her purse. She opened her phone and saw she had a new text message.

"Oh no!"

"What is it? What's wrong"

"No, no, no, no . . ." She began to cry as she fell to the

floor. "I need to go home. There's an emergency and I need to go home."

He walked toward her and took her hand, trying not to become alarmed by her reaction to the text.

"I will go with you, Serena. You don't have to be alone."

"You don't understand, Vincent. I need to do this alone. It's a friend and she needs me right now."

"I will respect your wishes, but promise me if you need me you will call?"

"I promise," she said, running up the steps to the bedroom where she could get dressed. "Could you please call me a taxi?" she yelled from up stairs.

"Why don't you take my keys, hun? You might get there faster."

"Thank you. We can finish this later." She smiled before planting a gentle kiss on his lips and heading out.

After gettting in Vincent's Maxima, she turned the ignition and left. She had been negligent, caught up in her own fantasies. How dare her to dream for herself when her friends needed her?

She had decided to head home and change, but somewhere in the middle of her journey, she decided to call Elizabeth. Upon hearing the news, she felt herself snap. She swerved recklessly to the side of the road and stopped suddenly. It couldn't be true. She couldn't find tears. Her mind sought some sort of answer, some justification for what she heard. Her hands shook violently and she couldn't hold on to the steering wheel.

"Please, let this not be true." Serena looked at her hands and willed them to be still. Putting her blinker on, she merged back into traffic and took off.

Cleo ran from the hospital as fast as she could, before the doctors and nurses began swarming around Cathalina's lifeless body. She couldn't risk getting caught, especially if those detectives were on their trail. She hopped into Natalia's Mini Cooper and thanked her lucky stars that she didn't drive her own car, which would have stood out like a sore thumb. She put the car in gear and headed toward Biscayne Bay, which led to Cathalina's upscale practice. She looked around cautiously and parked toward the back of the building. She waited to enter until she was sure there were no prying eyes. As she approached the door, she reached into her purse and prayed that she still had the copy of Cathalina's keys in there. She hadn't needed to use them since the others came on board.

She searched frantically, amidst makeup and small toys, brushing away a handcuff. Finally, she saw the spare set of keys lodged in the bottom of her purse. She breathed a sigh of relief and fumbled with the locks until they opened. Stepping onto the plush, white carpeting that was heaven for any foot, she fell to the floor and began to cry. Everything was signature Cathalina. Her unique style and touch, her class and taste in expensive furnishings and electronic toys were evident everywhere Cleo looked, down to the very smell of her, which was lingering in the air.

Cleo's large frame jerked and throbbed with each shattering realization that she would never see her friend again. In that moment in which she fulfilled her promise, she had also said goodbye. She would not be able to attend funeral services or explain to the others why she did what she did. In Cleo's eyes, this was the only sin she had ever committed. She looked at the time and realized that she had to pull herself together. She jumped to her feet, walked over to Cathalina's desk, and searched for the button to open the hidden wall areas for her wall safe. She found the button and set to work. The day was ebbing away and there was too much to do.

* * *

Dyania walked briskly next to Taylor, closing the car door behind them in the parking lot and heading into the building where Dr. Cathalina Shekhar held her private office location. They walked into the building and down the corridor to her suite.

"Nice place. It must cost quite a pretty penny to have an office at this location," Dyania observed, turning to look about her. "It's breathtaking." Taylor smiled as they stopped briefly to check the exact location they were trying to find.

"It is quite a place. She must do very well as a doctor. But I still don't know why you wanted to come here. She committed a crime of self-defense against a rapist in a sleazy club bathroom. Why are we investigating her?" His tone had gotten more somber as his thoughts raced.

"I don't know, Isaac. I just know that there's more to this. Worse case scenario, we find a next of kin to inform about her accident. So far we've only got Elizabeth, who we already knew of, and a few others who were noted in her Palm Pilot. But something just doesn't add up with her."

Cleo could hear voices outside in the hallway. She rushed through the shredding of the last of what she found in the safe, and scurried to put things back in order so it wouldn't be noticeable. She stuffed the shredded materials into a black plastic bag and wiped the glistening tears from her cheeks. She stopped momentarily to listen to the voices. She had an eerie feeling in the pit of her belly, then panic pushed her to move faster. She estimated that the people were right around the corridor, and soon they would be approaching Cathalina's office. She wasn't sure who they were, but at the mention of her friend's name, dread consumed her and she began moving as quickly as she could. She needed to get out of there.

Do they realize that Cath is dead? Are they coming after me? The thoughts were swimming around Cleo's head like a thousand ocean ripples against the shore.

"Let's stop talking and see what the good doctor can prescribe for us." Dyania didn't want to be out in the hallway much longer. She was eager to see if her hunches were on target. She tugged lightly on Taylor's sleeves to nudge him along. They were right at the bend in the hallway, and Cleo could hear them as if they were right in front of her.

"Dyania." She turned to look at his face and closed her eyes as he pressed his lips against hers. She opened her mouth and allowed his tongue to explore hers, and moaned slightly at the exquisite gentleness of his kiss.

Cleo grabbed her bag and the plastic bag full of the shredded papers and cracked open the door. She peeked around the corner and saw a man and a woman in a passionate embrace. The thought brought her back to so many moments she had loved and made love to Cathalina, the way her soft, small hands felt running down her spine. Fresh tears sprang to her eyes and fell to her shoulders. She gathered her things and quietly exited the suite. The door squeaked and she looked up, terrified that they had heard it, as they could now see her if they looked. But they were still locked in their kiss.

Slowly, Taylor pulled away from Dyania and her eyes opened to glow at him.

"That was nice."

"Thank you. I just wasn't sure if . . . I mean, I really wanted to . . ." Dyania placed a long, graceful finger to his lips.

"That was nice," she said again with a sexy half-smile that hinted at more than what she said in those three words. Taylor was pleasantly surprised at her receptiveness. She had been so locked into work, thinking about work, figuring out work, that he didn't even think she had noticed him. But she had.

Dyania had been staying at Taylor's place for the past week. And although she had her own bedroom and private bathroom, she had a roommate for the first time in her life, and this man behaved as if he didn't even know who she was. She was tired of the way the others fell at her feet and groveled as though she were beyond special. This man made her feel ordinary. She had been special all her life. With him, she felt normal and it felt good.

"Now, can we go so we can get to bigger and better things?" she winked at him and caused his heart to speed up to the rhythm of drum beats. He smiled shyly and allowed her to lead him. They turned the corner and looked at the door that read: DR. CATHALINA SHEKHAR.

"Wow! Now that is nice." He reached out to touch the exquisite engravings on the door and looked at Dyania. "Is that engraved on platinum?" His awe was obvious. "And no one stole it?" He laughed as Dyania nudged him in the side with her elbow.

"You know, you just crazy. Look around you. The people in this building do not need to steal. Can't you see that just about every suite has their information engraved in gold."

"Yeah, but this is platinum. Not white gold."

"Well, the lady has got taste and she wants to be different. What can I say?" she smiled. She knew there was something about Cathalina that she liked. She liked her even more as she ventured deeper into her life. The woman had stood up and said NO. It was gruesome and it was disgusting, but sometimes the message needed to be said in a way that was heard. She couldn't stop thinking about what kind of passion it would take to pull off that kind of job.

"Did you bring her keys from her purse?" Taylor asked as he fumbled around in his pockets and only came up with his own keys.

"I got you." Dyania dangled the keys to tease him playfully and then put the correct key into the lock. "Wait. This is strange." Dyania wrinkled her nose in concern.

"What is it?" Taylor asked, reaching to assist her with the door.

"It's already open, Isaac. Do you think she would leave her office open?"

"Somehow that doesn't seem likely. I mean, yeah the place is upscale, but inside here are her clients' information and private documentation," he reasoned.

Suddenly, Dyania's intuition picked up something. She wasn't sure why, but she began to run. Unknowingly, she followed Cleo's trail down the hallway and out the back entrance of the building. She got outside just in time to see a car take off. It was speeding so fast that there were tire tracks left behind. She wasn't sure why, but she just felt that person in the car had beaten them to something.

She walked back in to find Taylor waiting for her.

"What happened? You took off like a bat out of hell."

"The minute you noticed the lock, something was triggered in me. It was like an image, a thought, an idea. I'm not sure, but I followed it. Sometimes these impressions are so real it's as if I can see an infrared outline of what's happening or people who are no longer there." She paused and looked at Taylor, who eyed her peculiarly. She shook her head and walked away.

Damn, I cannot believe I said all that out loud. What's wrong with me? Shit, now he is going to think there's something wrong with me, she thought as she shook her head disdainfully.

"Are you saying you're psychic?" he asked playfully, but Dyania didn't see the humor in his comment, and it annoyed her.

"Did I say that?" she sneered. "Forget it!" She fanned her hand at him and walked back toward the suite. Taylor followed behind her, trying to figure out what he had said to piss her off when his pager went off.

"Oh crap!"

"What?" Dyania turned abruptly.

"Come on. Let's go. That's a code blue."

"What do you mean?" Dyania asked as they exited the building and headed back toward the car.

"Gotta call and find out. But it's urgent, and with this code, it's never good news," he told her as they got into the car, picked up the radio, and called into the station.

21

Elizabeth was awakened suddenly by the jerk on her shoulders. She groggily came to her senses to see Serena only inches away from her face.

"Serena." She called her name and then an emotional tidal wave took her. "Oh, Serena, where have you been?" she cried into Serena's shoulders as Serena tried to understand herself exactly what had happened to her. How could she explain to Elizabeth that she was caught up in rapture, that her dreams and fantasy for love and a normal life took her away from her responsibilities to her friends?

"I . . . I don't know, Elizabeth. Something happened to me."

"I missed you Serena." Elizabeth confessed. "I couldn't feel anyone. "Then the voicemail message. They're following me, Serena."

Serena sat down next to the disoriented and babbling Liz and tried to decipher what she was saying, while still trying to sort out the flood of emotions that had decommissioned her.

"It's Francesca. She sent them after me, and now they are

coming for me. Oh God." She broke down in tears and shook as she reclined back beneath he covers.

"Who's Francesca?" Serena's bewilderment eluded her.

"Don't you know, can't you feel her?" Elizabeth lashed out. "Why don't you understand? Cleo was right. You are not good enough. You have abandoned us. Me." Serena looked at the woman who was slowly losing her mind, and felt a piece of herself wither away mentally.

"Cleo? What do you mean, Cleo? Cleo don't know anything. She isn't even really one of us. She is an outcast."

At the moment the words escaped Serena's lips, Elizabeth's hands made contact so hard that Serena's lips bled.

"You are such a fucking liar. You don't know what you're talking about. Cleo is in love with Cath, you blind fool. Has been since forever. You are the one who fucked up. You are the one who Cathalina wanted, loved, and trusted. You are the one who disappeared. And now the police found her. She is in the hospital and I cannot even go to see her. Now she is in the hospital and . . ." She fell into a new wave of wailing and howling as Serena waved her hand to hit her back. Then Serena dropped her hand, realized that Elizabeth was really shaken up. She couldn't handle anything right now. She was more messed up than Serena was.

"I am sorry, Liz. I am going to fix this, I promise. Everything is going to be fine. Wait and see," she told her as she rose to leave. Elizabeth calmed for a moment and shook her head, confirming that she understood. As Serena walked from her bedroom, she was suddenly stopped by a huge object that came flying at her. Elizabeth had grabbed her phone from the nightstand next to her and hurled it at Serena.

"It's all your fault, Serena. It's all your fault," she accused and fell into another fit of bawling. Serena stopped for a moment and wondered what had happened to her life, her dreams. Instead of accomplishing anything, she had fallen deeper into a depth of dysfunctional and unhealthy behavior.

"Just look at what's going on around me. I have failed." She chuckled at the sad realization as she turned away from Elizabeth and walked toward the door. There was nothing more she could do there right now.

Dyania and Taylor were shocked to arrive at the hospital and learn about Cathalina's death.

"Damn, what the hell is going on here?" Isaac asked as they stood outside of Cathalina's hospital room door. "There must be something we are missing, something bigger than just this." He turned to Dyania and the physician who had just explained to them that Cathalina's neck was broken.

"There were no signs of a struggle. The only scenario is that the perp is a friend," Taylor said.

"It would seem so, I guess," the doctor told them, tears glistening on his cheek as he attempted to conceal his deep sadness for the loss of Cathalina. He had watched her go though the ranks as she excelled. He was great friends with one of her undergrad professors. He remembered his friend's constant marvel at this one particular student who seemed to understand the plight of human flaws with such ease that he felt proud, even though he knew she had not even attempted to study. He remembered watching her career grow. As she finished her doctorate and opened up her own private practice, she single-handedly drew clients to her just from the name she had made for herself as a student and during her internship. Eventually, she took clients away from her very own mentors and professors. She was a shrewd businesswoman, but she could not be faulted. She knew her stuff.

The Indian doctor, who was a minority getting on in age, felt Cathalina was a joy to watch, even though they were in different fields.

"Who would do this to someone so wonderful, so young?" His old voice cracked under the pressure of his thoughts. Accomplished in his own right, he knew that if it was a friend who did this, there could only be a couple possibilities, but he kept those thoughts to himself, including the thought that maybe Cathalina didn't want to live.

"Well, friend or foe, this person is a murderer and some of these cameras must have caught something. There must be something to help us," Taylor rambled on, fury fueling his rage. He felt like punching something or someone. His muscles flexed with anger and Dyania watched him, fascinated by his intense emotions. She was glad he was as passionate about the cause as she was, but this was just another death, another casualty in the daily work of an officer.

Her thoughts were drawn back to the doctor, who signaled that hospital security was approaching. He coughed, gathered himself together, and forced a smirk to his face.

"Thank you, gentlemen." He nodded as he took the package from them and watched as they walked out of earshot.

"What's that?" Dyania reached for the large envelope.

"I had already requested the tapes that detailed all comings and goings in this area within the past eight hours. We could narrow it down to a closer time, but I think you might rather do that," he offered somberly.

"Thank you," Dyania said, realizing that the loss to this graying, sophisticated doctor was more involved than he was saying. She watched his aging profile as he walked as briskly and steadily down the hallway as a man in his mid twenties. He seemed to be in his late to early sixties, but from his strides, you could never tell.

"Let's get out of here," Isaac said without taking her hand

or reaching for the package. He just turned and expected her to follow. Dyania didn't like that, but she realized there were extenuating circumstances that she didn't understand, and she was very interested in finding out more about this Cathalina Shekhar, who had stirred up all this confusion here in Florida.

Outside, Isaac took a few deep breaths to quell his anger and Dyania watched him, observing the intensity of his emotions.

"What now?" she asked, wondering where his next thoughts were leading.

"Now we go and watch every second of those tapes until we find something to go on. I am not letting this one go," he told her as he walked toward the hospital parking lot and his car. Again, Dyania followed. She felt she was on autopilot and this would lead her to exactly what she came here for. They got in the car and drove quietly back to the Sunny Isles Police Precinct in North Miami Beach, Florida. She followed him into the station and watched as the officers from her previous encounter scattered from her presence with fear, while others, having learned about her since she first arrived, watched on with curiosity. She nodded at them politely and followed Isaac, who seemed oblivious to the rest of his precinct's reaction to her.

Cleo couldn't contain her grief and her anger when she returned to Sex Cell. She paced and pounded on everything in sight. She must have fallen asleep because she didn't feel or sense that there was anyone else there with her.

She was startled when she felt the gentle touch on her shoulder. She looked up to see Natalia, and was not surprised.

"What are you doing here? This is my private place."

"Yes, I know. This is why I am here. You need me." She smiled, trying not to swallow as she held her breath. She couldn't understand how Cleo seemed so comfortable. The place stunk.

"Get out of here, Natalia. Not only don't I need you, I don't even like your skinny, little, ugly KKK ass." She lashed out at her and the words stung Natalia. She had always thought of Cleo as more than a madam, and felt that the woman felt some fondness toward her. She didn't understand why she was saying this, but she held her ground and swallowed her pride. Cleo was all she had right now, and she was going to hold on to that hope.

"Yes, you do need me, and I need you. We have an agreement, remember?" Natalia reminded her. She was pushing the envelope with Cleo, and didn't want to focus at the moment on Cleo being emotionally distraught. She wanted her bastard sister dead and didn't realize she was teetering on the edge of Cleo's impatience.

"You don't seem to understand me. I DON'T need you. I don't need anybody now that Cathalina is dead," she emphasized. "But not to worry, Serena has hers coming, and she will be getting it very soon," Cleo told Natalia, somberly returning her head to the car's steering wheel.

"What do you mean dead? How?" Natalia was alarmed. It wasn't possible. Cathalina was the love of Cleo's life. She would have done anything for her. She reached back to Cleo, touched her hair, and saw her shoulders shake with grief.

"She's gone. What am I going to do? And now the police, those bastards." She went from vulnerable to angry in a breath and Natalia was left with a thousand questions running through her mind.

"Come on, Cleo. We have a lot of work to do. We can talk about this, but we have to keep moving." Natalia wanted Cleo to stay on track. She was on a mission and Cleo breaking down would not help either of them.

"Natalia, just go and leave me alone. I already told you

that things would be taken care of, so just leave me the fuck alone for a minute," Cleo flared, stopping Natalia's nagging for a moment and then enraging her.

"Cleo, you have to get up. You're wasting time." Natalia's frustration was reaching a boiling point and she reached to pull on Cleo's arm.

In that instant, Cleo's arm went flying and connected with Natalia's nose. The power of her anger was so strong that immediately Natalia flew backward, falling on her posterior with her mouth open wide in shock. She squeezed her eyes shut as she felt the crackling of human bones beneath her, and she knew that she could be among them if she did not tread lightly. She touched her nose for evidence of the blood she felt slowly staining her face.

"You have crossed the line one too many fucking times, Natalia. You have been given too much leeway, and your disrespect is about to cost you your life if you don't watch your fucking step."

Cleo glared at Natalia so hard that goose bumps invaded the woman's flesh. Watching Natalia sit on the floor where she had landed with a bleeding nose, put a smile on Cleo's face. She looked to her right where her animal pets were and looked back at Natalia as the thought crossed her mind to feed her to them. She felt her anger bubble over, and her smile became sickeningly creepy. Suddenly, Natalia had become a part of her problem, her annoying nagging having irked Cleo for the last time. She needed to remember who she was playing with and who was in charge. Cleo walked over to her and kicked her hard in her stomach with her spiked leather boot and watched as Natalia doubled over in pain, gasping for air.

"Go get my whip, Natalia, and return here with it immediately." Cleo paced around Natalia like a vulture on the attack. She was so blinded by her fury that the very sight of Natalia ignited her anger. And knowing who Natalia really

was—a descendant of people who once enslaved her an-
cestors, and a carrier of the bloodline of hooded cowards
who thought her people inferior—only served to enrage
her further.

"Get up," Cleo demanded once again, watching Natalia's
struggle.

Natalia obeyed, rising tentatively to her feet, knowing full
well that Cleo's rage could flare again and send her back
down. She scurried to the spiral staircase as best she could,
nursing her wounded ribs and aching belly. She made her
way to Cleo's office, retrieving the cat-o'-nine tails with the
biting snake heads. As she walked back to Cleo, her own
anger flared. She was better than Cleo, above her. Why
should she do what Cleo told her to? She looked at the
weapon in her hands, dropped it to the floor, and ran to
the private room Cleo had set up for her friends. As the
steel doors shut behind her, she turned and looked around
the conference room where not so long ago, she watched
Serena turn into a monster and drop Cleo like a bag of lard.

She admired Cleo's taste and appreciation for seclusion
and privacy. The woman was ingenious at coming up with
secret hiding places. If Natalia didn't know that this room
was there, she would never have thought to look. There
was no way she would allow Cleo to continue to boss her
around. She was going to get Serena with or without Cleo's
help, and she would make Cleo pay for touching her in
anger if it was the last thing she did.

She had to get out. Sneaking out the back entrance of the
conference room hideaway, she was free. But where would
she go now?

Cleo waited and waited for Natalia to get back so she
could take out some of her anger on her back, but she
never returned, making Cleo's anger bubble and fester. She
ran up the spiral staircase and found her whip on the
ground where Natalia had dropped it upon deciding that

she would not allow herself to be punished anymore. Fury surged through Cleo as she raced out and jumped into Natalia's car. She'd had enough. Natalia was right. She *did* have a lot of work to do, and she was going to do it if it was the last thing she did, and she would take care of Natalia later. She smiled as she thought about the young girl. She had nowhere else to go.

22

"Listen, Taylor, I have to go. There has to be a way for me to check on the one and only other contact we knew that Cathalina had before she was murdered." Dyania became restless looking at the videos in Taylor's precinct. She hated the feeling of everyone watching her and she was uneasy.

"Wait. I think you're moving too quickly. Check this out." He pulled her closer to him and shivered as she leaned in, closing the space between them. Pulling himself together to regain his focus, he pointed to the video screen.

"See what time is registering on the monitor?" He turned slightly to look at her. "What time did the coroner say was the time of death?" He was wondering if she saw what he did, but she didn't seem to get it.

"Just tell me what you see, Isaac. I want to go pay Elizabeth a visit. I came to Miami for her, and right now she's the only connection to your dead bodies," Dyania voiced absentmindedly.

"Look, the coroner recorded her time of death as approximately 3 PM, correct?" He made eye contact with Dyania and she nodded her head. "The monitor is showing this woman . . . look, pause the tape," he told her as he pointed at the video. "There, this woman, fair skin tone, short hair, overweight." They had the video paused as Cleo looked through Cathalina's hospital room door with a tear-streaked face.

"She seems distraught. Are those tears?" Dyania's interest was now sparked.

"Look at the time that was recorded—2:50 PM She was the last person to go into the good psychologist's hospital room before the doctor died. Now start the video again. See there," he said excitedly, stopping it again. "At 3:10 PM she left the room. No one else was seen coming or going after that." With his eyes wide with enthusiasm, he looked at Dyania, who finally got it.

"We've got her. Now we can go see if she signed in to get a visitor's pass. We might get lucky with a name we can track." Dyania hugged him eagerly.

They both jumped up, ran out of the precinct, and got back into his car. As they drove, there was another code blue called over Taylor's radio, but this time he didn't have to go far and was already headed in the right direction—an attempted murder to investigate at Larkin Community Hospital.

"When it rains, it pours," Dyania said as she shook her head, annoyed at yet another detour. As she watched, Taylor called in as the closest reporting homicide detective in the area.

"Well, she's not dead," he commented humorously. "Probably a case of domestic violence. We just need to show up so the abused feels better. She will refuse to press charges and we will be on our way." He tried to comfort Dyania, who only stared out the window and fondled with her necklace. It helped her to think when she felt uneasy. "You OK?" he asked, pulling her out of her thoughts.

"Yes, I heard you." She turned to him and smiled reassuringly as he sped to the hospital.

They walked to where the hospital staff directed them and saw a slender woman sitting alone shivering outside the triage area, watching as two male doctors whispered amongst themselves. When the doctors saw Dyania and Isaac walking toward them and flashing their badges, they stopped and greeted the officers.

"This woman claims that she was beaten by Serena Kowtow," Dr. Media whispered, only for the two detectives to hear. Taylor chuckled and Dyania was jolted by the news.

"Come again?" Taylor asked, not believing his ears.

"This woman claims that our esteemed Florida State Judge Serena Kowtow assaulted her for having an affair with her manservant," Dr. Hernandez clarified. "We don't know what to believe. She is beaten up pretty badly and she described the judge and her home with such detail that it's hard to believe she is making it up. Yet . . ." He paused.

"Yet it seems so unbelievable," Dr. Media finished. "She claims the judge tried to kill her and she escaped."

Dyania listened to the exchange while carefully eyeing Natalia. She seemed genuinely distraught. She walked over and carefully sat down next to her.

"Hey." Dyania smiled. "Are you cold?" she asked, observing Natalia's ripped shorts and smeared T-shirt, and the goose bumps rising on the woman's arms from the blasting air conditioning.

"A little," Natalia answered suspiciously.

Dyania stood up, walked over to the triage window, and whispered to the nurse.

"May I have a blanket for this patient, please?" she asked, pointing to Natalia. But Natalia was not shaking because she was cold. She was shaking with fear, wondering if she had gotten herself in too far over her head, and if she could pull this off. She had no idea that Cleo had such powerful friends. Until the doctor asked her if she meant State Judge Serena Kowtow, she didn't know that was who she was. Now she had to follow through with the plan.

Dyania returned and gently placed the blanket over Natalia's shoulders.

"That's better," Dyania said and smiled again.

"Are you going to arrest me?" Natalia asked.

"Why would we do that? You are the victim here. If someone tried to kill you, it does not matter who they are. They have to be held accountable according to the law," Dyania told her confidently, but had a strange feeling that her words were not comforting to the woman. "Are you afraid of her?"

"Yes." Natalia dropped her eyes, afraid to make eye contact with this woman who had gently piercing eyes that might see right through her.

"You don't have to be afraid. We will just ask that you accompany us to the judge's home where you last left her. We will take it from there." Dyania looked up to see that Taylor was wrapping up his conversation with the two male doctors.

"Hi. I'm Detective Taylor. I'm sorry about what happened to you." He stooped down before her.

"Ready?" Dyania asked, and he nodded.

"We're going to need you to come along with us. We'll get to the bottom of this."

Natalia looked at Dyania before looking back in Taylor's direction, dropping her eyes to the floor, and nodding.

Dyania helped Natalia to her feet and released her arm so she didn't feel like a prisoner while walking opposite her with Taylor sandwiching her on the other side.

Serena fought to control her urges to transform as anger and resentment filled her while she drove back to her Coral Gables home. The ride there was not as tranquil as it once was, the vehicle not the luxury transport she had become used to, and her life was falling apart. She drove slowly, absorbing Elizabeth's words and how torn apart she had looked. She felt horrible, as though a part of her had left her. She felt lost.

As she neared her premises, she knew something was wrong, but was not able to identify the emotion. She slowed down. The usual safety and serenity she felt when driving up to the scaling moss and ivy covered walls was no longer there. As she punched in the codes to the entrance of her home, tears came to her eyes. She felt overwhelmed, and she didn't notice the Mini Cooper parked a little way down the street from her home. As the gates pulled open, she drove in and slowly came to a stop at the end of her long driveway leading to her front door.

Something was different, and she knew it. She sat still and looked at her home, which now seemed strange and empty to her, the void so overpowering she felt as though she was being filled to explosion. Her emotions and psyche became gorged and swelled. She felt totally off balance, and the hot and cold flashes she felt, the surges of anger, empathy, and fear were eating at her. She felt paralyzed where she sat and was not sure whether she should go in or stay in the car.

She got a sudden flash of the moment when Cathalina felt Cleo break her neck, and couldn't stop the sounds of anger and pain that gushed through her brain. The voices were crushing her brain and the tremendous loudness and the demands of them were irresistible. She placed her hands to her ears to stop the chilling sounds from violating her mind, but she couldn't get rid of the voices. The dam on her tears loosened and salty drops of water rolled down her face. The spider's poison and her hormones chaotically blended as she became psychologically disheveled.

Cleo got out of the car, walked to the gate, and stood

there watching, wondering if Serena would get out from where she sat inside the car. She already knew the code, a perk of going through Cathalina's things. She would get Serena if it was the last thing she did.

Cleo looked up from her obsession as a car neared the semi-private premises and watched as it slowed down. She began to move around so as to seem inconspicuous, looking to the ground as if she had dropped something. She wondered why this vehicle was driving so slowly. She looked up and inadvertently made eye contact with Natalia as the car pulled over and parked directly across the street from Serena's residence.

Sensing the unusual vibration of energy, Dyania perked up and paid closer attention to the woman who she rode beside in the backseat. Then she looked curiously at the woman across the street who was attempting to find something in the grassy area located in front of the premises.

"Is that the judge?" Dyania asked Natalia and looked to Taylor for confirmation. Natalia swallowed hard and shook her head.

Cleo stood up and began making her way back to the car parked behind the strange vehicle with Natalia in it. Her heart raced and she wondered why Natalia had followed her and brought people with her. She feared that Natalia may have some friends and brought them to hurt her, or had reported her and blown the cover off of Sex Cell after disappearing. Even though Natalia shook her head, Dyania's instinct told her there was something more to the woman. She got out of the backseat and walked slowly toward Cleo, whose palms had begun to sweat. She hadn't had a run-in with the cops in years. She despised them, and this one had cop written all over her. This whole situation stunk. If she got her hands on Natalia, she was a dead woman.

"Hello," Dyania greeted, flashing her badge. "Do you

know the resident of that home?" she asked nonchalantly. She noticed that the woman looked like the same woman on the tape, but didn't make an immediate connection.

"No, I don't," Cleo answered, trying to keep the harshness of her tone under wraps.

"So why were you loitering in the area?" Dyania asked again, not looking up as she reached for a pen and grabbed her notepad from her jacket vest pocket. As she began to write recognition set in.

"Wait a minute." Cleo stopped briefly, wondering what would come next.

"When has it been a crime to walk on the sidewalk?" Cleo's annoyance got the better of her.

"License and registration, please?" Cleo moved to get into the car. "You can get it from the passenger side."

Dyania realized that this was the same woman they were looking for, but decided to play it way cool so she wouldn't realize they were on to her.

"It's OK, I won't bite." Dyania's intuition went into overdrive. She could smell the fear on this woman.

"Please stay here." Dyania walked back to Taylor's vehicle and asked him to run the license and license plate number, which she wrote down. She also told him that Cleo was the woman on the tape at the hospital and asked him to stay calm. As she began walking back to Cleo, she heard Taylor's urgent request for her to return. Cleo flinched. She knew she was caught.

Dyania rushed back to Taylor as he began cuffing Natalia in the back of the vehicle.

"This vehicle is registered to our guest here, Natalia Kowtow. Isn't that right?" Taylor asked rhetorically, sarcasm dripping with every word.

"But that's the same last name as the judge she alleged attempted to murder her. I don't get it," Dyania said, the magnitude of the situation all clumping together. "That car seems so familiar to me, and now it's apparently being driven by a friend of Natalia, who just accused a notable judge of attempted murder, and that judge just *happens* to bear the same last name as her accuser?" Dyania ran the scenario off out loud to make sense of it, and watched as Cleo made an attempt to make her way around to the driver's side of the car for a quick getaway.

"I don't know what's going on here, but it's going to get figured out mighty fast," Taylor insisted, but Dyania had already taken off to catch Cleo. She was banging at the door for Cleo to open it, but Cleo had other intentions. She placed the key in the ignition and started the vehicle. Taylor jumped out of his car to try to assist Dyania, but Cleo pressed on the accelerator and almost ran him over.

Dyania dropped her gun and began running. Her speed gradually accelerated as if her feet had grown wings. She grabbed onto the driver's side mirror, and with all her strength, she used her elbow to bang into the driver's side window, shattering the glass and causing Cleo to lower her head behind the dashboard to protect her eyes. The car swerved, sending Dyania's legs flying as she held on to the mirror for dear life. The brief moment of loss of control for Cleo gave Dyania some leeway and she reached in and grabbed Cleo by the neck. She felt the scales on Cleo's neck rise and her fingers began to slip. Dyania grabbed for the neckline of Cleo's top and tried to pull herself into the car, causing Cleo to turn sharply, spin, and make a wide circle, turning the car back in the other direction toward Taylor, who was in the car with Natalia, calling for backup.

The car moved fast, swinging Dyania from side to side uncontrollably, and then, just as suddenly, went into a reverse. As soon as the vehicle slowed, Cleo tried to throw herself over to the passenger's side so she could get out of the car, but Dyania grabbed onto her arm from where she was hanging through the driver's side door. Cleo kicked at her, accidentally putting the car back into drive. They both looked at each other with alarm, but Cleo figured that she had nothing to lose at that moment. Natalia had blown the cover off her operation, and Cleo had just killed her lover. She was not going back to jail.

Dyania sensed what Cleo was going to do and tried to stop her. Suddenly, the necklace Dyania wore, the gift from her dead parents, began to burn the mark of three interwoven spiders into her flesh. Still half hanging out the window, Dyania's body gave off the smell of burnt flesh. Cleo's eyes flung wide open. At first she thought the car was on fire, but then she realized that it was only the woman who was hanging on to her.

Cleo used the moment of the detective's hesitation to her advantage and pressed her foot to the gas, causing the car to go skidding off the street. Cleo braced herself as she was thrown from the driver's seat to the passenger's side of the car when the car rotated. The car skidded onto the sidewalk and crashed with a bang into the wall of Serena's private premises.

Hearing some kind of commotion, Serena got out of Vincent's car and started to walk back down her long driveway to see what was going on, but then something stopped her. She looked back toward her house where there was no commotion.

Why hadn't Jason come to the window to see what was going on? She had been sitting at her front door for a while now. Why wasn't he there ready to open the door at her beck and call, ready to perform his services? Then she remembered the dispute when Vincent came by and how ugly that was. She turned back and began walking toward her door. He was probably still pissed, she reasoned. Then she heard screaming and a loud crash.

She started to go see what was happening. This quiet,

residential, upscale neighborhood did not see or hear much commotion, but Serena was distracted and distraught. She had her own issues to deal with and she needed to figure out how she was going to make Cleo pay for what she did to Cath. Jason would help her. He was always great to talk to and had some wonderful ideas. Why didn't she think of that before?

Her spirits lifted as she turned back toward her large front door and stood there as she collected herself. She was a mess, but she hoped Jason would take care of her. He would clean her up, make her a hot bath and a cup of hot cocoa, and make her feel better. Maybe he wasn't angry any more. Maybe he just needed some time to think. She turned the knob and put a smile on her face. She couldn't wait to see Jason's deep dimples and long, neat dreadlocks when she opened the door. His rich, deep, cocoa-colored skin would glow at the sight of her, and his eyes would shine with love and adoration. Yes, she would be OK as soon as she was on the other side of her door.

23

The ambulance and police cruisers rushed to the scene of the accident. No one in the crashed vehicle moved. Taylor rushed over to Dyania, but was held back. He was working closely with her, and although he was used to seeing gruesome scenes, it was different when it involved a partner or loved ones. Natalia couldn't stop screaming. They had to administer tranquilizers. She was psychologically traumatized after seeing her car crash with the only person who had ever helped her inside.

When the paramedics cleared the debris from the car and pulled Dyania and Cleo from the rubble, they were shocked to find that neither was fatally injured.

Cleo had broken both her legs, had a few crushed ribs, and had knocked out when her head hit the dashboard. They took her out and rushed her to the nearest hospital.

Dyania had a few scratches and bruises but was also OK. She was a little dazed when they touched her. She brushed herself off and walked over to Taylor, who was staring at her with his jaw hanging open. She reached for his face with her left hand, and shook his head back and forth.

"Hey, anybody there?" she joked. He closed his mouth and swallowed hard. "Why are you looking at me like you've just seen a ghost?" she asked, oblivious to the fact that she had walked away from a car wreck that should have broken her body in half. Taylor continued to stare at her, dumbfounded. He couldn't find his voice.

"We have a lot of work to do," Dyania said. "Let's go check out what's going on inside the honorable judge's house. It is all too strange that Natalia and the judge have the same last name. Maybe Judge Kowtow knows something about what's going on here." She spoke nonchalantly to Taylor with her back turned to him, and then began walking toward the gate.

As she approached the alarm, Dyania began to press numbers that corresponded to letters and just kept trying certain codes until she got it right. The gate buzzed softly and began to retract.

"You coming?" she asked Taylor, as if what she did was as natural as opening her eyes.

Still a bit shaken by the day's events, Taylor could not find words to speak, so he just followed her, leaving the cops and paramedics to clean up the mess they left behind.

"Dyania!" he finally called, finding his voice. "Do you realize you just walked away from an accident back there?" He caressed her arm and moved his hands around her face and neck to feel for himself that she was really going through with this.

"Stop it, Isaac. You're embarrassing me and we are not in private," she teased.

"I'm sorry. I didn't mean . . ." He began to blush and realized she was poking fun at his concern.

"Listen, I really just want to do this now before I cave, OK? Seems like someone is home and I have a few questions I would like answered."

"How do you know someone's here?"

"This car's not cold, and the tire tracks are fresh." Taylor followed her to the door.

Pushing open the door that was already ajar, they were shocked to be met with the scene of Jason's decaying body that had been hanging from the chains for days. Taylor couldn't take it. He had seen many a grisly scene, but the events of the day had weakened his stomach and he began to vomit. Dyania moved like a pro as though she was expecting his sudden reaction. She grabbed him and led him to a wall where he could find support and recover.

"Come when you are ready," she told him and walked away. She surveyed the entrance. Female clothing was strewn across the floor, all the way down to white lace panties and a bra. She whistled as she looked at the large, extravagant interior and then turned to Taylor.

"Beautiful, isn't it?" she asked. He looked at her as if she had lost her mind. She was behaving as though she was just taking a leisurely tour of the home.

Taking out his handkerchief, Taylor wiped his mouth and forced himself not to vomit again. Suddenly, Dyania looked up and her eyes focused on an opening that seemed to be a hidden door in the stone wall. From where she stood, it was dark. With determined steps and purposeful strides she walked up to the opening that was an entryway leading down into darkness. She felt for the stairs as her eyes adjusted to the darkness. Taylor ran to catch up with her. She seemed to navigate through the darkness with ease as though she had climbed up and down those very stairs a million times before, while Taylor had to feel for the wall since there was no banister to prevent an ugly fall.

The stairs ended at a clearing of what seemed to be nothing more than a domesticated cave, like something out of the *Flintstones*. Dyania's sudden halt caused Taylor to bump into her back as they stared into the cave. He was once again met with one of the most horrific death scenes he had ever seen. A woman, naked with caramel-toned skin and beautiful, bountiful, curly, auburn hair lay on one of two stone beds in the middle of the room. Glass cages inserted into the walls in the four corners were empty, but coming from everywhere, crawling in every direction, there were spiders. Three distinct species covered the woman's body so completely that not one inch of her face could be seen. Her body shone white beyond the dark blanket the insects made over her. There were so many of them that it seemed as if the woman had walked into a nest. They crawled all over the walls, the floor, the ceiling, and fell like rain as they tried to fight each other for a morsel of their dinner.

Dyania began to walk inside the room, and Taylor reached for her arm to stop her. She turned to him and smiled warmly, but the cold look in her eyes would be something he wouldn't soon forget.

"What are you doing? You can't go in there."

"I have to get to her, maybe we can save her."

"I don't think so, Dyania. It's too late. Look. They've surrounded her.

"But . . ."

"No, please, let's go." He panicked when he saw that the animals noticed their presence or maybe just a way out and began swarming them. He started to run, but was afraid to leave Dyania.

"All right, I will go with you."

"Hurry and shut the door before they get out."

"Wait, get something to brush them off, they're coming out!"

"Here, use this." Talor handed her his blazer and took off his shirt to help fan them away. He noticed that some were already climbing on Dyania's feet and crawling toward him.

"Oh God, please protect her. Please let her know what

she is doing," he prayed, not knowing at what point he fell
to his knees. He had never been a religious man, but at that
moment he found faith.

He saw her brush the last of the spiders from her and he
jumped to his feet quickly to run out with her. She closed
the door and turned to walk back toward him. Taylor
looked up at her and in the center of her chest the pendant
fell away. Slightly above it a red outline, like a glowing flame,
burned in her chest and seared her flesh. She reached for
the door, and in one motion she pulled Taylor to his feet
with ease and led him back up the stairs.

"I don't think there is anything else we can do for these
two. Let's get to the precinct and find out what we can from
Natalia, and then I would like to go visit Ms. Chung in
North Miami Beach. She is not too far from the precinct."
Taylor didn't have to say a word and couldn't. As they ar-
rived at the car, Natalia began coming to.

"What hap—" before she completed her questions, Dyania reached behind her and slapped her so hard she passed
out again.

"Nothing more from you for now," she stated and nodded that Taylor should continue his call for the coroner to
return to the address for the two bodies they had left behind.

EPILOGUE

Cleo was verbally abusive and brazen in the hospital as they worked to heal her wounds. She refused to talk to the cops and behaved insanely every time they threatened to arrest her.

When Dyania and Taylor showed up at the hospital and told her that Liz was dead, Cleo really lost it. They didn't want to tell her the details, but she insisted on knowing how her friend had died. The last time Cleo saw her, Elizabeth was alive, although distraught.

"But she was not OK, Cleo. You said it yourself. She was upset about not being able to contact Cathalina, and her conscience was eating away at her about what happened back in Georgia with Francesca."

"I don't give a shit about any Fran bitch," Cleo spat. "You killed her!" she accused.

She became so violent they had to tranquilize her daily. She was monitored around the clock and her hands were strapped to her bed to protect her from herself and to keep her from harming visitors.

Dyania walked out of Cleo's room after speaking to her about Liz, and sat next to Taylor.

"Did you tell her Elizabeth Chung slashed her own wrists in the bathtub and bled to death?"

Dyania felt a profound loss with Liz's death, but couldn't express it to anyone.

"No, I only told her of her death when she flipped out on me." Dyania hung her head. "Something is still missing. I just don't know what else to do now. It's almost time to return to Atlanta. I need to write up my report and put this Francesca case to rest."

Taylor was not sure what he could say to help, so he gently placed his arm around her shoulder and she gratefully rested her head on his strong shoulders. They sat there in silence for what seemed like forever before a group of doctors, psychologists, and psychotherapists approached them.

"Let's go." Dr. Mariano smiled understandingly at them. Her old, wrinkled face was filled with wisdom and her light, hazel eyes glowed with truth. Her hair, which was completely white from age, was pinned elegantly in a bun. She stood strong and tall and walked away exuding pride and elegance.

Dyania and Taylor stood and followed the esteemed group of physicians to the conference room where the police chief, a representative from the mayor's office, and a few other esteemed attendees waited anxiously to understand why they never knew about these women who had been the cause of so many unsolved deaths and missing persons for more than a decade. Everyone wanted Cleo's head on a platter. Natalia was their star witness, after helping the police to uncover all the dirt behind the Sex Cell. The gators and crocs in the hidden dungeon were taken away by animal protection, and the bodies were being checked by forensics for identification.

Having searched the home of the Honorable Serena Kowtow, and finding all the gruesome things left behind in the aftermath of her death, everyone was still spellbound that all this happened and no one had known about it.

"Dr. Mariano, can Cleopatra stand trial?" the police chief asked, silencing the pandemonium of discussion between individuals.

"We don't know yet. We still need to keep her under observation," she answered, the sadness of the situation visible on her experienced face.

"How could people like this function, have normal lives, be accomplished, successful, and beautiful women, and pull off one of the most ghastly and horrific string of serial killings that has ever occurred in Florida, without anyone figuring it all out?" the rep from the mayor's office asked.

"That's simple," one of the worlds's most noted psychoanalysts answered. "These women are functional psychopaths."

"What the hell does that mean?" a member from Miami Police Investigations asked, annoyed at what seemed to be the runaround.

"That just means that the same way we have functional alcoholics who can be drunk and go about their normal lives, and functional drug addicts doing the same, there are also functional psychopaths. Functional alcoholics and drug addicts are still alcoholics and drug addicts. They still crave that fix and that high. They still will beg, rob, steal, and kill for that one fix when they are fiending," the analyst explained.

"These women," added another of the therapists among the group, "are actually some of the most brilliant women. Look at their profiles," he suggested as he shifted through some papers and everyone in attendance followed suit, trying to find what this man was making reference to. "Ah," he said, finding it. "Turn to the second to last page in your folder. Our honorable judge was the first black woman to become a Florida State Court Judge at such an early age. Had she stayed on that path, she would have continued to make history. Now turn to the previous page. Cathalina Shekhar was a well-accomplished psychiatrist in her own right. Elizabeth Chung, a noted off-Broadway star, born with what would be considered a deformity, excelled in her chosen field. Even the patient we have here, Cleopatra, for whom we have yet to find any relatives or loved ones, well, look at the empire she created. She has Swiss bank accounts and monies we have yet to total. Don't you find it fascinating that you and I, who are standing here in judgment of these women, and accusing them of wrongdoings, could not even begin to fathom the inner workings and greatness of their minds?"

The group of more than twenty people became quiet as the realization of the hurts and pains these women must have suffered to have done what they did overwhelmed them. Some teared up and others didn't bother to wipe the drops of sadness that dampened their faces and smeared their makeup. But the chief of police was appalled and showed no sympathy. His anger boiled at the way everyone seemed to be eating up every word these doctors said.

"Bullshit!" the police chief yelled. "They are not great at anything. They are the scum of the earth, and Cleopatra, or whoever the hell she is, will pay. She is stupid. All her friends abandoned her, leaving her to take the blame." He snickered, causing a wave of chaotic discussion amongst the group.

"Listen to me," Dr. Mariano said softly, training her eyes on Dyania whose eyes were filled with remorse and sadness, and Taylor, who acted as the pillar of strength Dyania needed to lean on.

"I have had enough, Doctor," the chief said, reaching for his hat and gathering his papers.

"You need to understand this from the victim's point of view, from the medical point of view," Dr. Mariano continued. "These women are sick, just like many other ill people out there, walking around without getting the proper treatment. I am sure as we investigate this further and in the years to come, we will learn that these women were hurt badly. Statistics show that most predators were once victims themselves. We are in a state of distress and need to break the silence and deal with this. These women represent the extremes of such travesties, but how many more men, women, and children are being raped, abused, and told to keep their mouths shut? How many are still afraid because of the shame they think they will bring to themselves and their families if they tell?" she shook her head as her voice cracked. Looking at Dyania again, the doctor swallowed hard, fighting to regain her composure.

"This is true." Another medical professional jumped to Dr. Mariano's aid. He quietly walked over to her and stood tall. "There have been studies to prove that it's a terrible cycle of abuse, just like domestic violence and spousal abuse. We already know that abused children often grow up to be abusive parents. Though this is the most extreme case of a perpetual cycle of abuse we have ever seen, it is still what it is," he said calmly, forcing the group to listen more intently.

"I don't care what you say. This does not excuse their responsibility for what has happened," the chief said.

"No one said it did," Dr. Mariano responded.

"Well somebody is going to have to pay, and answer for all this mayhem that I now have to deal with," he retaliated angrily.

"I understand, Chief. I understand." Dr. Mariano reached for her papers and pulled a chair out from the head of the conference table. Her legs were tired and had given way. "I understand," she said again to his retreating back, and then reclining in her chair, she focused once again on Dyania, who sat quietly.

The youthfulness of Dyania's face cut through the hard edge and façade she had displayed earlier when dealing with Cleo. Dr. Mariano nodded her head. She would need to talk to that woman soon, before it all started all again.

GLOSSARY OF TERMS

1. **Ativan**—brand name for lorazepam; used to treat anxiety, insomnia, and alcoholism.
2. **Amphetamines**—are potent psychomotor stimulants. Their use causes a release of the excitatory neurotransmitters dopamine and noradrenaline (norepinephrine) from storage vesicles in the CNS. Amphetamines may be sniffed, swallowed, snorted or injected. They induce exhilarating feelings of power, strength, energy, self-assertion, focus and enhanced motivation. The need to sleep or eat is diminished. The release of dopamine typically induces a sense of aroused euphoria which may last several hours: unlike cocaine, amphetamine is not readily broken down by the body. Feelings are intensified. The user may feel he can take on the world.
3. **Hallucination**—perception of objects with no reality usually arising from disorder of the nervous system or in response to drugs.
4. **Barbiturates** are often called "barbs" and "downers." Barbiturates that are commonly abused include amobarbital (Amytal), pentobarbital (Nembutal),

and secobarbital (Seconal). These drugs are sold in capsules and tablets or sometimes in a liquid form or suppositories.

5. **Malignant eroticized transference**—In a seminal paper Blum (1973) differentiated between the erotic transference, which is ego-dystonic and which the patient realizes is not reasonable, and the erotized transference in which the patient is flooded with erotic preoccupations and fantasies about the analyst and hopes fervently that the analyst shares them. Pregenital factors may actually dominate but the patient resists interpretations and wishes to enact urgently the gratification of sexual desires with the analyst. Blum insists this phenomenon is not always pregenital or uninterpretable, and he correctly points out that often there has been sexual seduction and over-stimulation in the childhood of such patients. Erotized transferences have multiple determinants and a variable course.

6. **Childism**—A reference to the hatred of children which is shown from the abuse they suffer from adults.

7. **Labia majora**—The large outer lips of the external sexual organ of the female (vulva). The labia minora are the small inner lips which come together to form a hood over the clitoris.

8. **Gonorrhea** is a sexually transmitted disease (STD). Gonorrhea is caused by *Neisseria gonorrhoeae*, a bacterium that can grow and multiply easily in the warm, moist areas of the reproductive tract, including the cervix (opening to the womb), uterus (womb), and fallopian tubes (egg canals) in women, and in the urethra (urine canal) in women and men. The bacterium can also grow in the mouth, throat, eyes, and anus.

9. <u>Syphilis</u>—is a sexually transmitted disease (STD) caused by the bacterium *Treponema pallidum*. It has often been called "the great imitator" because so many of the signs and symptoms are indistinguishable from those of other diseases.

10. <u>Anti-Serum</u>—An Animal or human blood serum containing one or more specific ready-made antibodies and used to provide immunity against a disease or to counteract venom.

11. <u>Passive Aggressive Behavior</u>—Behavior which is characterized by negativity. A person with this condition will at times fluctuate between going along with a plan and actively resisting it by voicing complaints or doing some other act which more or less is a display of unreasonable reluctance.

12. <u>Pedophiles</u>—An adult who has sexual desire for children or who has committed the crime of performing sexual acts with a child whether consensual or by force (rape).

13. <u>The Sistine Chapel Painting</u>—A painting done by Michelangelo Buonarroti in 1512 in Rome to show the creation of man and his history up to Noah.

14. <u>Genital Herpes</u>—Sexually transmitted disease (STD) caused by the herpes simplex virus type. It is passed from one person to another through sexual contact.

15. <u>The Black Widow</u>—this spider has potent neurotoxin venom and is considered the most venomous spider in North America.

16. <u>Brazilian sandering spider</u>—(*Phoneutria spp.*) is regarded by some as the most dangerous spider in the world. It is highly venomous and kills some 5 people across the world annually. It is named as such because it was first discovered in Brazil, though this genus is known to exist elsewhere in South and Cen-

tral America. This spider is a member of the *Ctenidae* family of wandering spiders.

17. **The Brown Recluse**—The brown recluse spider is a venomous spider, *Loxosceles reclusa*, of the family Sicariidae (formerly of the family *Loxoscelidae*). It is usually between 1/4 and 3/4 inch, but may grow larger. Coloring varies from light tan to brown. Differing from most spiders, which have 8 eyes, recluse spiders have 6 eyes arranged in pairs. Only a few other spiders have 3 pairs of eyes arranged this way and recluses can be distinguished from these as recluse abdomens have no coloration pattern nor do their legs, which also lack spines. The brown recluse spider is native to the United States from the southern Midwest south to the Gulf of Mexico.

18. **Crocodiles**—Crocodiles are found in the warmer waters of Africa, Asia, Australia, and America. Crocodiles are often confused with alligators, but you can tell them apart by the shape of their tapered snout, and by the way crocodiles' lower teeth stick out when their jaws are closed.

19. **Nymphomaniac**—A person who is considered uninhibited, who desires sex frequently or sex with multiple partners, usually participates in deviant sexual behaviors typically categorized as fetishes or freaky.

20. **Hermaphrodite**—A person born with both a vagina and a penis. Normally only one of these sex organs is fully functional, unlike Elizabeth Chung in the novel, who has both her vagina and penis operating equally.

21. **Eunuch**—A man born as a man who has no penis due to castration; a male without testicles and or penis.

22. **Victim**—Someone attacked or have malicious actions taken towards them. Someone who has been acted on and usually adversely affected by a force or

destroyed, or scarified under any of various conditions. A person that is tricked, duped, violently hurt.

23. **<u>Psychopath</u>**—Psychopaths are social predators who charm, manipulate and ruthlessly plow their way through life, leaving a broad trail of broken hearts, shattered expectations without the slightest sense of guilt or regret.

ABOUT THE AUTHOR

Denise Campbell began writing using poetry as her entry into the literary world as a pubescent adolescent, but began publishing in 2001. She is the author of *Spanish Eyes*, *Love Thy Sister Watch Thy Back*, *Ebony Passion*, and *By Faith*, in addition to which she is a playwright, speaker, activist, and entrepreneur. Denise Campbell is active advocate for children and organizations working to bring attention to crimes against women. She currently resides in New York City with her daughter, Cheyanne Campbell, and is at work on her next novel.

For more information, check out her website at www.DeniseCampbell.com.

Attention Writers:

Writers looking to get their books published can view our submission guidelines by visiting our website at:
www.QBOROBOOKS.com

What we're looking for: Contemporary fiction in the tradition of Darrien Lee, Carl Weber, Anna J., Zane, Mary B. Morrison, Noire, Lolita Files, etc; groundbreaking mainstream contemporary fiction.

We prefer email submission to: candace@qborobooks.com in MS Word, PDF, or rtf format only. However, if you wish to send the submission via snail mail, you can send it to:

Q-BORO BOOKS Acquisitions Department
165-41A Baisley Blvd., Suite 4. Mall #1
Jamaica, New York 11434

By submitting your work to Q-Boro Books, you agree to hold Q-Boro books harmless and not liable for publishing similar works as yours that we may already be considering in the future.

1. Submission will not be returned.
2. **Do not contact us for status updates.** If we are interested in receiving your full manuscript, we will contact you via email or telephone.
3. Do no submit if the entire manuscript is not complete.

Due to heavy volume of submissions, if these requirements are not followed, we will not be able to process your submission.